She was like a c... ...,
Gage thought.

Her red hair was caught back tightly at her nape, but he suspected that hair was untamable. She had probably hated it all her life.

Something long dormant stirred deep inside him. He wanted to step on it, squash it ruthlessly as if it were a snake. Instead, he faced it dead on. For the first time since—since *then,* he was seeing a woman as a woman, reacting to a woman as a woman.

If he had to start feeling desire again, he wished to hell it could be directed at someone besides Emma Conard. She was apparently a dyed-in-the-wool spinster who took strips out of the hide of any man foolish enough to approach her. And even if that weren't true, she wasn't the kind of woman who was meant for casual affairs, and he'd never again be in the market for anything else.

Dear Reader,

It may still be winter outside, but here at Intimate Moments, things couldn't be hotter. Take our American Hero title, for instance: Paula Detmer Riggs's *Firebrand.* Judd Calhoun left his Oregon home—and his first love, Darcy Kerrigan—in disgrace. Now he's back—as the new fire chief—and the heat that sizzled between the two of them is as powerful as ever. But there are still old wounds to heal and new dangers to face. Talk about the flames of passion . . . !

Rachel Lee is on tap with the third of her Conard County series, *Miss Emmaline and the Archangel.* It seems the town spinster has a darker past than anyone suspects, and now it's catching up to her. With no one to turn to except Gage Dalton, the man they call Hell's Own Archangel, her future looks grim. But there's more to this man than his forbidding looks would indicate—much more—and Miss Emmaline is about to learn just what it means to be a woman in love. Marilyn Pappano's *Memories of Laura* takes place in the quintessential small town—Nowhere, Montana—where a woman without a memory meets a man who's sure he knows her past. And it's not a pretty one. So why does sheriff Buck Logan find himself falling for her all over again? In her second book, *Dixon's Bluff,* Sally Tyler Hayes mixes danger and desire and love for a small girl and comes up with a novel you won't want to miss. Harlequin Historical author Suzanne Barclay enters the contemporary arena with *Man with a Mission,* a suspense-filled and highly romantic tale linking two seemingly mismatched people who actually have one very important thing in common: love. Finally, welcome new author Raine Hollister. In *Exception to the Rule,* heroine Layne Taylor finds herself running afoul of the law when she tries to defend her brother against a murder charge. But with Texas Ranger Brant Wade as her opponent, things soon start to get extremely personal.

As always, enjoy!

Leslie Wainger
Senior Editor and Editorial Coordinator

MISS EMMALINE AND THE ARCHANGEL

Rachel Lee

Silhouette® ™
INTIMATE MOMENTS®

Published by Silhouette Books New York

America's Publisher of Contemporary Romance

SILHOUETTE BOOKS
300 East 42nd St., New York, N.Y. 10017

MISS EMMALINE AND THE ARCHANGEL

ISBN: 0-373-07482-4

First Silhouette Books printing March 1993

Printed in the U.S.A.

Books by Rachel Lee

Silhouette Intimate Moments

An Officer and a Gentleman #370
Serious Risks #394
Defying Gravity #430
Exile's End #449
Cherokee Thunder #463
Miss Emmaline and the Archangel #482

*Conard County Series

RACHEL LEE

wrote her first play in the third grade for a school assembly, and by the age of twelve she was hooked on writing. She's lived all over the United States, on both the East and West coasts, and now resides in Texas with her husband and two children, who are both in college.

Having held jobs as a waitress, real-estate agent, optician and military wife—"Yes, that's a job!"—she uses these, as well as her natural flair for creativity, to write stories that are undeniably romantic. "After all, life is the biggest romantic adventure of all—and if you're open and aware, the most marvelous things are just waiting to be discovered."

For Dad

Chapter 1

Pain clawed at Gage Dalton with fiery talons, driving him from the stark emptiness of his apartment above the bar out into the dark emptiness of the misty night. The staircase from his door slanted down the outside of the two-story brick building, and his boot heels thudded heavily on the wood steps as he descended. The snowy alley was dark, deserted. Not even a cat prowled in the shadows.

At the foot of the stairs, he hesitated. The Friday night ruckus from the bar came clearly from around the corner, louder than it was even in his rooms, which were directly above it. Mahoney must have opened the double front doors to let in some of the refreshing, chilly night air. It wouldn't be long before a Conard County deputy would show up to quiet things down.

He stood there a little longer, listening to the noise, not wanting to be part of it, but drawn to the promise that a couple of shots of whiskey could dull his senses, numb his nerves, ease the pain. He seldom accepted that promise. Usually, he walked. There were times when it got so bad that he paced off every street in town, up one side and down the other. Conard City wasn't very large, but it was large enough that he could spend three or four hours that way without retracing a single step.

Tonight he decided to allow himself the whiskey. It would take the edge off the razor-sharp pain, would ease the chill of the night air. Turning the corner onto the sidewalk, he stepped into Mahoney's.

Silence spread around him in a slow, ever-widening wave as he walked unevenly to the bar. Gage Dalton was that kind of man. When he walked into a room, any room, other men instinctively gave him space. They sensed that he hadn't a damn thing left to lose, that he had forgotten the meaning of fear. That made him both dangerous and unpredictable. With a man like that, it was safer to leave him alone in a bubble of silence and space.

Mahoney saw him coming, and filled two shot glasses with good Scotch. Gage threw a few bills on the bar and downed the shots one after the other, like medicine. Then he turned and limped back toward the door, a tall, rangy man with a disfigured face and silver hair. Mystery hung around him like a pall.

Behind him, the silence slowly filled in with talk, but little laughter.

"Damn!" Emmaline Conard never swore, but she swore now, for the third time in as many minutes. Her car wouldn't start, it was late, and it was cold and she really didn't want to walk the five blocks to her house alone.

Which was silly, really, she told herself as she tried yet again to get the engine to turn over. The starter ground and groaned sluggishly, warning her that she was killing her battery.

"Damn!" she said again, and let her head drop against the steering wheel. She would have to walk. It wasn't as if she weren't properly dressed for the damp, cold night. Having lived in Wyoming all her life, she knew better than to go anywhere in December without adequate clothing because any unforeseen problem could become life-threatening in a climate this cold.

She was wearing boots and a parka, and warm wool slacks, sufficient for the short distance and a temperature that was only slightly below freezing. She could easily and safely walk home.

Except that she quite simply couldn't do it. She reminded herself that this was Conard City, that she knew each and every one of the five thousand souls who inhabited the county, and that she was as safe on the streets in this town as she was in her own bed. It didn't help. She had a fear of walking darkened streets alone that went far beyond reason and bordered on phobia.

So, she told herself, trying to be brisk and positive, she would just go back into the library and spend the night in her office. Or she could call the sheriff's office and ask for a deputy to drive her home. Nate Tate and his deputies were always wonderful about things like that, always ready to help a neighbor out. They wouldn't even think it odd that she didn't just walk.

Unfortunately, she also had a thing that bordered on phobia about being alone in a car with a man, even men as gallant as most of the Conard County deputies.

Nor did she want to call one of her friends, who would be bound to find it curious that Emma didn't just walk a distance that, by local standards, was insignificant.

She shuddered and tried one last time to turn the engine over. Just one more time before she gave up and faced the inevitable: an uncomfortable night on the floor in her office.

The fear was so deeply rooted in her that she had long since given up arguing with it. To this day she had no idea exactly what had happened to her, only that during her senior year at college she had awakened in the hospital to discover she had been so badly assaulted and beaten that she had been comatose for weeks. She had no memory of the days immediately preceding the assault, and only fragmented memories of the first few weeks after awakening. What she *did* have was an unreasoning fear of darkened streets and of being alone in a car with a man.

But until this very moment, neither of those fears had seemed particularly inconvenient. Now they closed around her like an iron cage.

Swearing again, she pounded on the steering wheel and gave the ignition one more try. This time the starter sounded like a windup Victrola that had completely wound down.

"Oh, damn." She sighed, sagging back against the seat. Suddenly she felt closer to tears than anger. Now she would have to cross the dark parking lot again. Admittedly, years of practice had made it easier. These days she was even able to cross it at a brisk walk rather than a dead run. But it was still a gauntlet she had to run, and once a day was enough. More than enough.

Suddenly, like a vision from her worst nightmare, a shadowy figure appeared around the corner of the library building. Emma drew a sharp breath, and her grip on the steering wheel tightened until her knuckles were white. Oh, God!

The figure stood there a moment, legs spread, backlit by a streetlight so that he was nothing but the pitch-black silhouette of a man in a cowboy hat. Then, with an uneven gait, he began to walk toward Emma's car.

Panic exploded in her head like a blinding light and she clawed desperately at the door handle. *Run!*

"Miss Emma?" The shadowy figure paused halfway across the parking lot. "Miss Emma, it's Gage Dalton. Are you having car trouble?"

Relief hit her as hard as the panic had. Gage Dalton. She knew who he was. Everybody knew who he was. The old biddies at church gossiped and speculated about him without a kernel of fact to go on beyond his disfigured face and limp. They said he looked like hell's own archangel. But everyone also knew that he worked part-time for Nate Tate at the sheriff's office, so he couldn't be a bad guy. Not a really bad guy. And at the moment, he was as good as a uniformed deputy, as far as Emma was concerned.

But relief had left her weak and shaking, and she couldn't seem to move or talk. All she could do was sit there with the car door half-open, and tremble and try to cope with the conviction that she had somehow just escaped the reenactment of a nightmare she couldn't remember.

"Miss Emma?" He stepped a little closer.

Everyone in the county called her Miss Emma. She didn't know how it had started—probably with the children who came to the library—but after nearly a decade as the Conard County librarian, she was addressed that way by nearly everyone.

"Mis-mister Dalton," she finally managed to gasp.

Her acknowledgement gave him permission to approach. He did so slowly, unthreateningly, hands safely tucked into the pockets of his leather bomber jacket. When he got to within a yard, he squatted facing her, his movement hesitant, betraying his pain. "Sounded like you ran your battery to death."

She nodded, still trying to get control of her breathing. "It wouldn't start, and I just kept trying, like an idiot."

"I've done that a time or two myself. Come on, I'll walk you home."

With those simple words he solved her entire problem. Emma rose on shaky legs and reached for her briefcase and purse. Gage took the briefcase from her with a polite "Let me," and waited while she locked the car.

As they turned the corner from the parking lot onto the sidewalk, the streetlight illuminated the disfigured side of Gage Dalton's face. His cheek looked as if it had been badly burned, and a jagged scar ran from his temple to his jaw. Emma snatched her gaze away, not wanting him to catch her staring. His limp concerned her far more than his disfigurement, anyway. It surely couldn't be comfortable for him to walk this distance.

The silence between them didn't seem to bother him, but it disturbed Emma. Having grown up in this county, she was accustomed to friendly conversation with everyone she met and unaccustomed to silence. Worse, it felt churlish and unneighborly not to be friendly when he was going out of his way to escort her home safely.

He was an... intimidating man, though. Not frightening, though she imagined he could easily be terrifying. At

the moment, however, he was simply...intimidating. Tall
whipcord lean, limping, disfigured. Dressed in black from
head to toe as was his custom—a custom well remarked on
by nearly everyone in Conard County. Hell's own archangel, indeed.

Well, hell's own archangel was walking her home, ensur-
ing her safety as if such gallantry came naturally to him. The
least she could do was be civil to him. She spoke.

"I appreciate your escort, Mr. Dalton. I know it sounds
silly, especially here in this quiet little town, but I don't care
to be alone on dark streets." Which was as close as she ever
came to admitting her terror.

"My pleasure, Miss Emma," he replied in that whispery
rasp that sounded more ruined than natural. "Small town
or not, it's an unfortunate fact that women aren't safe in this
country."

"That's a rather broad statement," Emma protested,
though she quite frankly felt that way herself.

"A true statement," Gage remarked. "It has been pro-
jected that three out of four will eventually become the vic-
tims of sexual assault, and statistics on other types of crime
are just as shocking. No, ma'am, this country isn't safe for
women."

My word! Emma thought, startled. "I had no idea!"

"Few people do." He paused at a corner, his stormy eyes
sweeping the intersection with automatic caution as they
waited for a car full of laughing teenagers to speed by. Then
he gently clasped her elbow and stepped into the street with
her. "The picture it paints of our society, of men in partic-
ular, isn't something we want to look at."

Emma stole a glance up at him, and he suddenly looked
down at her. Their gazes locked for a strangely intense moment. When she at last tore her eyes from his, she felt oddly
disturbed. Subtly irritated.

"I'm sorry, Miss Emma," Gage said after a moment. "I
guess that wasn't a good topic to bring up when you're
walking down a dark street with a man you don't know."

"Well, it's not exactly as if I don't know you, Mr. Dalton," Emma protested. "I mean...well, I know *of* you.

That you work for Nathan Tate. And I consider Sheriff Tate to be an impeccable judge of men." As had her father, Judge Conard, before her. For the moment she chose to ignore the fact that no one was infallible, not even Nate Tate.

For the moment it was simply miraculous that she was actually walking down this street. She might not know Gage Dalton, but his presence was amazingly like a magic shield, holding the darkness at bay, holding back the crushing weight of the night, making it possible for her to walk and talk and breathe as if she were a perfectly normal person.

Years ago, before whatever it was had happened to her, she had loved the darkness, loved the night. In the summers she had often been found on her back in the grass, looking up at the brilliant stars, dreaming of distant shores and alien worlds, wondering if in some backyard light-years away another girl was staring up at the infinite cosmos and dreaming, too.

Impulsively, she confided the memory to the man beside her, then bit her lip, wondering if she sounded like a ridiculously naive country bumpkin. Gage Dalton had lived his life elsewhere, and Conard County must seem like an incredible backwater to him.

"I liked to do that, too," he said, astonishing her. "My other favorite thing was watching the clouds on a summer afternoon. I can't remember exactly when it was I grew up too much, or got too busy...." His voice trailed off.

"I can't, either," Emma said when the silence became too marked. This man, she felt, was not accustomed to sharing memories, feelings, or any other part of himself. "Perhaps I'll try it again this summer. Only I think I'll lie on the chaise in my backyard, rather than the grass."

He glanced down at her. "Why? The grass feels better."

Emma wrinkled her nose. "Insects. The grass is crawling with them. That's what an education does for you, Mr. Dalton. All those precious books I love so well have made me conscious of the insects in the grass and the parasites in the beef I used to eat rare."

He astonished her again with a short, husky laugh. "Where's your sense of adventure, Miss Emma?"

She frowned thoughtfully a moment, then said, "I honestly don't believe I have one. Not these days, at any rate." She glanced up at him again and dared a question. "What made you decide to move to Conard City? It must seem like the end of the earth to most people."

They walked nearly another half block before he answered. The wind nipped coldly at her cheeks, and she pulled her collar up, wondering how her innocent question could have offended him. And it must have offended him, or he would have answered readily.

But he did answer, finally. Slowly. Sounding thoughtful. "It *does* seem like the end of the earth," he agreed. "That's why I'm here."

Which told her exactly nothing at all.

Emmaline Conard, while she suffered from a couple of phobias and some occasional squeamishness, was not, and never had been, a coward. Life had taught her a few lessons, lessons learned the same way a child learns to avoid a hot stove, but cowardice—timidity—was not her nature. Until given cause to feel otherwise, she feared very little. Consequently, she plunged right ahead and asked another question.

"Did you know Sheriff Tate before you moved here?"

Again Gage looked down at her. "Looking for some grist for the gossip mill?" he asked softly. Too softly.

Emma shivered at the silky note in that too-husky, ruined voice. The warning was unmistakable. "No." Her tone was sharp, the same one she used on the troublesome children in the library. "I don't gossip, Mr. Dalton. I was simply trying to make pleasant conversation with a new neighbor. It's rather hard to find something to discuss with a stranger!"

His grasp on her elbow remained gentle, but Emma battled a desire to pull away from his touch. The urge was childish, of course. The fact that the man was difficult didn't give her an excuse to act like a two-year-old. Besides, she thought, casting an uneasy look around, she didn't want to make him stalk off, not before they reached her house.

A half block later, the sound of his voice startled her into renewed awareness.

"I knew Nate before I moved here," he said.

As an olive branch, it left a great deal to be desired, but Emma readily accepted it. In a place as sparsely populated as Conard County, where everyone had need to rely on his neighbors from time to time, allowances were made for nearly every kind of eccentricity or quirk.

"I suspect," she said pleasantly, "that Sheriff Tate would make a wonderful ambassador. At least a half-dozen people have moved here because of him."

"He loves this place," Gage agreed.

Had Emma been less stubborn, she probably would have thrown up her hands right then. Trying to converse with this man was like throwing pebbles into a pool that refused to make ripples. Like throwing stones into a well and never hearing the impact. Ridiculous! Stubbornly, she made one more attempt. "Will you be at Deputy Parish's wedding tomorrow afternoon?"

"Won't everyone?"

Emma almost laughed at that. It was true. Micah Parish and Faith Williams had tried to arrange a quiet ceremony in Good Shepherd Church, but Reverend Fromberg had let the news slip to some of the Bible Study Group, and the next thing the couple knew, the whole county was in on the planning. The wedding ceremony would take place at Good Shepherd, but the reception, originally planned to be punch and cake at Nathan Tate's home, had turned into a covered-dish dinner in the high school gymnasium, with cases of champagne donated by several civic organizations. "Does Deputy Parish mind?" she asked Gage, knowing he worked with Parish.

"No." After a moment, he added to the unvarnished word, "Actually, I think both he and Faith are touched by it."

"Deputy Parish has earned a lot of respect in this county." Emma glanced up at Gage. "I hope he realizes that."

"I don't think that's something a man ever truly realizes."

That said a great deal about Gage Dalton, Emma thought. She wondered if he even suspected how much he had betrayed about himself with that simple remark. Probably not. She had the distinct feeling that he wasn't a man who ever consciously exposed himself.

And once again they had reached a conversational dead end. Emma wondered if this man was as maddening to talk to when you knew him well. If anyone ever even knew him well.

Well, it wasn't her problem. If he was simply going to respond to her gambits and make none of his own, then she might as well conduct the conversation with herself.

"I need to do something about a Christmas tree," she said. The thought had been plaguing her all day. "Ever since my great-grandfather, Eugene, built the house on Front Street, it's been traditional to have a large tree in the bay window. Lance Severn usually gets one for me and keeps it at the nursery, but he was sick this fall, and I never thought to make other arrangements."

"How big a tree?"

"Usually twelve feet. They built ceilings high in the old days, and anything shorter looks dwarfed." She sighed. "I guess I'll just have to put up a dwarf this year."

"Will Conard City be appalled?"

Startled by his teasing question, she darted a look up at him and found him smiling faintly down at her. Lord, it *was* possible for this cold, hard man to look friendly. Just a little. "Probably," she said, when she remembered the question. "It's a tradition. People come in from all over the county to see the decorations and trees on Front Street. On the Sunday evening before Christmas, the choirs from all the churches get together and go up and down the street caroling, and the homes are opened to offer hot cider and cookies to everyone who comes. It's one of the most beautiful events of the year."

And there was her house, thank goodness. She was hardly conscious of quickening her step in her eagerness to be indoors and safe, and away from this disturbing man.

They had only gone another dozen steps, not quite reaching the end of her shoveled driveway, when Gage gave a muffled curse. Startled, Emma looked up at him and then came to an abrupt halt.

The man was in agony, she realized. His entire face had turned into a rigid mask, and his lips had compressed into a thin, tight line. When she halted, he stopped immediately and closed his eyes. She longed to know what was wrong, but felt she had no right to ask. Instead she reacted with a woman's natural instincts, taking her elbow from his grasp and slipping her arm through his.

"Do you think," she asked quietly, "that you can make it a little farther? I'm sure I have some brandy."

His eyes snapped open and stared straight down into hers. His eyes burned, she thought uneasily, but couldn't look away. Their touch was like hot phosphorous. Hell's own archangel.

"Come," she said, instinct overriding conscious worries, and natural inclinations drowning caution. As spontaneously as she breathed, she slipped her arm around his waist and urged him forward. "Lean on me if it helps."

For an instant he stood rigid, resisting as if he had been carved on the spot from native stone, but then he stepped forward with her. His arm came to rest around her slender shoulders, and he leaned, just a very little, on her.

His limp had grown considerably more pronounced, Emma realized, biting her lip in distress. Lord, how could she have been so inconsiderate as to hurry the man the way she had? His pace had been slow from the outset, and if she had thought about it, she would have known that was because of his limp, not a gallant attempt to measure his step to hers.

And now, as he leaned a little on her and they moved so closely that her hip brushed his, she smelled the faint odor of whiskey on him. He must have been hurting fiercely, she thought, because Gage Dalton had lived long enough in

Conard County that if he was inclined to drink heavily, or even frequently, every soul would have long since heard about it. Therefore, he'd been drinking for medicinal purposes.

"Can you manage the steps?" she asked him as she guided him around back to the kitchen door. During the days, the rest of the house grew cold because she turned the heat way down, but the kitchen stayed warmer because of the water heater. Right now it was probably the only comfortable room in the house.

"Yeah." The word was clipped. He took his arm from her shoulders. "But I—"

"Oh, stuff it," Emma said impatiently. "You men are all such stubborn little boys at heart. You're hurting, Gage Dalton, and you may as well have a glass of brandy for the pain and warm yourself up a little in my kitchen. Then you can go back to being a macho idiot in a much more comfortable condition."

Silence greeted her speech, which was probably just as well, Emma thought as she fumbled her key from her purse and unlocked the door. She definitely needed to put a leash on her tongue. She was beginning to sound like her great-aunt Isabel, another Conard family spinster. Lord, what a horrifying thought!

Embarrassed by her own behavior, she hardly dared look at Gage as she waved him to a chair at the big round oak table and rushed about turning up the heat, starting coffee and stretching to reach the dusty bottle of brandy on the top shelf.

Without warning, a long, powerful arm reached past her and snagged the bottle.

And suddenly, for Emma, time froze as she found herself trapped between a large, hard, male body and the counter. Panic exploded blindingly in her head, and instinct caused her to twist away. The next thing she knew, she and Gage were on opposite sides of her kitchen, he frowning at her as he held the brandy bottle by its neck and watched her warily, she gasping as if someone had leeched all the air from the room.

After a moment Gage turned and reached for two of the snifters that had been on the same shelf. While Emma watched in disbelief and tried to regain control of her breathing and her hammering heart, he washed the two glasses at her sink and filled them with brandy. Then he sat at the table, placing one glass across from him for her.

"Claustrophobia's a terrible thing," he said, keeping his attention on his glass. "Sorry I crowded you." He lifted his snifter and sipped. "Great brandy."

Claustrophobia. That was all he thought it was. Relief that he had provided his own explanation and wouldn't question her weakened her. For nearly a minute she didn't move, simply stood and collected herself, more embarrassed than she had felt in years. First she had treated the man like one of the recalcitrant children she often dealt with at the library, and then she had turned crazy on him when he had simply tried to help her. Oh, Lord, Lord.

"It was kind of you to ask me in," Gage said presently, still not looking at her as she cowered in her corner. He stretched his left leg out and began to dig his knuckles into his powerful thigh muscles as if he could gouge out the ache. "The cold seems to make it worse."

Emma drew a deep, shuddery breath and tried to appear composed. "Do you hurt often?"

"All the time."

All the time? She couldn't imagine how awful that must be. Regaining control of her body, she moved to the table and sat across from him. The statement had been unvarnished, offering no further information, spoken matter-of-factly in a way that said he wanted no pity. An offering, she realized, to balance his discovery of her "claustrophobia." She wouldn't have expected such sensitivity from him. From any man, come to that. Emmaline Conard didn't have the world's highest opinion of men as a group.

She also owed him some kind of apology. "I'm sorry I lectured you the way I did about coming inside."

He looked up and met her gaze. His eyes, she noticed for the first time, were a stormy gray-green, like the sky before a bad squall. It was an unusual, beautiful color.

"That's okay," he said, and the corners of his mouth lifted in a faint, lopsided smile. "I'm used to it. When I was a kid, I don't think I ever got out of the library without at least one lecture from the librarian."

Emma was surprised to feel herself smiling back at him. "Was she such a dragon?"

"I always thought so, but in retrospect, I think I was a hell-raiser."

"I'm surprised you spent any time at all there, then."

Gage gave a small shake of his head. "I always loved books. Still do. All the lectures in the world couldn't keep me away from them."

Emma suddenly had a poignant vision of Gage Dalton as a small boy. There were a few young hell-raisers who came to her own library regularly, and they were all poor, defiant and wild, and starved for attention, affection and ideas. Once again, she didn't think Gage knew how much he had betrayed about himself.

"The coffee's ready," she said after a moment. "Would you like some?"

"Please. Black."

He looked at her then, but she forced herself to turn away and get the cups. He made her uneasy. Not the kind of uneasiness she felt in the dark, but something else altogether. His gaze was hypnotic, somehow. Fiery. Sulfurous. Brimstone. A startled laugh almost escaped her. Lord, how her imagination took off sometimes!

She was like a candle flame, Gage thought. Her red hair was caught back tightly into a clip at her nape, but he suspected that hair was untamable. Judging by the cloud of it below her barrette, it would, if freed, instantly become a springy mass of tight, wild curls, a halo of fire. She had probably hated that hair all her life long.

She was a little taller than average, sturdily built, not a fragile porcelain doll, but a strong woman. The kind of woman who would have pioneered the West and survived. No one would ever call her delicate, but the delicacy was there nonetheless. It was there in the fine grain of her pale skin, in the faint blue veins apparent through it. It was there in those smoky, soft green eyes when they darted his way.

Something long dormant stirred deep inside Gage. He wanted to step on it, squash it ruthlessly as if it were a snake. Instead, he faced it dead on. For the first time since—since *then,* he was seeing a woman as a woman, reacting to a woman as a woman. He wouldn't have minded it half so much if he had reacted this way to Molly Garrity, the waitress at Mahoney's. Molly was an uncomplicated woman who was ever ready to ease a man's physical needs.

Gage didn't particularly care whether he ever felt desire again, but if he had to start feeling it again, he wished to hell it could be directed at someone besides Emma Conard. She was apparently, by all reports, a dyed-in-the-wool spinster who took strips out of the hide of any man foolish enough to approach her as a woman. And even if that wasn't true, she wasn't the kind of woman who was meant for casual affairs, and he would never again be in the market for anything else.

He kept his gaze on the coffee cup as she carried it over to him and tried not to notice that her slacks and bulky sweater didn't entirely conceal a well-proportioned shape. "Thanks."

"You're welcome. Will you excuse me for a second? I want to get the mail from out front."

"Sure."

He allowed his eyes to stray for a moment, to watch her derriere sway gently as she passed through the door into a darkened room beyond. Then, in the brief privacy, he closed his eyes and tensed, inwardly battering down the wolves of emotional and physical pain that never stopped howling at the walls of ice behind which he confined them. His constant companions, they had long since ceased to frighten him, but they still tormented him, some times more than others.

The sound of Emma's returning footsteps alerted him. When she reentered the kitchen, she found Gage sipping his coffee. She tossed a small stack of mail on the table and sat across from him.

"I wonder what this could be," she said, pointing at a large brown envelope. "I don't get anything at this address except bills and junk mail." She gave him a small smile. "The good stuff all comes to the library."

He glanced at the envelope. It sure didn't look like junk mail. A stamp for the exact amount of postage sat crookedly in the corner, and the addressing had been done sloppily on a typewriter. "Don't mind me," he said. "Satisfy your curiosity."

She took him at his word. He felt a rare twinge of amusement when he saw her remove a letter opener from the drawer behind her to neatly slit the flap. He should have guessed she wouldn't be the tear-it-open type.

"The postmark is Laramie," she remarked. "I used to know some people..."

Her voice trailed off as she drew a large, glossy, black-and-white photograph from the envelope. As Gage watched, her expression changed from perplexity to consternation, and then to something very like shock. Her hand trembled until the photo shook like a leaf in the wind. Suddenly, she flung it from her. Closing her eyes, she covered her mouth with her hand.

"Miss Emma?" Gage immediately swung around in his chair and leaned across the table. A glance at the photograph told him it showed nothing but a hammered-metal dagger, probably an archaeological artifact. Nothing to cause such distress. "Miss Emma? What's wrong?"

"I...don't know." She gave a shaky laugh and opened her eyes. Gage noted that she was careful to avoid glancing at the photograph. "When I looked at that thing it was as if...I don't know. A chill hit me without warning."

He reached for the picture. "Do you mind?"

She shook her head and wrapped her arms around herself as if she was freezing. "Be my guest. I must be coming down with something."

The last was more a comment to herself, and Gage treated it as such as he studied the dagger. It was a simple instrument, crudely shaped at hilt and pommel, and scored with cross-hatching for decoration and grip. The blade appeared to be manufactured of the same beaten metal, but the edge had been honed on a whetting stone; fine polishing marks were visible. In the very top of the pommel, a stone of some kind had been set. It might have been glass or a gemstone of high quality. Impossible to tell in the gray tones of the photo.

"It looks like some kind of archaeological artifact," he remarked after a moment. "An old one, I'd think. It's crude." He glanced up quickly to take stock of her reaction and found her staring at the photo as if it were a live snake that might at any moment strike. "Miss Emma?"

She blinked. Slowly her hazy green eyes lifted to his stormy ones. "Sorry. That thing...that thing is hideous!"

Her reaction was extreme, but Gage didn't argue with it. "Was there a letter in the envelope? Somebody looking for contributions for a museum or something?" Her reaction was rousing his investigative instincts, he realized. There was something else going on here.

She reached for the envelope immediately. "Of course. Why didn't I...? Nothing." She dropped the envelope. "Of course. That's what it is. The letter just got left out. Why didn't I think of that?" She gave a brittle, short laugh. "Well, I'll just throw it out."

As she reached for it, Gage drew it back. "If you don't want it, would you mind if I kept it?"

She settled back on her seat, her eyes wide as they studied him. "Well, I...certainly not. You're welcome to it. But why?"

He shrugged. "It looks familiar somehow. I'd like to place the period. It's just an old hobby of mine."

"Please. Keep it."

"Thanks." He reached for the envelope, slipped the photo back into it and tucked the whole inside his half-unzipped leather jacket. "Great coffee, Miss Emma. We need you to come over to the sheriff's office and show us how to do it."

The color began to return to her cheeks, and while she didn't seem quite as relaxed as before, neither was she as uptight as she had been when she saw the photograph. A puzzle, Gage thought. A real puzzle. He was going to find out everything possible about that dagger and see if he could get to the bottom of it. He had never been able to resist a puzzle.

He would have liked to question her about her reaction, find out more about how the picture had made her feel, what connections she had made when she saw it, but he guessed she wasn't about to become a passive interrogation subject. No, most likely Miss Emma would throw him out on his butt.

And out on his butt was where he ought to be, he thought, tossing down the last of his brandy. Emma Conard had done a rare, neighborly thing when she invited him in, but she hadn't asked him to take up residence. A polite guest would take his leave now that he was a little warmer.

He gathered his muscles a little at a time, getting ready to stand. His slowness was partly reluctance, but partly the fact that, since the explosion that had turned his life into a living hell, the simple things were no longer quite so easy to do. These days, getting out of bed was an achievement.

Finally, feeling that he could rise without groaning or losing his balance, he shoved himself up from the chair. The redistribution of his weight always caused a sharp pain in his hip and leg, but he was prepared for that and hardly noticed it.

"My thanks for the brandy and coffee, Miss Emma. I'll say good night now."

She didn't argue; he hadn't expected her to. She thanked him for escorting her home and then watched him through the storm door as he limped down her driveway toward the street.

Once there, he turned away from the center of town, planning to walk until the demons subsided.

In her front yard, though, he saw a small, discreet sign sticking up from a snowbank, lettered in black on white: Room Available. He paused and looked up at her house, a rambling two-story frame structure with a wide porch. It sure would be nicer than the rooms above Mahoney's, he thought. Quieter. And it wouldn't stink like fry cooking and stale beer all the time.

Miss Emma would never rent a room to a man, he thought. Never.

But he turned anyway and limped back around to her kitchen door to ask. As he came back up the driveway, he could see her through the row of three windows beside the door. She was clearing the coffee cups and snifters from the table and carrying them toward the sink, but as she came back to the table with a dishcloth, she suddenly paused. For a moment she stared fixedly into space, and then she shuddered, closed her eyes and wrapped her arms tightly around herself.

Gage halted and hesitated, unsure whether to disturb her. Could she still be upset by that photograph? It seemed such a crazy thing for her to get bent out of shape over. But she *had* gotten bent out of shape. Seriously so. Something about that photo had first perplexed her and then frightened her. He wished he knew what connection her mind had made that had caused her to consider the picture such a threat.

As he watched, she shook herself visibly and then bent over the table to wipe it clean. Hesitating no longer, Gage strode up to her door. She jumped when he knocked, then showed utter relief when she recognized him. She hurried to open the door.

"Mr. Dalton! Is something wrong?"

"No, ma'am. I just saw your sign out front." He shifted his stance, wondering why the words were suddenly so difficult to speak. "I might be interested in the room."

"Oh!" She bit her lower lip and studied him. He was standing on the second step, so they were at eye level with one another, and waiting impassively for her answer. "Mr. Dalton," she said finally, "please don't take this personally, but I really don't think it would be wise for me to rent the room to a gentleman. This is a small town...." She trailed off, obviously at a loss.

Gage nodded and gave her a faint, crooked half smile. "Thought so. Never hurts to ask, though. Good night, Miss Emma."

As he walked down the dark driveway, snow began to fall gently. He heard the door close behind him, as so many doors had closed behind him in life.

Just another closed door, he told himself. That was all. Just another closed door.

Chapter 2

Emma watched Gage walk away and felt like a world-class heel. But really, she couldn't take a man as a roomer. The whole of Conard County would become convinced that the starchy Miss Emmaline Conard had suddenly developed a case of round heels. Some of them would probably even demand that she be removed from her job so that their dear little children wouldn't be corrupted by her influence.

Not that Emma cared about such narrow-minded people. She really didn't. The judge had raised her to set her own course and live up to her own standards; he had taught her that you couldn't please all of the people all of the time. But the judge had also taught her that appearances were everything. A man could be hanged for appearances, quite literally, and a murderer could walk away a free man for the same reason.

If Emma really had an affair, she wouldn't be ashamed if everyone knew about it, would hardly care what they thought. But she wasn't going to be hanged for a sheep when she was a mere lamb. No way.

Still . . . She bit her lip and watched Gage disappear into the dark. A few gently falling snowflakes caught the light from the kitchen and sparkled.

It was almost Christmas, and he looked so alone. Where would he go, what would he do, for the holidays? Did he have family somewhere he could join? Or would he spend the holiday treeless, cheerless, alone, going to Maude's diner for Christmas dinner?

Well, it wasn't her problem, she told herself as she finished straightening the kitchen. Not her problem at all. Gage Dalton was a mature adult, and if he was alone it was by choice. Just as she was alone by choice.

Snapping the light switch off, she headed for her bedroom at the rear of the house. As long as she didn't have a roomer, she kept the upstairs closed off to conserve on heat. Even after five years, it felt odd to be using her father's bedroom, but she really couldn't afford not to. Heating all of this old house all winter without a roomer to help with the expense would devour her savings in no time at all.

As a small child, she had come into this room to spend an occasional night with her widowed grandmother. Her father and mother had slept upstairs in a room right across the hall from her own, and her brother Gene had been right next door.

An invitation to spend the night with Grandma had been exciting, special. Magic. Even now, closing her eyes, she could remember lying in the big old bed with the blanket drawn up to her chin, watching as Grandma let down her astonishing hair. All day long she kept it neatly tucked into a roll under a net, but at night she brushed it out to her hips and then braided it for sleeping. To four-year-old Emma, that hair had seemed to come from nowhere, a surprising magician's trick.

When Emma had been six, Grandma had died. By the time she was eight, her mother and brother Gene were both gone, killed in an accident on a snowy road in the mountains. The old house, once so full, had become incredibly empty, and it was years before Emma grew used to having the upstairs to herself, used to Judge Conard sleeping in Grandma's room.

Nothing had changed. The walls were still covered in dark green silk wallpaper; the curtains were yellowing sheers that covered even yellower shades. The huge walnut armoire still covered most of one wall, the tall walnut highboy graced the other. The master bath boasted a black linoleum floor and a claw-footed tub that was probably worth a great deal of money.

And now Emma slept in the same bed that had served all her forebears since Grandfather Eustace came back from the trenches in France and announced he was leaving the ranch to his brother Ralph and going to law school. Ralph had lost the ranch during the Great Depression, but Eustace had prospered, eventually bringing his son, Eugene, Emma's father, into the law firm of Conard and Conard.

Emma's brother Gene had been destined to be the next Conard lawyer until he had died on that snowy mountain road. Emma had tried to fill his place, and the judge had encouraged her, but after she was assaulted she just plain couldn't do it. The judge never said anything, never criticized or bemoaned fate, but Emma had never been able to believe he wasn't disappointed in her. He had wanted a lawyer and gotten a librarian, and when he died, the law firm died with him.

Now she slept in a bed she had always felt too small for and rattled around in this big old house like the seeds in a dried up old gourd, and she was trapped, because she had no alternatives left. The world outside Conard County had proved itself evil and cruel. The mere thought of stepping outside the safety of this county petrified her. She told herself it didn't matter, that she didn't want to leave anyway, but occasionally she admitted there was a huge difference between staying because she wanted to and staying because she couldn't leave.

Gage Dalton wouldn't be the only person in Conard County spending Christmas alone, Emma thought wearily as she at last climbed between cool sheets. Nor would he be the only one doing so by choice. After a couple of misera-

ble holidays as the fifth wheel at friends' celebrations, she
had taken to turning down every one of the well-meant in-
vitations she received. It was easier by far to be alone than
to be an onlooker.

She was tired tonight, she realized as sleep swiftly sucked
her into a lazy whirlpool. So sleepy.

The golden dagger hovered above her, hammered metal,
gleaming evilly, the ruby on its pommel twinkling like a
teardrop of blood. Suddenly it lifted and flashed downward.

Emma screamed and sat bolt upright in the dark. She was
alone. The house was empty, silent save for the familiar
rattle from the heating ducts as hot air rushed through them.
Gasping, she fell back against her pillows and waited for her
heart to stop galloping.

That awful photograph must have set off a nightmare.
But what a nightmare! It had been years since she'd had
even a moderately bad dream. Years, in fact, since she had
even been aware of dreaming.

And it was silly, so silly, to have gotten so upset over that
photo. Certainly Gage had been right when he said it was
probably a fund-raiser for some museum. What else on
earth could it possibly be?

But her heart continued to pound in a painful rhythm,
and in the dark she kept seeing the flash of gold, now from
the corner of her eye, as if she couldn't quite bring it into
view. What was wrong with her? It was just an old artifact
of some kind or another, nothing threatening at all. But how
did she know it was golden? Why was she so convinced that
the stone on the pommel was bloodred? Why had a simple
photograph invaded her dreams?

Disturbed, she finally gave in and turned on the lamp beside her bed. The Tiffany shade, a treasure of her grandmother's, cast spangles of brilliant color around the room.
Just then the regulator clock in the dining room sounded the
hour with three deep chimes.

Surrounded by familiar and beloved sounds and sights,
Emma snuggled back under her blankets and waited for

sleep to return. It wouldn't be the first time in her adult life
that she had slept with the light on. What a bundle of fears
and nerves she was, and she couldn't even remember why
she had become this way.

But that was a blessing, she reminded herself. She never
wanted to remember what had been done to her. Never.
Traumatic amnesia was a heaven-sent blessing, and not even
to be relieved of her present fears did she want to remember what had caused them.

It was shortly after three when Gage realized he was once
again standing outside Emmaline Conard's house. The
hours of walking had finally battered down the grinding
pain in his leg and worn out the wolves that gnawed at his
soul. He had intended to return to his rooms above Mahoney's to rest up for Micah's wedding, but somehow he had
strayed this way.

Why?

Something was wrong. Something was mortally wrong.
God, he hated this feeling! Every time he got it, something
awful happened, and most of the time there wasn't a damn
thing he could do to prevent it.

Smothering a curse, he turned sharply away from the
Conard home and headed toward Mahoney's as fast as his
limp would permit. Never again, by God. Never again. Involvement carried a price he wasn't prepared to pay. Not
again.

Emma thought Gage Dalton resembled a black hole
amidst the swirl of wedding festivities. Nearly five hundred
people crowded the high school gym, snacking from the
smorgasbord of covered dishes everyone had brought and
dancing to the amplified sounds of the school principal's
pop-music collection. Gage, however, sat in splendid solitude in a dimly lit corner far from the hub of the excitement.

He had shed his customary black jeans and shirt for a
charcoal gray suit in honor of the occasion, but the change
did little to alleviate the sense of darkness and gloom that

traveled with him. For a wild instant Emma actually wondered if, like a black hole, he swallowed all the sound and light around him. Perhaps if she stepped close enough, she would enter the bubble of silence that seemed to shield him from the world around him.

For all that, she continued to ease her way through the crowd in his general direction, taking care to avoid Don Fenster as she did so. Childish as it was, she and Don hadn't spoken for nearly twenty years, ever since Emma had popped him in the nose. It wasn't that she was still mad at him, but every time he saw her, his lip curled in a way that killed any desire on her part to speak to him. He'd been a brat as a child, she thought now, and as a grown man he was still a brat. *She* would have been perfectly content to let bygones be bygones, but not Don. No, he wanted to turn a childhood argument into the Hatfields and McCoys.

Sniffing in unconscious disapproval, she returned her attention to Gage Dalton. Everyone else here was laughing and talking and having a wonderful time, and it seemed terribly wrong to Emma that he should be sitting alone in that dark corner.

Just as she approached the table, Jeff Cumberland, one of the county's most prominent ranchers, settled into a folding chair across from Gage. Emma reached them just in time to hear Jeff say, "Have you and Micah learned anything new about my cattle?"

Everyone in Conard County had heard that Jeff had lost three of his best cattle, two heifers and a prize bull, to the mutilations that were an on-again, off-again mystery from Kentucky to Montana. Periodically livestock were found with their genitals and tongues missing. Experts contended that the apparent surgical precision of the always bloodless wounds was due to shrinkage of the flesh, and that however strange the mutilations might appear, they were in fact normal predator activity. Farmers and ranchers were not so easily convinced that any predator would take only the tongue and genitals and leave everything else intact. Since nothing could be proved one way or the other, most people had come to an uneasy acceptance of the mutilations.

Last month, however, Jeff Cumberland had had three cattle mutilated in one short week. The Sheriff's Department evidently tried to keep things quiet but had failed. Ever since then, Emma had sensed a restless anger among the ranchers, a frustrated need to do something to defend their herds and catch the culprits.

When she pulled out a chair and joined Jeff and Gage at the table, the two men acknowledged her with distracted nods.

"Not one damn thing," Gage said in answer to Jeff's question.

Jeff's jaw tightened. "When the experts at the lab don't even agree—" He bit off the sentence, leaving it incomplete.

"The experts don't agree?" Emma repeated. She hadn't heard this before. "What do you mean, they don't agree? I thought they always said it was normal predation."

Both men stared at her as if they had just realized she was there. She hadn't been meant to hear this, Emma understood. Gage looked a little perturbed, and Jeff looked dismayed.

"They do," Gage said shortly. "That's what they always say."

Emma looked at Jeff, who nodded. "That's what they say, Emma."

"Then why did you say…?" Her voice trailed off and she looked sternly at Jeff. "I don't like being lied to, Jeffrey Cumberland, and I'm certainly no gossip you need to hide things from!"

Jeff threw up his hands. "Enough!" he said. "I've got enough on my mind, and I'm not going to be lectured to like a schoolboy by you or anybody else. You've turned into a scold, Emmaline Conard. Your daddy would shake his head!"

Emma watched Jeff snatch his hat up from the table and stalk away. Something inside her hurt, she realized. Jeff's angry words had wounded her. Had she really turned into a scold? Oh, Lord, what if she *was* turning into another Great-aunt Isabel?

Gage's voice pierced her thoughts. "It sounds as if you two go back a long way."

"Jeff is my cousin," Emma admitted, trying to stifle the hurt and appear unconcerned. "He's older, and when I was really little, he often used to look after me. But what about his cattle, Mr. Dalton?" She searched his impassive face, trying to find any clue. "I know as well as anyone how much Jeff has invested in his breeding stock, and it's a lot more than money. If someone is deliberately trying to destroy them—"

Gage silenced her in an instant by suddenly reaching out and catching her chin in his hard, warm palm. He turned her face up to him, and suddenly their eyes were only inches apart, their mouths every bit as close. Emma forgot what she had been saying, what she had been thinking. For the first time in a decade, she was close to a man, aware of a man, and feeling like a woman. Like a whole woman.

"Miss Emma," he murmured in that husky, ruined, *sexy* voice, "do you think we could discuss this someplace less public?"

Before she could find her voice, let alone an appropriate word in response to that utterly suggestive question, a mocking voice intruded.

"Better look out, Dalton. She'll take a strip out of a man's hide for a lot less than what you're doing right now."

The remark sounded teasing, but Emma knew better. She wrenched her chin free of Gage's grip and glared up at Earl Newton. Earl had been the person responsible for starting the rumor that Emma had succumbed to the blandishments of a traveling man while she was away at college, had even hinted that she had born this nonexistent man a child and given it up for adoption. Emma presumed Earl had started the nastiness because she had repeatedly refused to go out with him. At least, she could think of no other reason for starting such a vicious rumor. All that was a decade in the past, of course, but Emma still heard references to her "traveling man."

Oh, how she wished there were something she could say that would wipe the smirk off Earl's face forever! But she had learned, painfully, that the only way to handle Earl and others like him was to pretend they had no effect on her at all.

She averted her face, intending to ignore Earl as if he had suddenly fallen through the floor and vanished. Much to her amazement, Gage shoved his chair back from the table and rose stiffly to face the other man.

"Maybe," Gage said to Earl, "you'd like to try picking on somebody your own size, Newton. We could go talk this over *outside.*"

The words were softly spoken, but menacing nonetheless. Emma wasn't at all surprised when Earl suddenly shifted uneasily and claimed he'd just been teasing.

"Sure," said Gage. "Me, too. I don't think Miss Emma much appreciates it, though, and I can understand why."

Earl stole a quick look at Emma. "Sorry, Miss Emma. Just joking."

Emma watched Earl scuttle off and tried to control the urge to just run and hide in the nearest dark corner. No doubt Gage had heard about her "traveling man," and he'd been in town only a few months. No doubt he, too, had heard how she chewed up any man who asked her out.

"It's not true," she heard herself say. "It's really not true. I just...don't date." She couldn't even look at him.

"That's your prerogative, ma'am. None of my business. Or anybody else's." He shifted his weight and bent a little, as if he was trying to ease stiff muscles. "I need to get out of here. I need to walk."

The words were said in a forceful, blunt tone that deprived them of casualness. Emma looked up swiftly and understood that Gage was getting claustrophobic from pain. She had felt like that when she was in the hospital, as if the only way to cope with the agony was to move and keep moving. She rose.

"Would you like some company?" she asked. "I'm ready to go home, and my car's still in the shop. I'd like to walk, but if you—"

He cut her off with an abrupt wave of his hand. "Sure. Let's go."

They waited just long enough to see the bride and groom make good their escape, and then they escaped themselves into the cold late afternoon. The sun was nearing the horizon, ready to plunge Conard County into another long winter night. Last night's dusting of fresh snow crunched beneath their boots, and their breath puffed in white clouds.

"It's colder," Emma remarked. Colder than yesterday. What she really wanted to do was tell him that none of what he had heard about her was true. For years she had lived with the shadows of those rumors, had accepted her father's assurance that the people who really counted, the ones who knew her and cared, wouldn't believe any such trash. Gage Dalton, however, didn't know her. He was new to the county, and if he heard the rumors, he would probably believe them. For some reason, she couldn't stand the thought.

She sighed and told herself it was stupid to worry about such things at this late date. It was such an old story, and Gage wouldn't even care if it were true. Why should he? And why was she making such a mountain out of an old, old molehill?

"I apologize for the way I hushed you in there," Gage said abruptly. "Nate wants this business with Jeff's cattle kept as much under wraps as possible, and I think it's wise. Upsetting half the people in the county won't help anyone, least of all those of us who are investigating the matter."

Remembering the *way* he had hushed her, Emma felt momentarily breathless. Just because she was dedicated to spinsterhood didn't mean she didn't have a woman's normal drives. Gage had reminded her forcibly of that fact, though she was sure it had been the farthest thing from his mind. No, he had simply seized the quickest way of silencing her in such a public place, a way that would put an entirely different color on their conversation, should anyone wonder what they had been discussing. A brilliant move on his part, she thought. Brilliant. It had sure fooled Earl, whose approach had probably precipitated Gage's action.

"I guess I can understand why Sheriff Tate doesn't want everybody seeing aliens behind every bush and snowdrift," Emma said. The sky was taking on that deep, deep blue cast to the east, the dark brightness of evening. "But there *was* something unusual about what happened to Jeff's cattle. Everyone knows that, Mr. Dalton."

With automatic gallantry, he gripped her elbow as they stepped from the curb into a snowy street. There was surprisingly little traffic, Emma thought. Probably because almost everyone was partying at the gym. She stuffed her hands deeper into the pockets of her parka and tucked her chin down closer to her chest, trying to retain every bit of warmth she could.

They walked nearly two more blocks before Gage answered her. "Everyone *believes* that, Miss Emma. Nobody *knows* it."

"What did the lab say?"

He glanced down at her and then changed the subject with a ruthlessness that left her breathless. "Did you ever figure out why that photograph of the dagger scared you spitless last night?"

They passed Maude's diner and Good Shepherd Church, and were walking past the courthouse when Emma found enough breath to speak. "No," she said.

"I wondered."

And then, before good sense could overrule her, she blurted out the rest of it. "I had nightmares about it last night. Awful nightmares. I kept seeing it swing down at me, as if it was going to stab me." Oh, Lord, that sounded completely and totally neurotic! *Why* had she ever confided that?

"That's awful," Gage said after a moment. "I've had nightmares like that."

Startled, she looked up at him. "About knives?"

"About bombs."

Bombs. Oh, God. Bombs. She didn't need him to explain why he had nightmares about bombs. His scarred face was explanation enough. "But I've never seen that dagger before," she argued. "Never."

Gage remained silent as they walked by the library. "Maybe not," he said presently. "Maybe it reminded you of something else. Who knows? I just meant that I know about those kinds of nightmares, is all. No fun.''

"No," she agreed. She stole another upward glance at him, her gaze skimming the shiny burned tissue, the jagged scar that slashed his cheek. A bomb. She looked quickly away, not wanting him to catch her staring. He didn't seem to be self-conscious about it, but he might just be good at hiding the fact that he was. She was good at that herself. Most people never guessed just how thin Emma Conard's skin really was.

A bomb. Good grief. Had it been directed at him? Or had it been some kind of accident? What had he done during all those years before he came to Conard County? What had driven him to come to the "ends of the earth"? She wished she had the nerve to ask him, even though she knew perfectly well that he would never answer her. In fact, now that she thought about it, it was astonishing that he had even mentioned the bomb. She seriously doubted that Gage Dalton ever let anything just *slip*. So why had he told her?

He was silent so long that when he at last spoke, Emma was nearly startled.

"Is the dream still bothering you now?" he asked.

"A little," she admitted. "It's like I can't quite shake it. I'll be doing something else and suddenly see the dagger in my mind's eye." She gave a deprecating laugh. "It'll wear off, I'm sure."

"I'm sure," he agreed noncommittally.

When her house came within sight, still a block up the street, Emma saw her discreet black-and-white sign advertising for a roomer and thought of Gage's interest in it. It seemed odd, when she thought about it, that a bachelor man would have any desire to live under a spinster's roof. Surely it would crimp his life-style?

"Where do you live now?" she heard herself asking him.

"Above Mahoney's."

"Oh." How unpleasant. "I imagine it's noisy?"

"Until closing," he agreed. "It always smells like stale beer and fried food."

"How macho."

He glanced sharply down at her and caught the teasing twinkle in her hazy green eyes. Slowly, like the reluctant opening of a rusty door, he smiled. It spread from the corners of his mouth, where it drew a crooked, curved line, pulled off center by his scars. It crept up to the corners of his eyes, creasing them attractively, and then eased the bleakness of his gray-green eyes.

Emma caught her breath. It was like watching a glorious sunrise to see Gage Dalton genuinely smile. Night vanished, replaced by a warm glow.

"Are you a teaser, Miss Emma?" he asked softly.

"I'm afraid so," she admitted, giving him a smile in return. "You need to understand that I was raised here, but in a different way than most women. Men are men in Conard County, Mr. Dalton, but most of it is pure pretense."

"And you see through it."

She shrugged. "I never thought it made a man less of a man if he scraped the manure off his boots at the door."

"Your father never needed to scrape his boots, did he?"

"No, he was a judge. But he did all those other manly things, from hunting every fall to bending his elbow at Mahoney's. It's expected hereabouts. The difference between my father and many of the other men around here is that he was aware of what he was doing. It was politic, and he did it politically."

"Is that why you don't date? Because you think you see through them?"

"No." Her lips compressed tightly, and she quickened her pace, not caring if she caused him another spasm in his leg. His question had been mocking, when she had only been joking with him. "I have a very high respect for quite a number of the men in this county, Mr. Dalton. Sheriff Tate. Jeff Cumberland. Tom Preston. Shall I make you a list?"

He caught her elbow and stopped her. "I can't walk this fast, Miss Emma," he told her quietly. Frankly.

She felt like a complete and total jerk. She had been teasing, but she had come off sounding like an utter snob. Then, with an unforgivable lack of courtesy, she had hurried her pace, knowing full well she would cause him pain.

Slowly, ashamed of herself, she faced him and raised her eyes to his. "I'm sorry. I'm really not a snob, and I was only joking." She didn't say anything about walking too fast. He might mistake anything she said as pity, and she was far from feeling any pity for this dark, dangerous man.

He studied her a moment and then gave her a faint smile. "And I don't mind scraping the manure from my boots."

She didn't want to go home, she realized as they walked steadily closer to her house. Suddenly she didn't want to be alone there, didn't want to rattle around listening to the endless ticking of the old clocks, waiting for the regulator to chime six so she could start preparing her solitary dinner.

Just then her foot hit a patch of ice hidden beneath the fresh, undisturbed powder of last night's new snow. She gasped and tensed, expecting to land on her bottom, but strong hands caught her halfway down, catching her beneath her arms.

"Damn!" Gage whispered the word, a short sharp exclamation, and then sucked a hissing breath of air through his teeth as the pain swamped him. From his spine, it rolled through him in tidal waves of agony, until cold sweat beaded his face and even his teeth seemed to hurt. For an endless span of time that felt like an eternity but could only be a few seconds, he held Emma suspended as he was frozen in the grip of a pain so fierce it completely shut him down.

Then, gently, he lowered her to the ground.

Emma scrambled immediately to her feet, concerned because of the way he had sworn and then caught his breath. One look at him as he stood there white lipped and half doubled over, with sweat beading his face, told her just how much he hurt. She didn't bother scolding him for catching her, didn't bother asking what she could do. People in severe pain tended to get very impatient at that kind of thing.

So she simply waited for the worst to pass. When he started to straighten, she stepped to his side and slipped her arm around his waist just as she had last night.

"I still have that brandy," she commented. "And with the holidays coming, I went out this morning and bought a few bottles of good Scotch and bourbon."

Gage released a long sigh and let his arm come to rest around her shoulders as they continued toward her house. "I could do with a stiff Scotch," he said after a moment.

"I thought you might. But don't you have something stronger you could take? Some kind of pain pill?"

He shook his head.

"Why not?" She felt indignant. "Surely—"

He interrupted without apology. "I refuse to turn myself into an addict, Miss Emma. Any kind of addict."

She could respect that, but it didn't make her feel any better to think of this man hurting and unable to escape the pain for even a brief while. "Will it always be like this?" she asked.

"I don't know."

She hadn't turned the heat down earlier when she left for the reception, so she took Gage into the house through the front door this time. He settled into the Kennedy rocker with obvious relief, as her father often had when his back troubled him.

Emma hurried to fix him a Scotch, a double, though he didn't ask for it, and told him she would be back as soon as she started a pot of coffee.

He probably wouldn't mind being alone for a few minutes, she told herself. A few minutes to grimace and groan and shift around until he got reasonably comfortable would be welcome, she was sure. Maybe he would like to use the heating pad. And maybe he would be offended if she offered. Men could be so asinine about things like that.

Standing in the kitchen, waiting for the coffee to finish brewing, Emma suddenly had the feeling that she was looking through some kind of distorted glass. The familiar room looked different somehow, and the familiar sounds of the house seemed . . . threatening.

Uneasy, she rubbed her arms and looked around the room. It was as if . . . as if the house had been invaded somehow. Nothing appeared to be out of place, everything looked just as it always had, but the sense of invasion refused to dissipate.

Out of the corner of her eye, she thought she saw something move. Whirling around, her heart hammering, she looked toward the windows but saw nothing. Nothing. That didn't keep her from hurrying over and drawing all the café curtains against the night.

What was wrong with her? she wondered edgily as she hurried to prepare a tray with mugs and some leftover chocolate-chip cookies she had baked for the children's story hour. Nightmares, that ridiculous reaction to the photograph of what was surely some kind of historical artifact, and now this sense of...of...

Unseen watchers.

A shudder rippled through her even as she scolded herself for silliness. She didn't believe in ghosts or things that went bump in the night. Even as a child such things had never troubled her, except for that brief time when, at four, she had become convinced there was an alligator under her bed. She had lived alone in this house for five years now, and never once had she felt uneasy.

Shaking herself, she thrust her anxiousness aside and filled two mugs with hot, rich coffee. It was a blend she ordered specially, the one small indulgence she allowed herself on her tight budget. She hoped Gage liked it.

He was sitting in the rocker with his eyes closed, the empty highball glass in his hand. As soon as she stepped into the room, even though she tried to be quiet, his eyes snapped open. He didn't move, just watched her set the tray on the coffee table and settle herself on the couch.

He didn't want to move, she realized. He must have found a good position. Leaning over, she took the glass from his hand. "More?"

"No, thanks. That was plenty."

"Coffee, then?"

"Please."

She leaned over again to pass the mug to him, so he didn't have to reach.

"You're a kind woman, Emma Conard," he said, surprising her.

She glanced up from her own mug and found he had once again closed his eyes. "Not really. It's just that I know what it's like to hurt, and what it's like to find the one position on earth where it almost doesn't hurt. There were a couple of times when I might have killed a nurse if I'd had a gun."

A short, husky laugh escaped him. "I know all about that."

"I thought you might. Would you care for a cookie?"

What he really wanted, she thought a few minutes later, was to sleep. His eyes kept closing when the conversation lagged, and his head rested against the back of the rocker.

Well, this was ridiculous, Emma decided. Rising, she told Gage she would be back in a few minutes. Only she didn't come back. Instead, she went to her bedroom at the back of the house and changed into jeans, warm socks and a favorite green sweatshirt. She took her time brushing her stubborn hair into a relatively neat ponytail, scrubbing off the makeup she hated to wear and applied only for special occasions. And when at last she crept back to the living room, she found Gage sleeping soundly in the rocker.

Satisfied, she went to the kitchen and started preparing a considerably larger meal than she would have cooked for herself alone. It distracted her from the deepening winter night and the persistent uncomfortable feeling that she was being watched. That something terrible was about to happen.

When Gage awoke, it was to the golden glow of lamplight and the mouth-watering aroma of baking chicken. For an instant he wondered where he was, but then he remembered Emma Conard telling him she would be back in a minute. Judging by the enticing smells wafting his way, he'd been asleep for some time. Turning his head a little, he saw her. Looking all of eighteen, she was curled up in a corner of the couch, her feet tucked beneath her. Absently, she played with a corkscrew of her red hair while she read a paperback book.

He watched her turn a page and wondered why she had let him sleep like this and why she seemed to be so unperturbed by his rudeness. He must have been snoozing for a couple of hours. Most hostesses surely would have found some way to wake him. He certainly wouldn't have blamed anyone for shaking him awake and sending him on his way.

Now that he was awake, though, he should say something, apologize, take his leave. Instead, comfortable in the rocker as he was seldom comfortable, he sat perfectly still and watched her read.

That hair of hers was beautiful, he thought, and wished again that he could see it unbound. Her skin was creamy, like living satin, and he imagined that if he touched it, she would feel warm and smooth. Her mouth was generous, the kind of mouth that made men fantasize a million and one things, all of them erotic. Why didn't she date? Had she been mistreated by some boyfriend?

Suddenly, as if she felt his gaze on her, Emma looked up. When she saw he was awake, she smiled.

"Good nap?" she asked.

"You should have tossed me out, Miss Emma. That was incredibly rude of me."

She shook her head. "You needed it, and I didn't mind at all. Dinner will be ready in another half hour. If you don't want to move, I can bring you a tray in here."

Damn it, he couldn't believe this. The woman didn't even know him. Why should she go to so much trouble?

He was a hard man, she thought, and he didn't know what to make of her. So she told him. "Look, Mr. Dalton, you've been kind enough to escort me home on two occasions. Apart from that, you're a neighbor. You needed to sleep, you obviously found the rocker comfortable enough to sleep in, and I'd have to be some kind of twisted, heartless beast to wake you up and throw you out. Besides, I lived with a great deal of pain after my—after my accident years ago, and I know how difficult it can be to get any sleep at all. As for dinner, I was going to cook anyway, and it didn't take one bit of additional effort to throw an extra potato into the oven." She suddenly smiled with exaggerated sweetness. "Can you handle that?"

"Do I have any choice?"

She studied him a moment, doubtfully, and then realized he was teasing. Her smile broadened. "I guess I didn't give you one."

"And I'm glad you didn't." He allowed a smile to show. "I appreciate it, Miss Emma. I really do. And I think I'm going to get one of these rockers for myself. I had no idea how comfortable one would be."

She nodded. "They don't look all that great, but my father was partial to it because of his back. You didn't hurt yourself when you caught me, did you?"

The last words came out in a rush, telling him just how much she had worried about that.

"No. It's an old injury, and nothing that I don't feel a dozen times a day. Don't worry about it."

He must have been a truly charming man before he was hurt, Emma thought a short while later as she thickened the gravy. Flashes of that charm still broke through the abrupt, harsh, dark envelope that pain had wrapped around him. And he must have been sinfully handsome before his injury. The vestiges of it were still there in his bone structure, in the chiseled line of his jaw. The premature gray of his hair, a silvery color, merely added an additional dash of mystery to him.

Turning from the stove to add some more water to the thickener she was using in the gravy, Emma glanced toward the kitchen window.

And screamed.

Chapter 3

When he heard the scream and a crash, Gage hit the floor running. Automatically, his hand dived beneath his suit jacket, searching for the gun he used to always carry, and when he found nothing, he swore fiercely. No gun. No weapon at all, except himself. These days, that was no bargain.

Before the sound of Emma's scream had fully died, he kicked open the kitchen door and peered around the doorjamb to assess the situation.

Emma stood alone, pressed back against the counter, her terrified gaze leaping from the door he had just kicked open to the windows beyond which the world had turned dark. At her feet lay a mess of white paste and shattered ceramic.

"Emma?" Seeing no one else, Gage eased into the room. "Emma, what happened?"

Her eyes were huge as they sought him. She shuddered once, wildly, and then wrapped her arms around herself. "Someone was staring in the window."

Gage reached the door in two long strides and threw it open. Standing on the back stoop, he scanned the driveway, what he could see of the street and the snow beneath the kitchen windows.

"Do you see anything?"

Emma stood behind him in the open door, and he spared her a glance. "Not much. Have you got a flashlight?"

"I'll get it."

To see over the café curtains into the kitchen while standing on the ground, a man would have to be better than eight feet tall, Gage figured. Either that, or he'd need a ladder, and it was moot anyway, because the snow below the windows was undisturbed—except for some snow that had fallen off the roof. . . .

He snapped his head up and peered at the roof, just as Emma returned.

"Here," she said, and gave him the light.

The snow was disturbed along the eaves, Gage saw. Taking the flashlight, he descended the steps and backed his way across the driveway while shining the light at the roof over the kitchen. The snow was stirred up, but cats could have done that, and surely, if a man had been up there, he and Emma would have heard him scramble away to safety.

The Conard house had two stories, but the second story had been a late addition, Gage judged, and had been erected over only part of the house. The kitchen roof was at the single story level, not as steep as the peaked gables of the second floor, and easy for a man to get onto. Still, a fast dash across the roof would have made enough noise to tell the tale.

"Gage?"

Emma was waiting in the doorway, Gage saw, shivering from the cold and frowning. He limped back toward her.

"Nothing," he said. "Whoever it was is gone now. What exactly did you see?"

He closed the door behind himself, shutting out the night.

"It all happened so fast— Oh! The gravy!" She turned quickly to the stove and reached for the wire whisk. Another half minute and it would have been scorched.

"Did you recognize the face?" Gage asked

"No." She turned off the gas under the gravy. "Dinner is just about ready."

Gage was habitually short on patience these days. Constant pain did devastating things to a man's temper. "Emma, will you just look at me and answer my questions?"

She spun around to face him, anger bringing color to her cheeks. "I *am* answering you, Mr. Dalton! I am also trying to keep dinner from being ruined. Furthermore, I don't believe I gave you permission to address me so familiarly!"

"Familiarly? You don't know the meaning of the word. *Honey* would be familiar! Damn it, woman—"

"And don't you swear at me, either!"

The pain was building up again, thanks to his careless dash from the living room. A hot poker was jamming into his lower back and sending rivers of burning lava down his left leg. He wanted to ignore it. He tried to ignore it, hating the weakness, but accepting the agony as his due. He couldn't ignore it, however, when fiery talons gripped his thigh and dug in deeply. He drew a sharp breath and squeezed his eyes shut. He would be damned if he would let this woman see how much he was hurting.

But Emma saw. Suddenly she was beside him, slipping her arm around him, talking in the sweetest, gentlest voice, a voice that made him think of cool spring water bubbling over mossy rocks. He clung to the soothing sound as if it were a lifeline thrown down into hell.

"Let's get you back in the rocker," she said, gently urging him toward the living room. "You were comfortable there—oh, I just know you hurt yourself when you caught me. You should just have let me fall!"

"No." He scowled fiercely down at her, but it was a wasted effort, because all he could see was the top of her head. "I didn't hurt myself. I'm just having a bad day. Will you stop mothering me?"

The next thing he knew, he was back in the Kennedy rocker with two fingers of Scotch in his highball glass.

"I'll be right back with a tray," Emma said briskly. "Then you can question me to your heart's content while we eat."

It *was* just a bad day. Though he was never entirely free of pain, most of the time, with the aid of aspirin, he could ignore it. Periodically, though, his damaged nerves howled and all but crippled him. Usually he walked himself into exhaustion, but tonight he tossed off the Scotch Emma had poured. Damn, the woman was a human bulldozer. And it galled him that she was seeing him this way. When this spell passed off in a few days or a week, nobody would be able to tell that he hurt. It was only when it got this bad that he couldn't always hide it.

Emma opened up a pair of TV tables, setting one before Gage so he wouldn't have to move more than his hands to dine. He watched her over the rim of his glass, noting the way her full breasts swayed when she moved, liking the way the lamplight caught the gold highlights in her hair. She was, he thought, a striking woman. Neither pretty nor beautiful, she would always be memorable.

For the first time in many, many months, he wanted to touch a woman's breasts and bury his flesh deep in hers. He wanted to feel a woman's cool, smooth palms on his back and buttocks, wanted to feel the sting of her nails as she tried to get closer and closer. He wanted her twisting and writhing and sweaty and hungry beneath him. All female animal.

Damn!

He looked away as Emma bent toward him to set a heaping plate of chicken, potatoes and asparagus before him. Not now. Not now. Not ever. Giving himself a giant mental yank, he turned his attention back to the Peeping Tom.

"Just what exactly did you see out that window?" he demanded.

Emma bristled a little, but she understood his irritation. She *was* trying to avoid the subject. She really didn't want to think about it, but whether she wanted to or not, she knew perfectly well that, come midnight, she would be lying in her bed remembering it. Forcing herself to remain outwardly calm, she offered him the gravy boat and smiled when he scowled at it but took it anyway.

"I saw a face," she said. "A face. I didn't recognize it, but it was distorted somehow. I wonder if the person might have been wearing a stocking? No, it didn't look like that. It wasn't a squashing kind of distortion. No, it was...pulled somehow."

"Pulled?" He simply stared at her, trying to follow her line of thought.

"Well, that isn't a very good word, but I don't know how else... Yes! That's it. It looked distorted, as if it were on the other side of a fish-eye lens! Like looking through a peep-hole in a door. I don't think I would recognize my closest friend through one of those things."

Gage set down the gravy boat and slipped his hand into the inside breast pocket of his suit jacket to pull out a pen and small pad. He scribbled down a few key words. "What about colors? Hair, eyes, anything."

"What about eating your dinner before it turns stone cold? I think maybe there was dark hair, but it could have been a stocking cap. I don't know. It was all so fast...."

She sounded so calm about the thing that he wanted to shake her. *She* had been the one who had screamed, after all, and brought him tearing into the kitchen as if he was still able to deal with such situations. And now she sat here acting as if she were the queen serving tea, and he was an importunate subject. Yes, he wanted to shake her.

That was when he noticed that her hands were trembling.

Something tight and angry in him relaxed as he realized that Emma Conard was all bluff. Mirrors and smoke. And she was so damn good at it that she must have had a lot of practice at hiding her fear.

Why? Fear of what? Intrigued, Gage settled back in the rocker, tucked his notebook away and picked up his fork. First he had to deal with the Peeping Tom. Then he would look into the mystery of Emmaline Conard.

"This is really good," he told her after he had tasted everything. "Was the face in the window upside-down?"

"Thank you. No. Right side up. Why?"

"Kind of hard to hang down from the eaves and look into the window right side up."

"Oh!" She looked up from her own plate and watched him slice another mouthful of chicken. She wondered if any other man in the county would have used a knife and fork on chicken. Probably not. Around here, chicken was finger food. "Well, it was definitely right side up. I just assumed someone was standing out there."

"He'd have had to be eight feet tall or able to fly, and considering there aren't any footprints under the window, he must have been flying."

Emma's hand tightened on her linen napkin. "Are you being sarcastic?"

"Not at all. I'm serious. When I didn't see any disturbance in the snow beneath the windows, I assumed the peeper must have been hanging over the edge of the roof, but then he would have had to be upside-down, and you're sure he wasn't. Of course, maybe he was wearing a mask upside down. That would definitely explain that part of it. Now we only need to figure out why you didn't hear anybody on the roof. Unless you did?"

Emma shook her head. "No. Not a thing." Inwardly she quailed. This was awful. Who would have done such a thing, and why? She thought she knew everyone in Conard County so well that if any of them had a propensity for this sort of thing, she would know. And that was utterly ridiculous, wasn't it? Nobody ever knew his neighbors well enough to be sure of something like that.

Gage had been watching her more closely than she knew, and he read far more in the slight flickers in her face than she would have dreamed. At that moment he changed tack. "I'm sure," he said, "it was just a kid playing a prank. Who did you scold at the library in the last few days?"

Emma's relief was palpable, so palpable that it told Gage just how much fear she had been hiding. That, too, was another mystery to add to his list of mysteries about this woman. Why had she reacted so strongly to that photo of the dagger last night? Why did she find it necessary to hide her fear about the Peeping Tom?

"I'm going to call the department," he told her when he finished eating. "A deputy will keep an eye on your house tonight."

"But you said—"

He refused to look at her. This woman was beginning to get under his skin, and he couldn't allow that. "It probably was some juvenile playing a prank. That's the most likely explanation, given that we haven't had any other incidents reported. But in case he decides to come back and try to give you another scare, there'll be someone outside."

She rose with him, following him as he headed for the kitchen to use the phone. "But isn't that a little extreme?" Oh, Lord, she could just imagine the gossip. Miss Emma, starchy spinster, was starting to imagine lurking rapists behind every bush. She would be the laughingstock of Mahoney's. "Mr. Dalton . . ."

"Call me Gage." He had just reached the phone, but he turned abruptly to face her. "Look, Emma, I have a personal thing about cruds who pick on women and children. I won't stand for it. Not for one damn minute."

She looked up at him. A tall woman, she was accustomed to meeting most men at eye level. Gage was five or six inches taller, and the difference made her feel small. Delicate. Feminine. It made her notice that the dark stubble of the day's growth of beard had begun to appear on his uninjured cheek. It made her notice the broad-shouldered, slim-hipped way he filled out his suit. It made her notice his hands, dark, lean and large.

She caught her breath and backed up. For long years she had schooled herself not to notice such things, had taught her body to pretend it had no needs and never felt empty. Her walls and barriers suddenly felt weak and shaky. Abruptly she turned. "Fine," she said, and headed back to the living room to clean up from dinner.

Twenty minutes later a deputy arrived. Sara Yates was Conard County's only female deputy, and probably Emma's closest woman friend in the county. Sara took one look at Gage, and another at Emma, and grinned in a way Emma didn't at all like.

"What's this about a Peeping Tom, Gage?" Sara asked, turning away from Emma before the latter could say anything.

Gage explained the sequence of events rapidly, clearly, concisely, in a way that told Emma he had long experience of making such reports. Rumor in the county had it that Gage Dalton had been a lawman somewhere before he came here to work part-time for Nathan Tate, and it appeared rumor was right. Emma couldn't have explained things so well or clearly if she'd had hours to prepare.

Sara trained her spotlight on the eaves, and she and Gage together began a close examination of the scene. Feeling useless, Emma went back inside to wash the dishes.

She was just wiping the counters down when Gage and Sara came back inside. Gage looked cold, Emma thought. He should at least have put on his jacket.

"Well," he said, "we found out how it was done."

Sara held up a long piece of twine from which hung the shred of a balloon. "Just a prank, Emma," she said. "Gage and I figure that the hoaxster shot it with a BB gun when you screamed. Makes it spookier that way."

Gage and Sara had stayed to have coffee and pie with Emma, and then Sara had driven Gage back to his place.

Alone in the big, empty old house, Emma felt uneasy. Just a prank, she told herself, and forced herself through her nightly routine of checking locks and windows. While she showered, she tried to repress images out of *Psycho*—surely a movie no solitary woman should ever watch—and then she proved she could conquer her nerves by lingering to dust herself with talcum powder.

Finally, edgy beyond belief, she dived into her bed and pulled the covers up to her eyes just like a little kid who was scared of the dark.

And she *was* afraid of the dark, she admitted. Thirty years old, and petrified of the night, of shadows, of empty streets. Petrified of being wounded again the way Joe Murphy had wounded her all those years ago.

She and Joe had become engaged halfway through her senior year in college. Just two weeks before the assault that had changed her life forever. When she had come out of her coma and learned what had happened to her, she had naturally turned to Joe for understanding and comfort.

Instead, he had broken their engagement. "The whole point of getting married is having children," he'd told her. "You can't have kids anymore, Emma. What's the point?"

What's the point?

Tucked under her blankets now, with the light beside the bed blazing brightly to hold back all the terrors that had no names, Emma squeezed her eyes shut against an old pain that still felt like a spear in her heart. Over the years, she had come to understand that Joe had been the smallest of the losses she had suffered. Her real loss had been the loss of her womanhood. The thing that Emma believed most made a woman a woman, the thing that gave her meaning and purpose, that made her desirable as a mate, was gone forever, never to be recovered. And never again would she risk even the remote possibility that a man might reject her because she was barren.

Lying alone in her empty bed, she listened to mocking whispers that seemed to come from just beyond the range of her hearing. The feeling of invasion returned. There was something evil out there, something waiting. Something looking. For her.

Gage drooped over his coffeepot the following morning. Wearing nothing but his black jeans, zipped but not buttoned, he cursed the strangely wild mood that had led him to stop in Mahoney's last night after Sara dropped him off. Seeing him, Mahoney had poured the usual two shots, but Gage had lingered for another two, and then another. He had only a vague memory of eventually climbing the stairs and falling onto his bed.

Hell, he *never* did that. The last time he had tied one on had been just after... He squashed the thought before it could be born. Some things didn't bear remembering. Some things had to be buried before they drove you mad.

He swore at the coffeepot and wondered why it was so damn sluggish this morning. He swore at himself for getting hung over, though it was only a small hangover. He swore at his back for hurting, then swore at life in general. And when he got done with that, he swore at Emma Conard for being so sexy when she was so damn uptight. At this moment he would have bet a year's pay she was a virgin. He swore again. She must surely be the last virgin on earth over the age of eighteen. Why the hell did she have to cross his path?

Someone knocked timidly on the door. Gage glared at it over his shoulder. Probably Mahoney coming to find out why he was swearing so viciously. Mahoney lived downstairs, behind the bar.

The knock came again, stronger. What the hell?

"Door's open," he growled. "Come on in, Mahoney."

When he heard the soft gasp behind him, he knew it wasn't Mahoney. Hell's bells, he didn't even have a shirt on, and he knew what Emma could see. And knew it was Emma. Somehow he just knew, though why the devil she would look him up on a Sunday morning...

He turned slowly, certain he would find shock and horror. Burn scars sure as hell weren't pretty. He found the shock and horror, all right. And tears sparkling on the dark fringe of lashes that framed her misty green eyes.

"Oh, Gage," she whispered. "Oh, Gage."

"I'll get a shirt." He headed toward the bedroom, trying to keep his front toward her. His chest wasn't bad at all, hardly marked. He'd been heading away from the car, going back to get the forgotten diaper bag when... He choked that thought off, too.

"It's...all right," she said. "You don't have to. I know it's early and..." She blinked, and a tear ran down her cheek. "I'm sorry I barged in on you but...I need your help."

She turned her back to him and folded her arms around herself, and he knew in that instant how much it had cost her to come here and ask for his help. Emma Conard was a proud, independent woman who hated to admit any fear.

He hesitated momentarily, torn by an unexpected urge to go to her and comfort her. Instead, he dashed into his bedroom and grabbed a sweatshirt that was hanging over the foot of the bed. Tugging it swiftly on, he returned to Emma.

"What happened?"

She didn't turn to face him, but stared out the uncurtained window at the brick wall on the other side of the alley. "I went out to get my paper from the porch this morning and found ... a decapitated rabbit."

Something inside him froze. "On your porch?"

"On my porch. Anyway, what with that and last night and ... everything, I thought that if you were still interested in renting a room from me, I'd be awfully grateful not to be alone in that house."

He didn't answer immediately. "Did you call the sheriff?"

She nodded. "They came out and took the carcass, and Dave Winters suggested that maybe I could have a friend stay with me while they try to figure out if this is serious or just kids."

Now she turned and looked at him. "I can understand that you might not want the room anymore, but it really wasn't anything personal when I turned you down before."

"No, I understood that. It'll take me a couple of hours to box up my stuff, but I'll come."

"Thank you. I'm on my way to church, but I'll be back home in about an hour and a half. Come whenever you feel like it."

He reached out and touched her arm. "Let me drive you to church."

Her faced blanched. Damn it, he wondered, what the hell was it with this woman? Why should the offer of a lift drain all the color from her face?

"No, really, it's just a short walk," she said, backing up and giving him a fragile, forced smile. "I'll see you later."

He followed her to the door and watched her descend the wooden staircase, thinking that perhaps she shouldn't go anywhere alone until this thing was settled. Damn, what had happened to the deputy who was supposed to be watching her house? A decapitated rabbit went far beyond a funny face painted on a balloon, but, disgusting as it was, it still didn't exceed the realm of possible teenage pranks. Given that, he could hardly stick to her side like a watchdog.

But he could make certain she was safe when she was at home, he thought, as she disappeared around the corner of the building. He could make certain that if she didn't turn up where she was supposed to be, someone would notice it.

Turning his back on the cold, clear day, Gage shut the door. Forgetting his hangover, he poured himself some coffee and then went to dig out the boxes he had saved in the storage closet.

Damn, he hated this feeling that something terrible was about to happen. It clung to his neck and shoulders like chilly, wet leaves, ominous and foreboding.

Emma hadn't told Gage the half of it, mostly because she was sure she would look and feel like a fool if she did. The rabbit was a tangible thing, proof that she hadn't utterly lost her mind. She could call the sheriff to deal with something like that.

But she couldn't call the sheriff to deal with her nightmares. There wasn't anyone she could tell that she had dreamed of the dagger again last night. She couldn't tell anyone that its image had begun to haunt the edges of her mind, like a memory she couldn't quite grasp. She couldn't tell anyone about the other nightmare she had had last night, when the balloon face had become a real face, a face she seemed to know but not know. A stranger she remembered. A man who terrified her.

The man who had hurt her?

Dawn had taken a terribly long time coming this morning. Lights had blazed at Emma's house for hours, holding the night at bay, but only with the arrival of the sun did she feel she was again safe.

It was crazy, it was creepy, and it was something she couldn't tell anyone else about. She walked into the church that morning looking for a comfort that no one on earth could give her, because there was no one on earth she could tell.

Gage pulled his black Suburban into Emma's driveway shortly after noon. She heard his engine as he pulled up and hurried out to the kitchen to meet him. During the time since she had gotten back from church, her nerves had stretched tighter and tighter, and even the old regulator's ticking had become ominous. Nor did it do a darn bit of good to remind herself how many years she had lived quite happily in this house. It just didn't feel safe any longer.

She reached the door as Gage was climbing out of the Suburban. Inexplicably, her breath locked in her throat, and she froze in astonishment as the most unexpected yearning squeezed her heart.

He was dressed, as usual, in head-to-toe black: black jeans, black Stetson, black boots, black leather jacket. On the surface, at least, he was everything she had always avoided. He looked like a brewing storm, like trouble distilled.

That didn't keep her from wishing she could know what it felt like to be held by him. Every cell in her body suddenly ached just to feel his arms around her.

But that was ridiculous. Absurd. Unthinkable. Ignoring the ache, she opened the door just as Gage pulled the first of his boxes from the back end of the truck.

"Hi," she called, and felt her breath catch again as he looked up at her and smiled back. "What can I do to help?"

"Keep the rocker warm," he replied, climbing the steps. "My back's going to kill me after this."

"Let me—"

"No." The word was flat, unequivocal.

Emma stepped back to let him pass. "I can ask the boys next door—"

"No." He halted and turned to look at her. "I may hurt like hell, Emma, but don't ever mistake me for being helpless or an invalid."

She watched his narrow flanks as he walked away and wondered why she had never before noticed just how sexy a man's bottom could be in a pair of jeans. Suddenly she charged after him.

"Doing a job like this when you know it's going to hurt you is just plain foolhardy, Gage Dalton!"

He was already climbing the stairs. "So I'm a macho idiot. But once you start giving ground, lady, it's hell to get it back."

Emma stood watching him climb the rest of the stairs, thinking that he was probably right.

"Which room?" he asked.

"Take your pick. The front bedroom has the hardest mattress, though, if that's important to your back."

"Thanks."

Nice buns, she thought again, and almost giggled at her own foolishness. It was such a relief to have another person in the house that she was a little giddy.

Gage did it all himself, every last damn box and book. And he had a lot of books. They constituted the major part of his possessions.

"Emma?" he called down the stairs. "Would it be a problem if I took a bookcase out of one of the other rooms?"

She appeared at the foot of the stairs, wiping her hands on an apron. Delicious aromas were filling the house again. "Help yourself." The bookcases had been empty since she had donated the books—mostly very old novels—to Sweetwater Nursing Home. Her own books, and the handed-down ones that she treasured, filled the floor-to-ceiling bookcases in her study. "Do you need any help?"

"No, but thanks."

Well, that was the most gracious refusal he'd yet given her, Emma thought as she headed back into the kitchen to finish peeling potatoes. It had been a while since she had cooked a big Sunday dinner for anyone but herself, and she was enjoying it. She was enjoying, too, the noise from upstairs as Gage moved around and unpacked.

The house had been empty and silent for too long, Emma thought now. Her last roomer had been a middle-aged French teacher who had spent her time quietly and unobtrusively upstairs reading or grading papers. Emma had hardly known the woman was in the house. Somehow she didn't think she would be unaware of Gage.

Even the runner in the upstairs hallway didn't entirely silence his booted feet, and floorboards creaked under his every step. The sounds made the house feel alive once again.

He came down the stairs again for another load and sniffed appreciatively as he passed through the kitchen.

"It sure smells a lot better than Mahoney's," he told her.

"You're invited to join me," she said—casually, she hoped, because she suddenly didn't feel at all casual about asking this man to dine with her. "Roast beef, oven-browned potatoes, candied carrots..."

"Say no more. I'll be there with bells on."

He managed to get the last box upstairs without knuckling under to the pain that flayed him, but when he reached the room that final time, he knew he couldn't have made one more trip.

Leaving the last boxes untouched for now, he grabbed a couple of his towels and headed for the bathroom. What he needed was a long, hot soak, and that claw-footed tub looked big enough to hold him, unlike most modern tubs.

A twenty-minute soak eased the worst of the spasms. Back in his room, he stretched out on the bed, facedown, and groaned with sheer relief. God, he almost didn't hurt at all. Almost. Let it last, just a little while. Just a little while.

Emma hesitated at the foot of the stairs, wondering if she should call Gage down to dinner or go upstairs to get him. Things had been so quiet since he finished his bath that she thought he might have fallen asleep. If that was so, she didn't want to wake him. The poor man probably needed whatever sleep he could manage to get, and while he was asleep he wouldn't feel the pain.

After a few more moments of indecision, she decided to go up and peek in on him. If he was sleeping, she could save his dinner to reheat later.

The door to his room stood wide open, and she saw him lying facedown on the bed. Jeans and a black T-shirt covered him decently, but his feet were bare, and there was something about them that made him seem oddly vulnerable.

Emma hesitated on the threshold. "Gage?" She said his name softly, hoping not to disturb him if he wasn't awake.

"I'm awake, Emma," he said, his voice muffled, "but I think I'm paralyzed. Maybe you'd better eat without me."

"Paralyzed?" She stepped into the room, closer to him, and battled an urge to hurry over and touch him somehow. "Did you hurt yourself?"

"Naw. Actually, I don't hurt at all. Not at all. And I just discovered I'm a coward."

"Why?"

"I'm afraid to move."

She gave a small laugh. "I can sure see why. Okay, I'll save your dinner for you."

"You don't have to—"

"I want to," she interrupted. "I'd offer to bring it up here, but I don't see how you can eat in that position."

"Me, neither. Well, I'll be surprised if this lasts even another few minutes. Just don't wait on me."

Turning away was somehow difficult, but she did it, descending the stairs with her mind full of the look of him lying sprawled on the bed, her hands wishing they could have touched him.

Lord, Lord, Emma, what's gotten into you? Yes, he's a virile-looking man, an attractive man for all he's aloof and difficult at times, but he's not the first attractive man you've ever seen. Why are you reacting to *him?*

And why *shouldn't* she react? some other part of her wondered. Gage Dalton was no more interested in any kind of involvement than she was. Reacting to him was about as safe as such a thing could be. He would never notice her as a woman, not in a million years. And if he should, just maybe, make a pass at her, maybe she could succumb. After all, she would go into it with her eyes open, knowing from the first that that was all it would ever be.

There had been a time in her life when moral strictures would have prevented her from even considering such a thing. Even with Joe, she had never permitted any more than a few kisses, because she hadn't wanted to be a tease and she knew she wouldn't go all the way.

But now she was past thirty, facing middle age as a perennial spinster, and some part of her resented the hell out of that. Why shouldn't she taste the forbidden apple a few times? She would have the rest of her life to aspire to sainthood. But now, right now, Emma Conard felt a crying need for human warmth, a human touch, human contact.

She felt, she admitted, a crying need for a man's heat and desire. She wanted to know what it felt like to be swept away by the dizzying feelings she had read about, wanted to know what real passion was, what real desire meant, and how it felt to be wanted like that.

And then she wanted to be able to walk away with a whole heart.

She could have laughed at her own foolishness just then, except that it hurt too much. She felt as if she were drying up and blowing away. Someday little children would scurry out of her way and whisper behind her back the way they had with Great-aunt Isabel.

It was enough to make her want to smash something. There were just no answers for why life could be so unfair. No answers at all. She had done nothing to deserve the assault that had ruined her life. Nothing.

But then, Gage had probably done nothing to deserve what had happened to him, either.

There was just no explaining it. No explaining it at all.

Muffled by distance, she heard Gage swear suddenly. Well, he would probably be coming down for dinner, she thought, as she heard him swear again. His vacation from pain was over.

Chapter 4

"I need to go out on a case," Gage said.

Emma immediately glanced toward the window and the night beyond. In a few short days she had grown accustomed to Gage's presence in the house, to the comfort it gave her. He had offered to pay more to have his meals included in the rent, and she had accepted, but that hadn't kept him from going out and stocking the pantry on Monday. Since then he had helped with the cooking and washed the dishes every night. Then, as the evening deepened, he would settle into the Kennedy rocker in the living room and read.

Tonight a phone call had come just as they were finishing dinner, and now he had to leave.

Emma's insides knotted, and her heart sped up. This evening she would be alone. Alone with the strange, disturbing images that flickered around the edges of her mind, unrecognizable glimpses of faces, sounds not quite heard. All she knew was that these flickers, these glimpses of what might be distorted memories, frightened her. For the last several days she had kept herself continuously busy, trying to squelch what seemed to be a growing pressure just beneath the level of her waking thoughts.

And now Gage had to go out. Maybe she could persuade Sara to come over until he got back. Or maybe she could go over to Sara's. Or maybe, she told herself sternly, she could just stay home by herself as she had been doing these many years without any trouble at all. What ever was the matter with her?

"Want to go with me?" Gage asked.

"Hmm?" Emma looked up from the plates she was carrying to the sink. "I'm sorry, what did you say?"

"Would you like to go with me? It's a clear night, and a quarter moon is rising. It'd make a pretty drive out to the Bar C."

The Bar C was her cousin Jeff's ranch, and that was the first part of his speech that penetrated. "Oh, no! Not another mutilation!"

"Afraid so. Would you like to come with me?"

"Come?" And suddenly she understood. Alone in the car with him. With a man. Her hands started to shake violently, and she hurried to the counter to set the plates down. "I...I can't. Thanks anyway."

"Why not?" He hadn't missed the way her hands had started to tremble, or the way she had paled. "Emma?"

"I...just can't."

He ought to leave right now, he thought with a kind of aching desperation. He didn't need any more problems in his life, a life already so burdened with painful problems that he sometimes felt as if he were wearing a lead overcoat. It was a selfish thought, though, and it shamed him even as he had it.

"Emma," he said, "is it me? Or is it the car?"

"Just go take care of your case, Gage. I'll be fine."

"I don't want to leave you here alone."

She faced him then, attempting a smile. "I'll give Sara a call. I think she's off duty tonight. You don't need to worry about me."

"She's on duty. She's the one who called me." Frowning, Gage stepped closer. "Emma, tell me."

And somehow it just came blurting out. Nobody in Conard County knew what had happened to her, because her father had protected her secret. He hadn't wanted her to suffer the curious looks and the endless speculation, not to mention the callous or careless questions. So no one here knew a thing about the assault. Emma had been happy to leave it that way, so why was she now telling this man her deepest, darkest secret?

"When...when I was a senior in college, I was assaulted. I don't remember anything about it but...I was in a coma for weeks, and after I woke I needed all kinds of rehabilitation."

"My God." Gage barely breathed the words.

Emma closed her eyes, not wanting to see his pity. She shrugged, as if these were matters of no concern. "I still don't know what happened, and no one was ever charged with it, but I have a few silly fears I can't seem to shake." Again she shrugged. "I can't get into a car with a man. I just...can't...do it."

She expected him to say, "Well, all right, then," or something else equally dismissive, then leave. Instead, his ruined voice took on an incredibly gentle tone.

"That's all right, Emma," he said. "That's all right. Perfectly understandable. I'll get someone over here to keep an eye on things while I'm gone."

Her eyes popped open. "Oh, no! Oh, Gage, really...everyone will hear about it, and they'll start wondering if I've gone off the deep end. Don't bother. I'll be fine, really. It'll only be a couple of hours, right? And nothing else has happened since the rabbit." And why was she trying to talk him out of giving her exactly the comfort she needed? Lord, Emma, you really *are* losing your mind!

Gage hesitated, but finally he said, "Okay. I'll get back just as soon as I can."

At the door, though, he suddenly turned around and came back. But he didn't stop a polite distance away. No, he came right up to her, to within a foot, and took her gently by the shoulders, moving her away from the counter.

"I don't want you to get claustrophobic because you're caught between me and the counter," he said gruffly in answer to the questioning but incredibly trusting look on her face. He couldn't imagine why this woman should trust him at all. He couldn't imagine why he hadn't been able to get out that door without coming back to touch her. To kiss her. And for the moment he was past wondering about it.

When Gage's stormy gaze moved from her eyes to her lips, Emma caught her breath in agonizing hope. The last time she had felt like this, she had been sixteen, and Lefty Sjodgren, the school's star quarterback, had taken her to a movie. She had felt like this then, too, standing on her porch as they said good-night, hoping against hope that Lefty would give her her first kiss. That kiss had been a huge disappointment. Somehow she didn't think Gage's would be a disappointment at all.

His head bowed a fraction, then hesitated. He wasn't sure he should do this. Not sure at all. Nor was she, but she didn't want to miss it. There might never again be a chance to feel this man's lips on hers, and she was going out of her mind wanting to know. She lifted her mouth, just a fraction. Just enough.

A soft, husky whisper of sound escaped him, causing her insides to clench sharply. Pleasurably. A sensation she hadn't felt in years.

"I shouldn't do this," he muttered, and then his mouth covered hers with hungry heat. Not too much, he warned himself. Not too much. This woman was inexperienced and fearful of men. Just a little kiss, just a sop to the aching need to hold her tightly and bury himself in her slick, silky heat. Living with her was rapidly turning into a new kind of hell for him, a hell he had no desire to run from. Not yet, anyway.

Her hands fluttered uncertainly and then came to rest on his hips, holding him gently. He nearly groaned with sheer pleasure at the touch. It wasn't a sexy touch, or even a hungry one, but it wasn't rejecting him, either. It had been so long since he had been touched. So damn long.

He meant to break away, meant the kiss to be gentle and noninflammatory, but somehow it didn't stop there. His tongue slipped past his guard and ran slowly, tenderly, along Emma's lips, tasting the coffee they had just drunk, coaxing her to give him more. Stop. He had to stop. But, oh, God, it had been so long, and he needed the gentleness, the softness, the heat. The longing rolled over him, overwhelming him, sweeping him up in aching waves.

Emma felt the coaxing, enticing sweep of his tongue across her lips all the way to the soles of her feet. Long-untested instincts took over before she even knew it. Her hands tightened on his hard, narrow hips as she leaned even closer, seeking deeper pressure, and opened her mouth to take him into her. At the first hot thrust of his tongue, her entire body took flame. Hungers long denied, long buried, sprang to immediate life. When his hands slipped from her shoulders to enfold her in a tight embrace, she wanted to sob for sheer joy. Nothing had ever felt so good, so right.

Suddenly Gage tore his mouth from hers and pressed his cheek to hers. For long moments he continued to hold her snugly, and then his embrace gentled. "That got a little out of hand," he said softly. Slowly, gently, soothingly, he stroked her back from shoulder to waist.

Emma could feel him withdrawing, rebuilding his internal barriers brick by brick. She recognized the wisdom of it and knew she should step back now. But for a few seconds she remained within his embrace, paralyzed by an urgent need to burrow into him, to never again know the loneliness that lurked just beyond the magic circle of his arms.

Ridiculous, she told herself and, with a sigh, eased backward. Gage released her instantly. He didn't immediately leave, however. Instead, he reached out and touched her cheek with gentle fingertips. "I'll get back just as soon as I can, Emma."

She smiled. "I'll be fine, Gage, really. There's no reason to think there's any real danger from these pranks. I guess my nerves just ran away with me on Sunday."

He hesitated a moment longer, then nodded and left, grabbing his Stetson from the peg as he passed out the door.

Once he was out in his Suburban, however, he radioed the department and told them to keep a sharp eye on Emma's house. She might have grown sanguine, but he hadn't. For three days now he'd been trying to connect the decapitated rabbit with the cattle mutilations, then trying not to connect them, telling himself that the rabbit was just inspired by the cattle. Somehow that didn't feel right, though. Nothing felt right, and his gut kept insisting these were no ordinary pranks.

His hands tightened on the steering wheel as he thought of Emma alone in that big old house, and even knowing a deputy would keep an eye on the place didn't make him feel a whole lot better. There were plenty of ways to get around such surveillance. He himself was a master of them.

And then there was Emma herself. The outline she had stammered out for him tonight was ghastly even in its bare-bones form. It twisted something inside him, something that had been dead ever since…before. And, unfortunately, he'd seen enough of that kind of violence in his life to be able to fill in Emma's outline with gruesome images.

He shifted on the seat, seeking to ease the tension in his lower back before it became uncomfortable. Such adjustments of his posture had grown so automatic that he was hardly aware of them. The movements made him appear restless, though, even when he wasn't. Like a caged wolf.

He was a man accustomed to accepting the way things were, like them or not, but right now he experienced a vain wish that he hadn't kissed Emma Conard. He didn't like the feelings that had goaded him back across the kitchen and driven him to taste her mouth. He didn't like having feelings at all anymore. Feelings were a dangerous roller coaster with as many lows as there were highs. And some of the lows twisted a man inside out and left him smashed for good.

Having a personal and intimate acquaintance with the depths of hell, Gage had no desire to experience any new tortures. But Miss Emma's mouth had been sweet and warm, water to a man in a desert. Her inexperienced response had been instant and generous, and her hands on his hips had been a touch of heaven. Just remembering it made his loins clench sharply. Part of him, at least, was coming back to life in a headlong rush.

A wise man would probably bail out right now. When it came to some things, though, Gage had never been a wise man. For the time being, Miss Emmaline Conard needed his protection and the security his presence in her house gave her. Never in his life, not once, had he been able to walk away from that kind of need.

Emma sat in the middle of the living room surrounded by boxes of decorations she had dragged down from an upstairs closet. Traditional Christmas carols played loudly from the stereo, and every light blazed. The curtains were drawn tightly, letting not so much as a wedge of the night into the room.

She'd completely forgotten the tree in all the uproar this week, but tomorrow, she promised herself, she would find a large one. In the meantime she could put up the garlands and wreaths, and replace blue candles with red and green ones in all the brass sconces.

The rhythm of the familiar tasks soothed her, bringing back memories that alternately brought a smile to her lips or tightened her throat. So many Christmases past, so many memories, etched in the brilliance of the holiday season. Somehow those memories took on a brightness and a golden warmth that her other memories lacked.

Except for the last several years. Oh, she thoroughly enjoyed the festivities before Christmas, looked forward to the annual open house, when Front Street filled with carolers and good cheer. But, since her father's death, that was the extent of it. On Christmas Eve she still went to the candlelight ceremony at the church, but that had become a time when she mourned her father's absence. And Christmas Day always dawned gray for her, even if the sun shone brilliantly.

A lousy commentary, she told herself, and tried to shrug away the morbid thoughts. And still, glittering at the edge of her mind like shards of sharp glass, were the images and sounds she couldn't quite grasp. Feeling their pressure sud-

denly, like a volcano trying to erupt into her conscious
world, she stood abruptly and went to get herself another
cup of coffee.

Moving around would help. Maybe she would bake a pie,
get her mind off memories of Christmas past and onto
something productive, something pleasant. Like the way
Gage had dug into the blueberry pie she had served on Sunday.

Like the way he had kissed her tonight. A shiver ran
through her, a pleasant river of remembered sensation. She
couldn't imagine why he had done that. It had seemed to
come out of nowhere, without warning or provocation.

Absently, she began to cut shortening into flour to make
a pie crust, intending to use the canned cherry filling she had
in the pantry. It had been a while since she had made a
cherry pie.

The entire front of her body had been imprinted with
every hard line of Gage's, she thought. The zipper of his
jacket had pressed against her left breast when he had
hugged her, and she could still remember the way his hips
had felt beneath her hands. What if she had tightened her
hold? What if she had drawn those hips closer, had pressed
herself to them? Would he have answered her questions and
initiated her into the mysteries of lovemaking?

Another shiver passed through her, a shiver of longing.
Oh, Lord, Emma, this is dangerous! Do you really think
you're capable of having an affair without getting involved
emotionally? If you give your body, you'll give your soul
and your heart, and it'll be worse by far than what Joe
Murphy did to you. Because he'll leave, Emma. You know
he'll leave. He's not a man who gives much of himself, and
even if he were, what would he want with *you?*

It was ironic, she sometimes thought, that with all the injuries and damage she had suffered from her unknown attacker and Joe Murphy, she hadn't developed a complete
distaste for men. That her sexuality hadn't died, but instead had needed to be continually smothered over the years.
Given that no man would want her, why couldn't she have
learned to want no man?

An unladylike word escaped her beneath her breath. At the same moment, the tape playing in the living room came to an end and the house was plunged into utter silence.

The unexpected ring of the phone was a jarring note. Emma started and then wiped her hands on her apron. Not for the first time she swore she was going to replace that wall phone with one that chirped rather than rang. Her phone at work had spoiled her with its quiet buzzing, and she had gotten so she hated the way this one jangled.

Tucking the receiver between her ear and shoulder, she said, "Hello?"

The line was open, an echoing silence that told her someone was on the other end, listening. Then there was a click, followed by a dial tone.

Emma stood stock-still for a moment, listening to the hum of the empty line, and then slowly she placed the receiver back in the cradle.

A wrong number, she told herself. Someone without the basic manners to apologize, that was all. Just a social cretin.

She started shivering then, with a cold that seemed to come from deep within her. Inescapably, inexplicably, she felt *watched*.

Snow that had been crusted earlier in the day by the sun's warmth crunched under Gage's boots as he walked away from the brightly lit mutilation scene. Beside him walked Sheriff Nathan Tate, a burly, ruddy-complected man with a deep, gravelly voice.

"The skinning of the skull is a new one," Nate remarked.

"I've heard of it with mutilations in other places," Gage replied. "The bone is still pink, so it's pretty recent. We need to have the lab find out if there are any marks on the bone from whatever tool was used to do the butchering."

Nate nodded. "I wish Micah was here. I swear that Injun reads the vibes in the air around things."

Gage chuckled almost in spite of himself. "You're sounding like a product of the sixties."

"I *am* a product of the sixties."

"Well, Micah will be back next week," Gage said. "In the meantime, we'll have to rely on modern science."

"I haven't been real pleased with the lab lately. They can't even agree with each other about this."

"They sure as hell ought to be able to tell a tooth mark from a knife mark on that skull, though." Gage paused beside his Suburban and looked back toward the floodlit site. "It's beginning to feel like a vendetta against Cumberland and the Bar C."

Nate made a grunt of acknowledgement.

"They sure aren't being killed where they're found," Gage said presently. "There'd have to be at least *some* sign of struggle, and there never is. Where does all the blood go? Why aren't there ever any tracks going in or out from the site? Damn it, Nate, I'm beginning to believe in little green men."

Nate made another grunt. "Except that there's no sign of tissue cautery. The cases blamed on the little green men almost always include heat damage to the tissue, as if from laser surgery."

"That's right." Gage was becoming something of an expert on the subject as his investigation progressed. "My guy at the lab said that was the core of contention on the last carcasses we sent up. Without any heat damage, the argument over whether the flesh was torn or cut evidently got pretty hot. I'm pretty much settled in my own mind on this, though."

Nate poked a toothpick into his mouth. "Little green men?"

"More like ordinary human beings. I'm willing to bet the lab finds knife marks on that skull, not tooth marks."

"What if they don't find anything at all?"

Gage shook his head. "Then it's little green men. But there's still tissue on that skull, Nate. Mark my words, our culprit is human."

A short, rueful laugh escaped Nate. "Damn, I hope so. I don't relish Jeff's reaction if I have to tell him it'll take Buck Rogers to put a stop to this."

"I'd settle for Superman," Sara Yates remarked as she joined them. "Nate, Ed Dewhurst and I are going to keep the carcass company until we can get it loaded on a truck. You have any special instructions?"

Nate shook his head. "Just the usual."

"Wrap the head," Gage said. "Wrap it in something to keep it from getting banged up."

"Good thought," Nate agreed. He looked at Gage. "You get back to Miss Emma. I don't like the smell of that mess, either. Damned if I know what this county is coming to." Shaking his head, he walked back to the carcass with Sara.

Gage looked after him a moment, understanding Nate's frustration. Lately it had been one damn thing after another. It seemed not so very long ago that Nate had been urging him to come out this way, promising him all the peace and healing he could ever hope for.

Well, it wasn't as peaceful as Nate had promised, that was for sure. But it wasn't as taxing, agonizing and frustrating as working undercover, either. Given his choice, he would still take Conard County and cattle mutilations over his old job.

Heading back into town, he stepped on the gas a little, knowing he wouldn't get stopped, because his Suburban was familiar to all the lawmen in the county. That was new for him, that feeling of being known, of being part of the group. Working undercover, he'd taken his chances with the law like everybody else, and a couple of times he'd gotten batted around a little by cops who thought he was just another addict or pusher. Getting knocked around with a nightstick had done wonders for his credibility on the streets, but it had sure made him feel alone. And angry. He'd been born with a burr under his saddle, but working the streets had made him furious to the deepest corner of his soul.

It was a refreshing, wonderful relief to look out the windows of the Suburban and see miles and miles of pristine countryside gleaming beneath a blanket of sparkling snow. It was breathtaking to see deer and buffalo and cattle everywhere he went outside town, and to be able to walk the streets of Conard City at three in the morning and see nothing more unsavory than a drunk cowpoke sleeping at the wheel of his pickup.

Whatever was happening with Jeff's cattle didn't fit the Conard County he'd come to know in his several months here, nor did the rabbit on Emma's porch. He knew the scent of evil. He'd smelled it on too many filthy streets and in too many sleazy hallways. Something evil had come to Conard County.

Emma was removing the cherry pie from the oven when Gage pulled up in the driveway. She turned, holding the pie in her oven-mitt-covered hands as he came in the house.

He paused, leaning back against the door he had just closed, and astonished her with a sudden, unexpected grin, a crooked expression because of his scarred cheek. "My, my," he said. "Donna Reed, move over."

The teasing remark surprised a laugh out of her. She never would have imagined Gage Dalton to be a tease. He sure didn't look like one as he leaned against the door in his habitual black: leather jacket, boots, hat, jeans. He looked like a promise of trouble.

Still smiling, she set the pie on the cooling rack in the center of the table. "You're welcome to a piece when it cools a little."

"I like my cherries hot."

Emma froze for just an instant, wondering if that had been a double entendre, or if her imagination was running wild because the man had given her one little kiss—a kiss that she now assured herself had been meant to comfort, not to arouse.

"Not this hot," she retorted in her best librarian's voice. "What did you find at the Bar C?"

"A dead cow with a skinned skull."

Emma grimaced. "Grotesque."

"Yeah. And not very illuminating." Still leaning against the door, he watched Emma strip off her oven mitts and tuck them into a drawer. "Everything okay with you?"

She looked toward him and suddenly caught her breath. She had looked at him before, had noticed before how masculine he was, how very attractive despite his scarred face. But now she saw those same things while knowing how his mouth had felt on hers, how his strong arms had felt around her. Now she looked at him with eyes that knew just how easily he could spark her to flame.

Deep inside, down low, she felt a hollow ache, felt the weight of emptiness, and wondered how a lack could feel so heavy. Quickly she forced herself to look away, reminding herself that even if he wanted her, he would never want to keep her, because she was not a whole woman. He might make love to her, but he would never love her, and she would be a damn fool to set herself up for that kind of heartache.

"Emma? Are you all right?"

"I'm fine." Realizing she had frozen in place, just staring off into space, she flushed faintly. "Just preoccupied, I guess."

He gave her a brief nod and levered himself away from the door, wincing a little as he did so. "I've got some good news for you."

"You do?" Unable to imagine what that could possibly be, she faced him expectantly and tried not to notice again just how narrow his hips were. What was it about narrow hips on a man?

"I stopped at the Quick Shop for gas and ran into Lance Severn. I asked him where we could get you a twelve-foot tree on short notice, and he said he had one waiting for you and wondered when you were coming to get it. I said I'd be there in the morning."

"Oh, my! He remembered!" Emma felt herself getting all misty eyed. "He's been so ill, I never wanted to say a word. It never occurred to me he'd remember all on his own. He's had so much on his mind."

"Well, he remembered." He hung his hat on the peg and leaned over the table, sniffing appreciatively. "How long do I have to wait?"

Feeling suddenly happy, and touched by Gage's almost boyishly wistful look at the pie, Emma gave a little laugh. "Ten minutes. It'll take that long to make the coffee."

"For that, I can wait. It's cold out there and getting colder." He tugged at his jacket and winced a little as he shrugged it off. "You've been okay while I was gone?"

"Of course. I started putting up Christmas decorations. Go see the living room." The phone call was forgotten, and the uneasiness she had felt was too embarrassing to talk about. For a moment, just a moment, she *felt* like Donna Reed welcoming her husband home at the end of a long day. She'd never felt that way before and was sure she never would again, so she surrendered to the feeling with a kind of melancholy eagerness. As soon as she had started the coffee, she followed Gage.

"Damn," she heard him say softly as she came up behind him. He stood in the arched doorway of the living room, surveying the changes. Garlands of evergreen decorated with bright red and green bows graced the mantelpiece, and the Nativity scene her great-grandfather had carved and painted with painstaking care filled an entire corner beside the bow window where the tree would be placed. On every table red or green candles filled polished brass holders, and here and there were sprigs of holly. Even without the tree, the room had become very Christmasy.

When he realized she had come up beside him, he looked down at her with a crooked smile. "You've been busy. It's nice. Real nice." He looked back at the room.

Something was wrong, Emma realized. Something was terribly, terribly wrong. The tension in him was palpable. "Gage?"

"I...um...think I'd better pass on that pie and coffee." He glanced at her again with a faint smile that never made it past his lips. He looked like a man in mortal pain who was trying to hide it. "I'm, uh, tired and my back's killing me. I'll see you in the morning."

Perplexed, she watched him climb the stairs, wishing she could somehow help him, knowing there was no possible way. Something had happened, she thought again, and turned to look at the living room. Something in here had wounded him. Frowning, she stood there for a long time, trying without success to see what it had been.

* * *

He just hadn't been prepared for it, Gage told himself in the morning as he shaved his uninjured cheek and chin. Now he knew how it was going to hit him, and he would deal with it better. He would be braced for the blow now.

Two Christmases ago he'd been in the hospital, out of his mind on painkillers, half-crazed by his losses, past being reached by anything at all except a desperate agony nothing could help. Looking back, he had a vague recollection of a few friends, a few colleagues, showing up with a specially prepared dinner for him, but he was pretty sure he hadn't eaten it. Last Christmas... last Christmas he'd been holed up in Clint Maddox's cabin in the Catoctin Mountains and had missed the entire holiday season.

He just hadn't been prepared for the flood of rushing feelings, the sudden upsurge of memories. He hadn't been ready to face his ghosts. Maybe he still wasn't, but at least he would be ready to withstand the soul-ripping agony if they suddenly showed up again, summoned by the sight or sound of Christmas.

Downstairs in the kitchen, he was surprised to find the coffee ready and the pie in the center of the table with a yellow sticky note on the clear plastic cover. Emma's very precise handwriting informed him that she had an early meeting with the library governing committee. A second sticky note suggested he have the pie for breakfast, and if he really liked hot cherries, a minute in the microwave would do it.

A woman who suggested pie for breakfast? She must be unique, Gage thought in amusement. His mother would have been horrified. His wife would have—

Ruthlessly, he broke off that thought and turned his attention to the present. He slipped a large wedge of the pie into the microwave and kept an eye on it while he sipped a mug of coffee.

An early meeting. Emma was in for a long day, then, because she never finished up at the library before seven. Usually, she went in to open at ten, but here it was just seven-thirty.

Well, he could help her out a little, he supposed, by getting that damn tree from Severn's place and setting it up in the living room. The task would also give him a chance to face all the decorations without a concerned audience, a chance to test the memories and his own emotional soreness until he was sure he could cope in public.

He would do that right after he finished up with some things at the sheriff's office. And while he was thinking about it, maybe he would call Brian Webster to find out if he had received the photo of the dagger yet. Emma's dismay over that picture still pricked at him, like a jigsaw piece he couldn't quite place. He'd mailed the photo back East to Webster, who was an expert in such matters, and if that dagger wasn't some kind of Halloween joke, Webster would have it placed in no time. And placing it might put the mystery to rest.

Downtown, across from the courthouse square, Gage pulled his Suburban into a slot marked Official Vehicles Only and waved at Deputy Charlie Huskins, who was just backing out one of the department's Blazers.

Charlie rolled down his window and leaned out, grinning hugely. "That Suburban isn't an official vehicle, Gage."

"Nate probably wouldn't agree. He pays most of my mileage."

Inside the storefront offices, Ed Dewhurst was manning the desk and phone, and Velma Jansen, the dispatcher, was leaning back in her chair, blowing a cloud of cigarette smoke into the air. Velma was one of Gage's favorite characters in Conard County, a scrawny, leathery, sixtyish woman with a big mouth and a bigger heart. She stuck her nose into the business of all the department's employees, and nobody ever really seemed to mind it.

"'Morning, Velma, Ed."

"'Morning to you, too, Casanova," Velma said.

Gage paused midstep on his way to the private office Nate had given him and faced Velma. "What's that crack mean?"

Velma blew another cloud of smoke. "Rumor has it you thawed the ice princess."

Slowly Gage turned and limped back to Velma. "I'm renting a room from Miss Emma, Velma." He spoke the words quietly, but they held enough threat to cause Ed to stiffen when he heard them.

"Of course you are, Gage," Velma said. "That's what I tell any idiot stupid enough to pass the gossip on. Just thought you ought to know what's being said."

"I can't do a damn thing about what people are saying."

"Did I say you should? I just thought you should know. I hate the way the person being talked about is the last to know. If you start feeling like people are staring or whispering, you have a right to know you're not imagining it."

Gage looked down into Velma's face, a road map of lines and creases, and a sudden laugh escaped him. "Yeah, you're right. It feels weird to have conversations halt when you come into a room."

"Well, if it's any consolation, most of the speculation is friendly, not nasty."

Some consolation, Gage thought, heading again for his office. He doubted very much that Emma would see it that way.

Stalwartly ignoring the wreath somebody had hung on the closed door of his office at the back of the building, Gage left the door open and dropped into the battered leather chair behind the even more battered wood desk.

So Miss Emma had been right about people talking, he mused. He'd spent most of his life on the streets of big cities, where people were apt to be deaf, dumb and blind if you were murdered right before their eyes.

When you lived in the combat zone called the inner city, you didn't give a damn about anything as inconsequential as who was living together. You worried about whether the guy next door was a pusher, and if he was, you worried about how you could avoid seeing something that might get you killed. At least, when you were a kid you did. When you grew up, you either became a pusher or joined the army to get out.

And then, maybe, if you were a big enough fool, you learned to be tough and got yourself an education, and then you went back and tried to clean up the streets so some other kid wouldn't have to grow up like that. Yeah, if you were a big enough fool, you did something dumb like that. And found yourself living on the streets without even your own name to comfort you for months at a time, running the very risks you'd tried to get away from by staying on the right side of the law. Yeah, it took a big fool to do that.

So he was a big fool, and he'd paid a price for foolishness that was higher than he had ever imagined possible.

Sighing, he rubbed irritably at his temples with his fingertips. There was tension there, and it had been growing since he got up this morning. He had the unpleasant feeling that things were closing in, that he was going to have to deal with matters that were beyond dealing with. He was used to keeping himself compartmentalized, to dividing himself into two people with separate lives. Once before, his separate lives had crashed together in a cataclysm that had cost him everything. Now he felt that things he had deliberately buried were going to surface in another cataclysm, this one purely emotional.

"Hell." With one muttered word, he slammed the lid back down on the grave of his past and forced his attention to the present. First, he needed to call the state lab and tell Herm Abbott about the new cattle carcass they were shipping up to him. Herm, unfortunately, wouldn't perform the necropsy, but as a lab assistant he would have access to whatever the pathologist found. It was Herm who had told Gage that the two veterinary pathologists disagreed about the earlier mutilations of Jeff's cattle, and Herm who had promised to see that Gage was told everything, not just what one person or another considered to be reasonable or politic.

Fifteen minutes later, with Herm's assurances still ringing in his ears, Gage picked up the phone once again and this time punched in a number on the East Coast.

"Professor Webster's office," a musical female voice answered.

"Hi, Sally. This is Gage Dalton."

"Gage! My word, it's been a dog's age! Where are you? Are you in town?"

"No, I'm all the way out in the wilds of Wyoming."

There was the briefest pause, then Sally said, "Can I ask? Or should I just keep my mouth shut?"

"It's a change of scenery, Sally. A good change, I think. I'm working for the sheriff out here. I haven't seen a drug pusher since I got here. Or an addict, for that matter. There must be one somewhere, but I sure as hell haven't seen him. Is Brian around?"

"He's in class right now, and he's got a seminar directly after. Do you want him to call?"

"I sent him a large envelope last Saturday, and I was just wondering if he'd gotten it, and if he had any ideas about the picture I sent."

"I haven't seen it yet. I sure would have noticed a letter from Wyoming. Why don't you give me your number so he can call you later?"

Gage gave her both the office number and Emma's number, asked a few questions about her husband and the Airedale terriers they raised, and then hung up.

His hand was shaking and his palm was damp. He studied his reaction with a kind of detachment, recognizing that he had crossed one of the invisible boundaries he had laid between himself and the past. The voices of old friends brought back memories and erased some of the distance of time.

And once again he ruthlessly stepped on the rising tide of feeling. Picking up the phone, he called Lance Severn to find out if he would need to bring someone to help load the twelve-foot tree onto his Suburban. Lance said his son would help.

Now, Gage thought, pushing back his chair and reaching for his jacket and hat, now he would go face the ghosts of Christmas past.

Chapter 5

Lance Severn's son, Walt, was a strapping college football player who was home on semester break. He handled the twelve-foot tree as carelessly as if it weighed nothing, leaving Gage with little to do except help tie it to the tailgate.

"I'm not sure I'll go back to Laramie for the spring semester," Walt told Gage. "Spring's a busy time for the nursery, and Dad'll worry constantly about the things he's not up to doing. Like this tree. He fretted and fretted about it. I kept telling him Bill Hascome could handle it, but Dad was convinced nobody but him could pick out a tree good enough for Miss Emma. Finally I came home two weeks ago and took care of it myself."

"It's a beautiful tree, all right," Gage acknowledged as he helped tie it down. "Miss Emma will love it."

"I went out to the Fenster ranch to get it. The old man planted a stand of trees to make some extra money. Up until he died three years past, he did it all himself. Now his widow has the grandson staying with her, and he keeps after it somewhat. Trees are getting a little ragged, though. Not what they used to be."

"They don't just grow this way naturally?"

"Nope. Need pruning and trimming to get 'em full like most folks want. And around here, they need a lot more water than nature provides. Don Fenster, the grandson, isn't regular enough about it. Guess he's caught up with those friends he's got staying with him. Bunch of creeps, if you ask me."

A faint smile of amusement came to Gage's mouth. Walt Severn sounded exactly like his father, a man who was nearly forty years older. And probably half of Conard County was talking about Emma and himself in the same casual way. The realization damped Gage's amusement and made him feel honor-bound to press Walt about Fenster's "creeps," and maybe get him to admit he was exaggerating.

"What makes you so sure they're creeps?" he asked Walt.

Walt shrugged as he tied another knot in the jute rope. "They've been living off that old woman for months now, and that just isn't right. They didn't even act neighborly when I came out to get the tree, just sort of stared and smirked." He gave the knot a final yank. "Creeps, that's all. We don't need that kind in Conard County."

Gage had a sudden vision of Walt twenty years down the road, helping tie Miss Emma's tree to some vehicle or other and talking just the same way. Ten years ago, even five, Gage would have thought such a life was wasted. Now, he looked at Walt Severn and envied him.

"I'll follow along in my truck," Walt said. "We'll have this tree set up before Miss Emma comes home for lunch."

Gage hesitated. "I'm not sure where she wants it, Walt."

"I am." The husky young man flashed a huge grin. "The Conards have been putting their tree in exactly the same place at least since I was born, and probably longer."

Later Gage sat cross-legged on the floor before the un-decorated tree and stared blindly up into its branches. With Walt's help, it really hadn't taken long to position and brace the tree. Walt must have helped his father with this job in the past, because he had even known that the tree stand was out in the detached garage.

Emma had brought out all the decorations last night, and Gage had forced himself to look through the boxes for the light strings so he could test the bulbs, a task that had traditionally been his at home. Somewhere in the process, though, he had fallen into the past. The strands of lights lay around him, winking gaily, completely forgotten.

A band was tightening around his chest, making breathing difficult, and his throat nearly closed as the tide of memory poured over him. Good memories. Happy memories. Lost memories. The ones that cut him to the quick with their simplicity and their hopefulness. Their blind innocence. The little things. The touch of a child's hand and the sound of a child's laugh. The warmth of a woman's arms closing around him as she laughed and wept at the same time. The joy of bringing joy to another.

Lost. Gone. Buried.

Ah, God! He drew a ragged breath, trying to expand his chest until the band of tightness would snap and set him free. It was in vain. Nothing, nothing, could set him free of loss.

"Gage?"

The sound of Emma's voice reached him but failed to penetrate the walls of grief that confined him. He drew another painful breath, struggling to break loose.

The sight of Gage's face struck Emma to her core. Wet trails of tears marked his cheeks, but he appeared oblivious of them, of her, of everything but whatever pain racked him.

She reacted instinctively, dropping to her knees beside him, putting her arms around him, pressing her soft cheek to his injured one. "Oh, Gage," she whispered. "Oh, Gage, tell me what I can do."

"Nothing...nothing..." His words were little more than a rusty, cracked whisper, but even as he refused her, his arms closed around her, squeezing until her ribs ached. She didn't care. Tightening her own arms around him until she couldn't hold him any harder, she pressed her face into the warm flesh of his neck and gave him what comfort closeness could.

"I'll be all right," he whispered roughly. "I'll be all right."

But she felt the shudders rip through him, shudders that would have turned into wrenching sobs if they had been hers. His grief became a palpable thing for her, so real she could feel it. This was not the pain, the agony that afflicted him physically. This was emotional and spoke of terrible losses. Just so had her father shuddered when he stood beside the graves of his wife and son.

"I'll be all right," he said again, but he didn't loosen his hold on her. When he lay back on the rug, Emma let him take her with him, let him hold her tightly against him and press his wet face into the softness of her shoulder. She forgot she needed to get back to work, forgot she had come home only to grab a sandwich and freshen up a little. She forgot everything except the man she held, the man who held her as if she was a lifeline.

Her fingers found their way into his silvery hair and caressed him soothingly, telling him with their touch that she was there, that she cared. It was little enough to do.

How many minutes passed, neither of them could have said. One last shudder passed through Gage, and then his arms slackened. Emma immediately loosened her own hold but found herself hoping against hope that he wouldn't pull away from her. Not yet. It felt so good to lie like this, to be held like this, to be so close to the warmth of another human being. She might never again be this close to another person, to a man, and she wasn't ready to relinquish the comfort.

Gage stirred. She kept her eyes closed when he shifted against her and bit back the protest when she thought he would leave her. But he didn't leave. A sigh escaped him, a heavy sound, and his arms moved, changing the way he held her against him, but not releasing her. Content that he wouldn't go just yet, she unconsciously snuggled closer.

Gage shifted again, abruptly, rolling onto his back and carrying her with him so that she lay on top of him. Suddenly the whole character of the embrace had changed. Emma's eyes snapped open, and she found herself staring down into eyes the color of a summer squall that were set in a face suddenly as hard as iron.

He didn't say anything. Not a word. She felt his hands at the nape of her neck, pulling at the barrette that bound her hair. Suddenly the clasp opened and her hair was free, springing up with a life of its own until it made a sparkling halo of fire around her face.

It was every bit as curly, kinky and wild as he had thought it would be, and every bit as soft and silky. He reached up and burrowed his fingers into it, luxuriating in it, finding her scalp with fingertips that seemed to have grown excruciatingly sensitive. She was warm, and she was alive, and he needed her vitality desperately.

The touch of his fingers on her scalp sent wild shivers trickling through Emma, running down her back to the base of her spine and then settling in her center like an uncertain edginess. She should stop this now, she thought. Whatever was happening, she should call a halt before she got in any deeper.

But her body was busy noting every hard angle of Gage's frame beneath her. She had never before been pressed this intimately against a man, and her nerves were taking a pleasurable inventory, awakening senses she hadn't known she had. Her breasts felt the hardness of his chest beneath them and began to ache in a way that made her want to rub herself against him to find ease. Her softer stomach fitted perfectly within the hard hollow of his, and his hard, narrow hips wedged against hers as if they were custom-fit.

And there, way down low, right against her most secret place, she felt the equally secret bulge of his manhood. Awareness sent an exquisite sizzle along her nerve endings, springing from the meeting of their thighs to every other point in her body.

Common sense dictated she should get out of this dangerous position right now, but common sense fled before the lava flow of desire that began to pour through her. Passion, never before experienced, made her a prisoner to her senses and paralyzed her will. Pinned by need, she stayed.

"Beautiful," Gage whispered hoarsely. "Why do you pull it back when it's so beautiful?" He fluffed her hair even more around her face and watched how it seemed to cling to his fingers.

She could have told him that she'd spent her life trying to get that hair to behave like hair instead of some wild thing with a mind all its own, but the words wouldn't come. The stroking of his fingers, the intensity of his gray-green gaze, deprived her of speech. The only sound she wanted to make, or was even capable of, was a whimper of pure pleasure. She retained enough sense to swallow it.

But then he pulled her startled face down to his and covered her mouth with a soft, wet kiss. "Let me in, Emma," he whispered roughly. "Let me in. God, I need to—"

He never completed the thought, because her lips parted, opening to receive him as if his will was hers. She knew, in some deep, aware corner of her heart, that he was using passion to exorcise his demons, that he was subduing pain with pleasure. Even this understanding failed to restore her good sense. She needed to give what he was taking. Her naturally generous nature wanted to give him any kind of surcease, and her long-denied femininity felt it was taking as much as it was giving.

She needed to know what a man's hunger felt like, needed to know what it meant to be desired, and he needed to replace his pain with that same hunger. For a little while they could each take what they needed. There could be no harm in that.

His kiss deepened, his tongue roughly stroking hers as if maybe, just maybe, he could find complete satisfaction in this if only he just thrust hard enough, deep enough, rhythmically enough. Never in her life had Emma dreamed that a kiss could be so passionate, so intimate, so arousing, or that something so near violence could be this erotic. A whimper escaped her as she opened her mouth wider and gave him back thrust for thrust. In her innocence she had no notion of the symbolism of her response. She knew only that she wanted to make him feel all that he was making her feel.

She was sure as hell making him feel. Gage had felt nothing but pain of one kind or another for so long now that he was nearly stunned by the sudden upsurging of desire. He had forgotten what it was to want something besides escape.

Some gentlemanly instinct tried to rear its head, reminding him of Emma's inexperience and his obligation to keep matters from getting out of hand, but he stepped ruthlessly on it. He was no gentleman. He was a street fighter from the slums, no white knight to protect a lady from herself. When she whimpered and pressed closer, the internal battle ended completely. She wanted him, too. It was enough.

"God, Emma," he whispered roughly in his ruined voice, breaking the kiss but holding her head close so that he could suck and nip at her lips. They were swollen and wet, and very, very sweet. She would be like that everywhere, he thought. Fresh and clean and sweet....

Her hands curled on his chest as he kissed her, kneading him until he thought he would lose his mind from wanting deeper, harder touches. *Slow down,* he told himself. *Slow down.* The last thing on earth he wanted was to frighten Emma.

But her fingers suddenly dug into him as he thrust his tongue roughly into her mouth once more, and then words spilled from him. Demands. Needs.

"Open my shirt, Emma."

She lifted her head a little and blinked sleepily down at him, her soft green eyes almost dazed looking. "Your shirt?" she repeated huskily. The mere thought made everything inside her clench pleasurably.

"I need your hands on my skin."

She drew a sharp breath and lowered her gaze to his chest. "Oh, yes..." she breathed. Without further hesitation she grabbed the front and ripped the snaps open with an eagerness that reached out and touched him somewhere deep inside.

And when her palms spread out on his chest, he unleashed a deep sound of pleasure. He'd forgotten how good it felt to be touched, to feel skin on skin. "Now your blouse, Emma. Open it."

The husky, hoarse command sent a jolt of excitement racing through her that turned her legs numb. It was followed immediately by a rushing tide of modesty that paralyzed her.

"Emma?" Gage looked up at her, and what he saw pierced his sensual preoccupation. The tart Miss Emma, who was reputed to strip the hide from any man who treated her like a woman, was trembling and blushing and making him wonder yet again if she was indeed a virgin. And he was treating her like a . . . like a . . . oh, hell.

He rolled suddenly, causing Emma to gasp in surprise, as she found their positions were reversed. Emma lay on her back on the rug, looking up at Gage, who propped himself on one elbow and held her in place by the simple expedient of resting his powerful thigh across both of hers.

Looking down into her confused and embarrassed face, he felt like the crud he probably was. Gently, he touched her cheek, brushed the wild, beautiful mane of hair back from her face. "I'm sorry, Emma," he said softly.

"F-for what?"

What a hell of a question, he thought with an unexpected burst of amusement that erased the last of his tension. He would have thought that was self-explanatory, given the circumstances. "I'm sorry I embarrassed you," he said. "Sorry I shocked you." But not, damn it, sorry he had touched her or discovered the passion she kept so well hidden. It was going to increase his misery while he shared her roof, but he couldn't regret it. Couldn't regret, either, that he had just discovered he was capable of feeling again. Not at this moment, anyhow. Later he would probably regret it like hell.

Emma's blush deepened, and her gaze lowered, only to dart quickly away from the bare expanse of his chest. Soft, dark hair covered his pectorals, and now she knew how that hair felt. Wanted to feel it again. "I...wasn't shocked," she admitted, her honesty springing from innocence. She never

dreamed the electric effect that truthfulness was having on
the man who hovered over her. "I liked touching you."

"You looked like a frightened rabbit," he said gently, ignoring the demands of his body in favor of treating this
woman the way she deserved. Street fighter or not, he
loathed anyone who preyed on women. He felt self-disgust
that he had even for an instant forgotten himself enough to
take advantage of Emma.

"I was...I never..." Her blush heightened painfully, and
she averted her face.

That was when he stopped suspecting and knew for sure
that Emma had never been with a man before. The surety
filled him with a tide of tenderness. "I know," he said
softly. Catching her chin in his hand, he turned her face
back to him and waited until she opened her eyes. "That's
why I'm apologizing. I got carried away. I wanted to feel
your hands on me, and I wanted to touch you the same way.
Anyway, I was moving too fast and I asked for too much,
and I embarrassed you. I'm sorry."

And her chance to find out what it was all about was
slipping away, Emma thought ruefully, because she was too
inexperienced to know how to take advantage of it. What
irony! If only there was some way to tell him that she wanted
more but didn't want to go too far. That she wanted to experience these wonderful, new things but not get into any
trouble with it. Oh, Emma, wish for the moon, why don't
you!

But Gage was incredibly alert to the least little signal, and
Emma was practically broadcasting. Her eyes strayed again
to his chest, and she licked her upper lip with a slow sensu-
ality that threw him almost instantly into overdrive.

"Emma?" His voice was a husky whisper, and he felt almost as he had at sixteen when he tried to talk a girl into
making out a little. Eager, impatient, terrified that the edgy
longing in him would go unanswered.

"Hmm?" Slowly, reluctantly, her eyes drifted upward
from his chest to his face. She didn't feel at all afraid, and
embarrassment was beginning to fade as the air around her
seemed to thicken again. All her awareness seemed to be

flowing from her brain into the rest of her body, making her
conscious of a growing heaviness, a strange, nervous anticipation.

"Want to... play a little?" he asked hoarsely.

"Play?" Understanding speared downward through her,
causing a deep clenching inside her, followed by a heavy
pulsing.

He saw her comprehension, and something in him knotted hungrily. "Just... explore a little."

Explore. She licked her lips. Hell's own archangel was
seducing her in tiny little steps, and she didn't think she gave
a damn. *Explore.* In childhood that word had somehow become associated in her mind with forbidden pleasures.
Somebody at some time must have said something.... *Explore.* The word alone was enough to make her tingle from
head to toe.

"Emma?" He bent his head, ignoring the ache in his
lower back as he responded to the one in his loins. "Yes or
no, Emma, but you have to say something."

She drew a shaky breath. "I don't want to go too far." It
sounded stupid, and even in her agitated state she thought
she sounded like a child, but it was a line she felt she had to
draw while she could still draw one.

"I know." He barely breathed the words as he found her
mouth with his and brushed a gentle, persuasive kiss there.
"I know. I swear I won't hurt you, but damn it, lady, we
both need some touching and holding."

Yes, she thought. Yes. That was exactly what she needed.
Touching and holding. Closeness and comfort. He needed
to forget his pain, and she needed to feel wanted. Surely they
could give each other that much.

"Yes," she murmured shakily. "Just a little."

"Then touch me, Emma. Any way you want to."

Before she could do more than register his command, his
mouth took hers again in a deep kiss, making her feel that
he simply couldn't get enough of the taste of her. In, out, his
tongue moved surely, strongly, and she never knew exactly
when her hips picked up the rhythm and began to rock ever

so slightly in response. It wasn't much of a movement, but it drew a groan from Gage.

He lifted his head and looked down at her from a face gone hard with passion. His eyes, though, those stormy eyes, were sleepy, gentle, reassuring. "Ah, Emma," he sighed, "you're a witch."

"And you're hell's own archangel," she heard herself say. She regretted the words almost as soon as they escaped her, but he surprised her by laughing softly.

"So I've heard," he murmured. "So I've heard." His hand slipped away from her shoulder swiftly and captured her breast through the silk of her blouse before she realized what he was doing. Her reaction was instantaneous, sharp, exquisite. She arched and whimpered softly.

"Yes," Gage whispered near her ear, causing another shiver to run through her. "Like that, Emma. Just like that."

He made her feel as if she was doing something wonderful for him when, in fact, he was the one giving her pleasure. No one had ever trespassed so far with her, and she had never imagined such a touch could feel so good. Even through the layers of her blouse and bra, the hardening point of her nipple could be felt, and Gage's fingers zeroed in on it, stroking back and forth until she bucked almost wildly beneath him.

"That's good, Emma. That's good. Just feel."

But she wanted more than to just feel what he was doing. She wanted to do a little exploring of her own. To that end she reached up and tunneled her fingers into his chest hair, reveling in the softness of the hair, the warmth and smoothness of the skin beneath. With every movement of her hands, she tested him and found iron-hard strength.

When her fingers accidentally grazed the hard peak of his small nipple, he caught his breath, telling her that in that way, at least, he was no different than she.

Gage's fingers froze on Emma's breast when he felt the heat of her breath on the aching point of his own nipple. "Yesss..." he hissed and instinctively leaned closer, encouraging her. The touch of her lips and tongue sent a zap of electricity straight from his nipple to his groin and was followed by a convulsive shudder of pleasure.

The sound of his groan, the tightening of his hand on her breast, thrilled Emma. Never had she imagined herself having such an effect on a man. It gave her an incredible sense of power to realize that she could imprison him in the same exciting web that he was weaving around her. It made her feel vital and alive to be able to evoke such pleasure. It made her feel incredibly generous and giving to know that she was making him feel so good.

And it loosened some deep-rooted inhibition within her. She was not alone in what she was experiencing and doing, and so she was no longer afraid or embarrassed. Trust blossomed for the man who was sharing himself as intimately as he was asking her to share herself. She forgot, for the moment, that no man could want her for long. She forgot she was crippled in an essential way. Forgot that her woman's purpose had been torn from her, and that her worthlessness had been thrown up into her face by a man she had loved.

She forgot how a man could wound her.

"Damn it, Emma..." The sound was one of sheer sexual enjoyment, torn from deep within Gage. His breath was ragged in her ear, and hers was ragged in his. "So sweet," he whispered, his breath catching. "So sweet...."

She wound her arms around him, wanting him closer, wanting to feel him with every cell of her being. She wanted his hands on her breasts, then his mouth, and when she felt him at last—at long last!—fumbling at the buttons of her blouse, excitement exploded like white heat within her.

And then the phone rang.

Reality washed over Emma in an icy, embarrassing tide. She snatched her arms away from Gage as if he burned her and squeezed her eyes shut. Oh, Emma! Lord, Lord, how could you have?

She wanted to sink through the floor, to die, to disappear, to do almost anything but face the man she had moments ago been kissing and holding and exploring. How could she have forgotten herself like this? It wasn't as if she

even knew him, because she didn't, not really. She had be-
haved like a shameless wanton.

"I'll get it," Gage growled as the phone rang yet again,
then again. "You stay right here. Don't you dare run. We
need to talk."

Talking was the last thing she could imagine herself doing right now, and certainly not with the man she had forgotten herself with. He couldn't actually mean to discuss
their intimacy, could he? Or to resume it?

As soon as Gage reached the kitchen, she scrambled to her
feet, determined to somehow escape. She had an extra
parka, an old one, in her bedroom, and a spare set of car
keys. She could slip out the front door while he was in the
kitchen....

"Emma, it's for you. It's Linda."

Her assistant at the library. No doubt wondering where
she had disappeared to.

She slipped past Gage into the kitchen, miserably aware
of the disheveled state of her hair and clothing. She must
look like a trollop, and by now Gage must certainly think
she was one. He probably had her figured for a desperate
old maid who would do anything at all to snare a man. Hu-
miliation burned her cheeks and thickened her voice when
she answered the phone.

"I hate bothering you," Linda said briskly, "but you said
you'd be back in a half hour, and I was getting worried."

"I'm sorry, Linda. I . . . had a little problem. I'll be there
shortly."

"No rush," Linda said warmly. "There's only me and
Mr. Craig here, and I can handle things. I was just worried." She hesitated almost audibly. "Emma, really . . .
is everything okay? You sound funny."

"I'm fine. Maybe just getting a cold." Emma said goodbye and hung up the phone, wishing she could crawl under
a rock and hide. Anything but turn around and face Gage,
who was standing behind her. She could feel him, as if his
presence changed the very atmosphere. Hell's own archangel. Maybe that was brimstone she smelled, because she'd
sure come close to succumbing to temptation.

"Emma."

That husky, ruined voice felt like black velvet on all her nerve endings, sending shivers through her that she now recognized as being purely sexual. She didn't want to turn, yet she did, facing him with downcast eyes. What was it about this man that overrode her good sense and caused her to do things she ordinarily wouldn't do?

"Emma, don't."

He was suddenly standing right before her, and he placed a finger beneath her chin, urging her to look up. Emma stubbornly refused.

Gage sighed. "I'm sorry," he said harshly. "I apologize. That should never have happened. It won't happen again. You don't have the experience to handle a man like me, and I damn well know it. I took advantage of you."

That wasn't entirely true, and Emma knew it. She might be utterly lacking in experience, but what had happened between them had happened with her complete cooperation. She couldn't understand why he was shouldering the whole blame himself.

Slowly she raised her green eyes and met him look for look. "There's enough blame to go around," she said stubbornly.

Her remark surprised him. He stared at her a moment, and then a slow smile creased his cheeks. "Guess so, Miss Emma. But right now you look good enough to eat, and I'm feeling like hell's own archangel on a weekend pass. Maybe you better freshen up while I make you a quick sandwich so you can get back to work."

Good enough to eat! My word, Emma thought as she hurried back to her bedroom. My word!

A look in the mirror brought her embarrassed blush back full strength, though. Her hair was tousled and wild around her face, and her blouse was wrinkled beyond hope. She would have to change. Well, that was all right. It would make a good excuse for her tardiness in returning to work. She could tell Linda she had spilled something on herself.

Good enough to eat. My word!

And what had he meant, *a man like him?*

* * *

It was snowing again, lightly, when Emma locked up the library for the day. She glanced out the tall, mullioned windows as she switched off the lights and saw the familiar sparkle of falling flakes. Downstairs, when she stepped out into the back parking lot, she found that nearly an inch of fresh powder had accumulated. A nearby streetlight turned some of the falling flakes into whirling glitter.

For a long moment Emma just stood there, watching the snow fall, reaching into herself for some of the Christmas spirit she seemed to be sadly lacking this year. Trying not to remember that she had to go home and that Gage would be waiting. How was she ever to face him again? How did two people ever look one another in the eye when they had actually... gone all the way? The question was undoubtedly indicative of her naïveté.

Sighing, she drew up the collar of her coat and took the plunge she always dreaded, the step into the dark, empty parking lot.

The instant she moved away from the building, the back of her neck began to prickle. It always did. She always had the uneasy, uncomfortable feeling that someone was about to seize her from behind. Unconsciously, she quickened her step.

It had been terrible today, she thought. The library had felt like a huge, echoing cavern, especially after Linda had departed at three, leaving Emma by herself. Even Mr. Craig, an elderly gentleman who spent most of his days in the reading room, had abandoned her, saying he had things to do for Christmas. She should be used to this by now, she told herself. December was her quietest month. Except for the children's story hour, which was always especially well attended at this time of year, she could have closed up shop entirely. People had no time for reading just now.

Except for Emma herself. She had scads of time for reading. And she might well have lost herself in the latest horror novel if her life hadn't begun to feel as if she were caught in one. Perhaps she needed to speak with Dr. MacArdle or Dr. Randall. Maybe one of them could reassure her about the feeling of pressure that kept growing in her mind. Maybe they could explain the flashes of glittering gold she kept glimpsing from the corners of her eyes, the voices that sounded like distant mumbling on a poorly tuned radio.

She was beginning to feel as if she was haunted, and the feeling quickened her steps even more. Glancing over her shoulder, she scanned the lot hastily, making sure she was still alone. The snow would have to be wiped from the windshield. She hated that. It made her feel so exposed to the night, to anyone who might come upon her.

It had been snowing just like this the night she was attacked. She had been walking down the street toward her dorm, hurrying because of the way the wind cut—

When had she remembered that?

Emma froze in place, blinking into the dark and the swirling snowflakes, cast back in time to a night she hadn't been able to remember since it happened. The memory was there as if it had never been gone. Vivid. Cold. Not yet terrifying, except that now she knew that the most terrifying events of her life had been about to happen.

Oh, God, what if she remembered the rest of it? She didn't want to... didn't want to, didn't want to didn't want to didn't want—"

"Miss Emma?"

Whirling, she saw a man emerge from the shadows and the falling snow.

"Emma?"

Gage. It was Gage. He drew closer, and she could see the white flakes on his shoulders, on his black Stetson. Closer yet he came, and she could see his scarred cheek and the dark pools of his eyes beneath the shadowing brim of his hat.

"Emma?"

She closed the last two steps between them as if he was the only shelter from the Furies. All her embarrassment was forgotten. Gage promised protection. How she knew that, she couldn't have said. She just knew that she could count on him.

"What's wrong?" he asked as she flew to him. There was no hesitation in the way he wrapped his arms around her and hugged her close, no reluctance in the way he bent his head to look down at her. "Emma?" And then, as if he understood, he pressed her head to his shoulder and held her snugly. "Shh...shh...shh."

"I remembered. I remembered. Gage, I don't want to remember any more. I don't want to remember what happened. I don't! I don't, I don't, I don't...."

"Shh...hush, baby. Hush. Let's get you home. We'll get you warmed up and get you a shot of brandy, and then you can tell me what's happening. Come on, honey. Come on...."

Little by little, he urged her toward her car, and finally he got her in the passenger seat, the seat belt buckled around her. With a couple sweeps of his arm, he wiped the fresh snow from the windshield.

When he came around to the driver's side and started to slide in behind the wheel, she screamed. "No!"

He froze, half in and half out of the car. "Emma?" Damn it, he'd forgotten that she couldn't stand to be in a car with a man. Now how the hell were they going to deal with this? He didn't think she was in any way fit to drive at this moment. She was, unless he missed his guess, very near hysteria.

He backed out of the car and squatted, looking in at her as she pressed back against the car door and watched him warily.

"Emma, you know I won't hurt you. Not intentionally."

"I...know," she whispered. "I know. But when you...I just...something happens, Gage! I don't know why."

"Well, then, I'll just walk back."

"No!"

He sighed and pushed his hat back on his head. "Emma, I don't think this is the time or place for a course of desensitization therapy. It's cold out here, and the longer we hold still, the more we'll feel it. I'll just walk back to the house."

He started to straighten, but Emma called his name. Slowly, ignoring the protest of his back and leg, he squatted again.

"I think . . . I think I can control it for the length of time it'll take us to get back to the house."

"You screamed the last time I tried to get into this car. If you don't mind, I'd rather not have to explain to half of the Conard County Sheriff's Department that I wasn't trying to assault you."

Emma blinked rapidly, battling an urge to weep. "Gage, please!"

"Aw, hell." He sighed and wondered if he would ever in his life learn to resist the plea of a sad or frightened woman. "Okay. I'll try to get in once more, but, Emma, if you can't handle it, that's it. I'll walk."

"I can handle it," she said raggedly, already growing tense at just the prospect. "I can handle it."

To Gage it sounded as if she was trying to convince herself more than him. He waited a moment, then straightened and once again attempted to slide into the car.

Her tension was enough to make the air crackle, he thought as he settled onto the seat. She gulped air as if she had just run a marathon, she hugged the car door as if she might slip far enough away to feel safe, and her hands were knotted into white-knuckled fists. Wonderful. It sure made a man feel good to make a woman feel like that. Sort of like Attila the Hun, or Bluebeard.

Before he closed the door, he accepted the keys from Emma's trembling hand and started the engine. He looked at Emma once more. "All right?"

She gave a short, jerky nod. Gage reached out and closed the door. Only Emma's sharply drawn breath testified to her increased tension when she was closed up with him. Releasing the brake, Gage edged them out of the lot, taking care on the slick, fresh snow.

Emma spoke breathlessly. "However did you manage to be right there when I needed you?" As soon as the words were out, she wished she could snatch them back. They placed unnecessary significance on Gage's appearance in the parking lot and revealed too much of how relieved she had been to see him.

"I walk a lot," he said. "It distracts me."

From his pain, Emma thought, and tried to loosen her grip on the door handle.

"I saw the lights at the library go out, and I came around the rear to make sure you reached your car safely," Gage continued. "I'm glad I did."

Emma was, too. She wondered how much longer she was going to be able to endure the impossible tension that gripped her from being closed in the car with a man like this, and thought that she could endure it at all only because it was Gage.

"Almost there, Em," Gage said a few moments later.

"This is humiliating!" The words burst from her as she battled back yet another impulse to fling the door open and jump out.

"Why humiliating? You can't help it."

"But it's such a small thing, and it's so stupid!" She drew a deep, shaky breath, battling to appear in control of herself when everything inside her was shrieking at her to run. "I hate to be stupid."

"I don't think you're being stupid at all."

Stupid or not, the minute he pulled the car to a halt beside his Suburban at the rear of the house, Emma bolted. She couldn't stand another minute in the car, not another ten seconds, and she scrambled out as if the demons of hell were after her. Then, utterly embarrassed, she hurried into the house with every intention of hiding in her bedroom, away from this disturbing man who had seen parts of her soul that had never before been exposed to anyone.

But Gage caught up with her halfway across the kitchen and swung her around, catching her to him and holding her as she struggled.

"Stop it, Emma. Stop it," he said sharply. "We have to talk, and you damn well know it. If you're remembering, I need to know what might be coming so I can help."

"Help? What kind of help . . . ?" She pushed at him, trying to get away.

"What if you remember in the dead of night, Emma? Who's going to be there for you if you remember what that man did?"

She froze, and then slowly, unhappily, lifted her wide, frightened green eyes to his. "I don't want to remember, Gage. I don't!"

"How are you going to prevent it, Emma?"

She shuddered. "I don't know."

"You can't prevent it. You can't. It'll happen. You're sitting on a time bomb, and if you've started remembering any of it, then the fuse is a short one."

She turned from him slowly, and he let go of her. "I'm going to change," she said tonelessly. "I need to make dinner."

Damn, Gage thought. He never would have pegged her for an ostrich. Did she really think that if she pretended it didn't exist, it would just go away? The lady was riding for one hell of a fall. One *hell* of a fall.

At the kitchen door she turned to look at him. "Who was there for you, when *you* remembered?"

When he didn't answer, she turned away and left him alone in the echoing silence of the kitchen.

Chapter 6

Gage, too, had experienced traumatic amnesia, though probably not for as long or to as great a degree as she had, Emma thought as she changed into her jeans with shaky hands. How else could he be so sure that she was about to remember all of it? How else could he be so sure that she was going to need someone when it broke? How else could he believe that she had really forgotten what had happened to her?

In retrospect, she realized how odd it was that he never questioned or doubted her when she had told him she couldn't remember. On the several occasions years ago, when she had tried to discuss it with a few college friends, she had met first with disbelief and then with all kinds of questions about what it felt like not to remember.

Gage hadn't questioned her, which meant he knew, and the fact that he knew meant he was probably right that she was verging on complete recovery of her memory. Oh, Lord!

She found Gage in the kitchen, reheating the soup she had made last night and slicing a loaf of bakery bread.

"Sit," he said quietly. "I'm taking care of dinner."

They ate in silence, neither one of them too terribly hungry, and then Gage poured them both mugs of coffee. When he settled into the chair facing her, pain flashed across his face, twisting his once-handsome features. Emma resisted an urge to reach out to him. The last time she had reached out, she'd wound up rolling around on her living room rug in a very improper fashion. There was, however, a burning question she couldn't smother.

"What did *you* forget?" she asked him.

Gage's head jerked, almost as if she had slapped him. A long, tense moment passed before he looked at her. "Sounds. I forgot the sounds. I never did see—" He cut himself off and looked away. He dragged in a deep breath before he continued. "I assumed—everyone assumed—that I'd been immediately knocked unconscious by the blast. When I started to remember . . . I thought I was losing my mind." *There was never a chance. Never.*

"Sounds? You mean the explosion?"

His gray-green eyes suddenly bored into her. "Screams. I mean the screams."

Emma's hand flew to her mouth, and she suddenly felt as if she would be sick. She should never have asked. She should never have disturbed this man's ghosts.

Gage sighed and looked down at his mug. Let it go, he told himself. Just let it go.

"What were you before you came here?"

He looked up again, tempted to tell her to drop it. He didn't want to discuss his past. His past was a closed book as far as he was concerned, and the more tightly closed he kept it, the better. When he walked the streets and traveled the roads of Conard County, people might stare at his disfigured face and wonder, but they didn't look at him with pity. They didn't whisper about him, because he gave them nothing to whisper about. He was as anonymous as a man could be when he stayed in one place.

But he was going to ask this woman to tell him things nobody in the county knew about her. As far as he had been able to determine, nobody in Conard County—with the possible exception of Nate Tate, who wouldn't betray a secret even at gunpoint—had any idea that Emmaline Conard had anything darker in her past than the assumed traveling man.

He needed to know more than she had already told him, though, because if her memory returned, somebody in this damn county would need to know what was happening. Somebody was going to have to hold her and listen to her and reassure her, and the lot would probably fall to him simply because he was sharing her roof.

Besides, he thought with grim resignation, she was going to need someone who would understand what was happening, and he was probably the only person around here who could.

"Okay," he said. "Okay. I worked for the Drug Enforcement Administration. DEA. I operated undercover in several major cities against drug kingpins."

"And one of them tried to kill you with a bomb?"

Such a simple, bald statement, he found himself thinking. It couldn't begin to convey what had actually happened. "Yeah."

"But if you were undercover—"

"My cover was blown. It happens." God, he wanted to get away from this now, before they edged any closer to the abyss of pain that was always just a single misstep away. "I'd appreciate it if you wouldn't tell anyone what I've just told you."

Emma nodded. "You have my word. I suppose you still have enemies?"

"A few." He would let her think that was the reason he wanted his secrets kept. Personally, he didn't care a bucket of hog swill if one of those guys came looking for him. It would be a swift way out of hell.

Except that hell didn't feel quite so empty and quite so cold with Emmaline Conard sitting across the table from him, her tightly bound hair like a candle flame in the dark. "Let your hair down, Emma."

She blinked. "I don't think that would be wise."

"Damn it, woman, are you always wise? Always cautious and careful and proper?"

Her lower lip quivered, just a little. "No. I certainly wasn't being proper or wise or cautious when I...when you...when we..." Oh, Lord, Emma, how could you bring that up? But her chest ached beneath a great weight, a weight compounded of unmet desires and loneliness. Of a feeling that even this man who had swept her halfway to the stars could see only an uptight old maid. Of a feeling that life had conspired to deprive her of everything that mattered, that this man scorned the walls she had needed to build to protect herself.

"Oh, hell." Gage looked quickly away and then moved so swiftly that she nearly jumped. Reaching out, he captured both her hands and held them tightly. "I'm sorry, Emma. Really. Talking about the past turns me into a bastard. Besides, I don't know how to deal with a woman like you."

"Like me?" Her lip quivered even more perceptibly. "What's so unusual about me? I'm just a woman like any other."

"No, you're not. Damn it, lady, I was raised on the streets like a wild dog. My mother was hooked on heroin by the time I was five, and my dad was knifed to death in a fight when I was six. Nobody ever taught me a damn thing, and all I ever learned I got out of books, once I could read. The army taught me table manners and how to keep clean, how to fight back with something besides a knife and a broken bottle. They sent me to school and taught me I could be something besides a punk. Then I joined the DEA and went back on the streets. I know about hookers and runaways and junkies, and about the hopeless ones who keep trying to avoid the muck, but I don't know a damn thing about satin and lace and churchgoing ladies."

"So because I haven't lived on the streets, I'm a different species?"

Her eyes were sparking angrily at him, and he was almost relieved to see it. It was a vast improvement over the quivering lip. "I didn't say that. I just mean I don't know exactly how to talk to a lady like you. I'm rough and blunt, and sometimes I'm coarse."

"You've done just fine so far, Gage Dalton."

"Good. Then maybe you'll get around to telling me what it was you remembered today. And what exactly it is that you're so afraid of remembering."

Emma's hands tightened in his. "You really think I'm going to remember it all?"

"That's what usually happens, they tell me."

"I don't want to." Her voice was thin, uncertain, totally unlike the Miss Emma who had most of the males in the county terrorized. "I don't see why I need to remember it. It was years ago, and apart from a few small fears, it doesn't affect me at all any longer." Except for one small but essential biological lack. What would Gage think of that? she wondered, and then told herself it didn't matter in the least, because it would never become an issue.

"Maybe you don't need to remember it, but if you remembered something today, then you're probably going to remember everything."

Emma tugged her hands from his, telling herself that, yes, his skin was warm and dry and callused from hard work, and that she would probably cheerfully fling her virtue away if he wanted to put those hands on her flesh, but that she really didn't need anyone to hold her hand. She had coped this far, and she could continue to cope. She had her pride, after all.

"What did you remember, Emma?"

"Nothing, really." She looked down at her mug. "It was—I was walking back to the dorm from the campus library. It was late at night, cold, snowing like it was tonight. I'm not sure how I know it was right before . . . it happened. I just know."

Gage nodded. "You just know, Emma. The rest of the memories are there, but you can't reach them. It's all in context, though. Your unconscious mind knows exactly what comes next."

Emma nodded and lifted her gaze to his. "I knew. You're right. Standing out there in that parking lot tonight, I knew exactly what would come next."

She wrapped her arms around herself, feeling cold and wishing she were a small child who could crawl into a parent's lap and find all the comfort she needed in a hug. That kind of comfort had vanished from her life when her mother died. Besides, she told herself sternly, adult problems couldn't be handled so simply. All the hugs in the world couldn't comfort her now.

"Talk to me, Emma," Gage said softly. "What do you know about what happened to you?"

The weight in her chest grew crushing. She drew a ragged breath, and then another, and wondered if she could even make herself say the words.

"Th-they told me he grabbed me when I was walking back to the dorm. They f-found a lead pipe with my blood and hair on it beside the sidewalk, so they think he must have stunned me by hitting me over the head once or twice."

Gage muttered an oath. "No prints?"

Emma inhaled deeply, slowly, battling for calm and control. "No. It was winter. He was wearing gloves."

Gage froze, struck by the way she had said that. "You remember that, don't you?" he asked softly.

Emma looked startled. "I-I guess I do. I see leather gloves. Black leather. Big hands. I don't know how I know that."

"It's all right, don't worry about it. What else do you know?"

"That he was—that he—oh, God, Gage, I *can't!*"

He reached out, capturing her hands again, squeezing them reassuringly. "It's all right, Emma. It's okay. You're safe now."

"I've never told anyone about it! Never. Even if I can't remember it, it's awful to even say it, to talk about it.... I don't think—"

"Did he rape you?" He didn't really want to be so blunt, but he had to know what she would be facing when the time came, and if he let Emma back off now, he would never find out. If she couldn't tell him, he'd ask outright.

Emma gasped. "No!" She tried to jerk her hands free, but he wouldn't let go. His expression was fixed, hard, not at all reassuring.

"Did he torture you?"

Emma stiffened and grew utterly still. Expression vanished from her face, leaving her to look as if she had been carved from palest marble. "Yes." It was a mere breath of sound.

Gage recognized what was happening, because it had happened to him countless times. Something in her had drawn back from all the uncomfortable, painful feelings. She had distanced herself.

"How badly did he injure you, apart from the coma?"

"Badly enough," Emma said tonelessly. "He left me for dead in one of those large trash bins. Somebody saw something and was suspicious and called the police. They found me before I froze or bled to death."

Gage muttered a string of curses, one after another, quietly but emphatically. Rising, he limped around the table and drew Emma up from her chair and into his arms. There was more here, he thought, as he held her close and offered what little comfort he could. Something had happened that she hadn't told him, something that was keeping this fresher in her mind than it should be when she couldn't even remember what had been done to her. Something was keeping her raw.

He thought of taking her into the living room because it was a cozier environment than the kitchen and might help soothe her, but then he remembered the undecorated Christmas tree. It wouldn't soothe *him* to sit in there. That left the library or study or whatever the hell Emma called it, with its ceiling-to-floor books, big old desk and leather sofa. Emma would probably feel comfortable there, and as long as he didn't have to deal with Christmas, too, Gage didn't give a damn.

"Go on into the study," he told Emma as he released her. "I'll bring the brandy."

Numbly, Emma obeyed. The calm that filled her was not natural, and in some detached fashion, she knew it. It was the calm of muffling barriers slammed into place to prevent emotional overload. Even the urge to run, to somehow escape, was silenced.

Gage joined her on the sofa with the brandy bottle and two snifters. "Here," he said, thrusting a filled snifter toward her. "Take it like medicine. You can sip the next one."

She tilted her head, studying him dispassionately. "I never get drunk."

"Tonight you're getting sloshed."

"Why?"

"Because if we're both lucky, you'll go to sleep and stay that way until morning. Frankly, Emma m'dear, I've had enough emotional turmoil for one day. If I can postpone the next round for a little while, I will."

She studied him solemnly and opened her mouth to ask what had made him weep earlier, but bit back the words before they escaped. Instead she tossed off the brandy and then held her glass out for more. He was right, she thought. They would both be better off if she could just knock herself out. Neither one of them wanted to handle any more.

"Slowly now," he cautioned her when he had refilled the snifter. "I don't want to give you a hangover."

"What the hell difference does it make?" Emma asked, and then clapped a horrified hand over her mouth. She *never* talked like that!

Gage astonished her by laughing. Honestly, truly laughing. "You're cute when you forget yourself, Emma. You ought to do it more often."

She said nothing, afraid she would only dig a deeper hole for herself. Waiting for the embarrassed blush to fade from her cheeks, she watched Gage ease himself into a more comfortable position on the couch. His every movement spoke of caution, as if the slightest wrong move could cause him severe pain.

"I can bring the Kennedy rocker in here, if you like," she offered. Comprehension was a little late in coming, but she suddenly understood that Gage had a problem with Christmas. Nothing else could explain his reaction to the living room last night, his tears before the tree this morning, and his desire to sit in here this evening.

"No, it's all right," he assured her. "It just takes me a little time to settle, that's all."

Emma leaned her head back against the couch and watched him without a thought for how rude it was to stare. He didn't seem to notice, anyway. His eyes roamed the bookshelves, and from time to time he shifted restlessly, as if he couldn't quite get comfortable.

So he had been raised on the streets. Like a wild dog, he had said. She couldn't imagine it. She could, however, imagine how defiant and angry he must have been. What had happened, she wondered, to turn him into this mature, contained man? If he had ever been a punk, no sign of it remained, except possibly in his preference for black leather.

"What's it like, working undercover?" she heard herself ask.

Slowly, Gage turned his head and looked at her. "Terrifying. Exciting. Boring. And sometimes it's the biggest ego trip on earth."

"What exactly did you do? Make buys on street corners?"

Gage shook his head. "Sometimes. The last few years, I infiltrated the bigger drug organizations. I wasn't interested in the street pushers then."

"How did you do that? I mean, I wouldn't know where to begin to look for a street pusher, let alone one of the big guys."

"It's easy when DEA backs you up. I'd just move into an area and start my own drug operation. I'd start really small and grow just fast enough to be noticed. After a while, I'd appear to be infringing on the big guy's territory, and his thugs would pay me a little visit. I'd be cooperative enough to let them know I'd be willing to discuss business, but that I wasn't going to be frightened away." A simple, clear explanation of what was, in reality, a complex, dangerous game of emotional and psychological chess. A game that in an instant could turn violent and bloody.

Emma shook her head. "I can't imagine doing anything that nerve-racking. How did you ever stand the tension?"

Gage sighed. This woman was going to pry every one of his most personal secrets from him, but somehow he couldn't bring himself to lie. He'd lived in the shadows of half-truths for too damn long. "I'd think about my brother. He OD'd a couple of weeks after our father died. Cort was eight."

"Eight? Your brother was only eight?" Emma was appalled beyond words. She was aware such things happened, of course, but they happened elsewhere, to people she didn't know. Until this very instant, such things had seemed distant, like a war in another country.

"You're very fortunate here in Conard County," Gage remarked. He took another sip of brandy and shifted yet again as the hot poker in his back took another jab at him. "Drugs are becoming a problem in even the smallest towns."

"I've heard. I think we need to thank Sheriff Tate that it isn't a big problem here. He started that drug-education program in the schools ten years ago, even at the kindergarten level. May I have some more brandy?"

Gage glanced at her empty glass, and one corner of his mouth lifted. "Lady, it's your bottle. You can have as much as you want." He poured a generous amount into her glass.

"It's relaxing me," she admitted.

Right to sleep, Gage hoped. All afternoon he'd cursed his carelessness with Emma. She was about as sexually innocent as a woman could be, and there was no getting around the fact that he'd taken advantage of her innocence. Carried away on new feelings, she hadn't even begun to realize her danger or how much at his mercy she had been. Gage had enough experience to know, though. He hadn't even unbuttoned her blouse, yet she'd been within moments of giving him any damn thing he wanted.

That unexpected responsiveness had haunted him all afternoon, making him feel both guilty and hungry. He didn't like to think of himself as a seducer of innocent women. All his experience had been with women who knew the score

and how to handle both their emotions and their bodies.
Even his wife . . .

He cut that thought off before it could blossom into pain.
It wasn't to the point, anyway. The point was, he had no
business taking advantage of Emmaline Conard.

But, he admitted, he sure would like to. The woman was
like tinder, ready to burst into flame. She made him eager
and nervous and horny as hell just by walking into the room.
Now he was plagued with the knowledge of her responsiveness, the way she arched toward him and begged with her
body for more. Now he knew that kissing her was incendiary, that her breast was made to fit his hand, and that in a
mere five minutes he could probably have her naked and
writhing beneath him.

Damn!

Slowly he turned to look at her again and found her
snuggled into her corner of the leather couch, her head loll-
ing back, eyes closed, stockinged feet tucked beneath her.
Something in him ached, and he wished he *could* reach out.
Just to hold her, he told himself. Just to hold her.

How the hell had a woman like her escaped marriage?
Why did such a passionate woman avoid men? He couldn't
believe all the cowboys around here were dead blind, so Miss
Emma herself had to be the sole cause of her unattached
state. And there had to be a damn good reason for that.

"I'm scared," Emma said abruptly. She set her empty
snifter down sharply.

Enough booze for now, Gage thought. "Scared of
what?"

"Of remembering. Of going to sleep."

"Sleep? Why sleep?"

"I keep having nightmares. Terrible, terrible dreams."

Gage could have told her that was part of it, but he forgot what he meant to say when Emma suddenly crawled
down the couch and curled up against his side, trying to
burrow into him. Without a thought for the consequences,
he wound his arm around her slender shoulders and pulled
her as close as he could get her.

"There's a dagger," Emma said shakily. "Like the one in the picture I got in the mail. You remember?"

"I remember." He tensed, sensing importance in this.

"I keep seeing it in my dreams, only it's golden, and there's a big, bloodred ruby in the pommel." She gave an unhappy little laugh. "I even see it when I'm awake, out of the corner of my eye. I keep jumping, expecting it to stab me. I'm losing my mind!"

"No...no...you're perfectly sane, Emma, I swear." And tomorrow morning, first thing, he was going to call Brian about that damn photo. He was beginning to think that there was more to it than mere fund-raising. "Does it hurt you in your dreams?"

"No..." She sighed. "I always wake up before it hits me. Sometimes I wake up screaming. I've been afraid that you heard me."

"No, I never heard you. Maybe you only think you scream."

"Maybe. I hate it, Gage. It's happening every night, and I just wish it would stop! I sleep with the lights on, and it's getting harder and harder to fall asleep, because I know it will happen again."

He hugged her and brushed a comforting kiss on the top of her head. Then, damning himself for a fool, he brought his other arm up and released her barrette. Time to distract her, he told himself.

"I love your hair, Red," he said gruffly. "It's almost alive."

She sighed. "I hate it. I've never been able to style it or make it behave."

"It's beautiful just the way it is." Slowly, gently, he fluffed it. "It looks like living fire, and it feels so soft." Gently he stroked it, and from time to time his fingers brushed the delicate, satiny skin of her neck. When they did, she sighed, and his groin tightened.

Playing with fire, he thought, and kept right on doing it. Hell's own archangel was accustomed to flying close to the flame, he thought wryly. He'd certainly done it often enough.

Emma was completely lost in the pleasure of being held by Gage. At the moment she didn't care that tomorrow she would be embarrassed by the way she had crawled into his arms. Just now, all that mattered was that he held her and stroked her and made her feel safe and welcome.

Beneath her cheek, his chest was hard and his heart beat strongly. He was warm, and he smelled wonderful, of soap and of something deeper, darker. Something exotic and erotic. Something that made her want to turn her face into him and nuzzle him, something that made her want to climb into his lap and press herself to him in ways she could barely imagine.

And, quite naturally, her embarrassment dulled by brandy, her thoughts drifted back to what had happened at lunch. How silly, she thought now, that she'd wasted the entire afternoon wishing it hadn't happened. Truth was, she had loved every minute of it and wished she knew how to ask for more.

"You're playing a dangerous game, Miss Emma." Gage's voice was little more than a rough, low whisper.

Emma suddenly realized that her fingers had slipped between the snaps on his black shirt and were absently stroking the skin beneath. Instantly she grew still. Her wits were muddled by the brandy, but not so muddled that she didn't know what he meant. She had, however, lost her usual sense of caution.

"I'm sorry," she said. "I was thinking about . . . earlier." She shouldn't have admitted that, she thought hazily, and tomorrow she was going to be upset that she had, but now, at this moment, it felt like the right thing to do. *This* was right, she thought a little dizzily. Being close to Gage like this was the most natural thing she had ever felt.

"Damn it, Emma, why don't you try a little prevarication once in a while?"

"Why?" She raised her hazy green eyes to his darker gaze.

But Gage was beginning to feel as addled as she was— from her closeness, though, not the brandy. He had hardly touched the stuff, but now he wished he had drunk enough to dull his senses. "Did you like what we did earlier?"

"Oh, yesss..." The words escaped her on a tremulous sigh.

Oh, no. Gage looked into her upturned face, into her sleepy eyes, and felt everything inside him tense with an urge to pounce. Slowly his gaze drifted downward to her soft, sweet lips, lips that were already slightly parted, lips she now moistened with a maddeningly sensual sweep of the tip of her tongue.

The worst of it was, he thought, that she didn't have the faintest idea what she was doing to him. In her utter innocence she was absorbed by what she was feeling and totally oblivious to the havoc she was wreaking. It was the sexiest damn thing he'd ever seen in his life.

His whole body was pulsing in time to his arousal, and a devil whispered rationalizations into his inner ear. Just a kiss or two, the demon whispered. What harm was that? A couple of kisses, maybe a feel or two. She would enjoy it every bit as much as he would. He could make them both throb a little, ache a little, yearn a little, and then he could send her safely to bed, because he would be damned if he'd take advantage of a drunken virgin. He'd committed a lot of sins in his misspent life, but that was one he never wanted on his conscience.

But a kiss or two? She was asking and he was willing, and if he didn't let it go any further, what harm could there be?

So easy, he thought, to sell his soul. Bending, he touched his lips to hers, felt the warm rush of her breath as she sighed her pleasure. That sigh nudged him even closer to the edge. Even the ever-present pain in his back and leg faded away before the uprush of aching passion. He wanted this woman. He could never have her, had no right to ever take her, but he wanted her like hell on fire.

"Emma...oh, damn, woman..." She felt so good in his arms, seemed to fit every angle and plane of his body as if she had been made for him. She filled a hole, made him feel like a man, made him feel like he had thought he would never feel again. Briefly, he rejoiced in life.

"Oh, Gage," she sighed shakily between kisses. "Oh, Gage..."

He ran his tongue along the smooth edges of her teeth, along the satiny, sensitive insides of her cheeks and lips. He felt her restless stirrings against him and suddenly lifted her so that she straddled his lap.

"Oh!" Startled, she opened her drowsy eyes and looked straight into his.

"It's okay, Emma," he whispered roughly. "We're just playing a little, remember?"

She nodded, hardly caring whether they were playing or deadly serious. Her knees were on either side of his narrow hips, making her acutely aware of how exposed her most private place was. And she was made even more restless by the growing ache that found nothing to answer it, and by the need to clamp her thighs together, a need he had completely stymied.

"Come closer, Red," he whispered, hell's own archangel seducing her with coaxing words. "Come closer." His hands closed on her hips, pulling her down until her femininity rested squarely against his engorged manhood. "That's it," he whispered. "Closer, Em. Closer."

She came closer, needing it as much as he, and when his hands slipped behind her to cup the roundness of her bottom and press her into him, she could do nothing but moan in utter relief.

"That's good, isn't it?" he whispered right into her ear, causing a sinuous shiver to run all the way to her toes. Gently, he pressed her into him again. "So good... What a temptress you are, lady. That's it. Just press against me whenever you feel like it.... Ahh..."

Dimly, he realized he had gone far past the couple of kisses he had intended. And then he wondered what the hell difference it made; he was already damned anyway. One more sin could hardly matter. When Emma rocked her hips against him again, slowly, deeply, catching her breath as she did so, he stopped thinking at all.

"Sit up, baby... sit up for me."

When she straightened, she pressed herself even more tightly to him. The sensation caused her to draw a sharp breath of pleasure that almost distracted her from the popping sound as Gage ripped his shirt open. She recognized the sound, though, and opened her eyes just a little so she could look at him through her lashes. He was beautiful, she thought, so beautiful, like a dark angel. Archangel.

He took her hands from his shoulders and laid them on his naked chest. "Touch me, Emma," he demanded. "Touch me."

Without the least hesitation she began to knead his powerful chest muscles with gentle movements. "I like the way you feel," she murmured unsteadily. "Smooth and rough all at once...."

Her blouse was open almost before she realized what he was doing, and when she felt the warm brush of his fingers against the soft skin of her midriff, she merely sighed and looked down. Dark hands reached for the front fastening of her simple white bra, and the sight was so erotic that everything within her clenched sharply. "Gage..."

He heard the way her breath caught, and his own caught in response. "Has anyone ever touched your breasts, Emma? Or kissed them?"

She gave a jerky negative shake of her head and then, as the bra clasp released, closed her eyes against a shaft of feeling so strong she didn't think she could bear it. She knew people did such things, but for years she had refused to even think of them, because such thoughts always made her feel so achy and empty, so lonely and alone.

"Oh, Emma," Gage breathed huskily as he stared hungrily at the satiny globes he had just revealed. She was small but full, and her nipples were rosy and already erect. Gently, knowing the sensation would startle her, he reached up and touched her with a careful fingertip.

"Oh!" She jerked as feeling speared through her, and her eyes flew open. "Oh, Gage!"

"It's fantastic, isn't it?" Leaning forward, he wrapped his arms around her hips and ran his tongue slowly, enticingly, in a circle around her knotted nipple. "Mmm," he growled deeply as he felt shivers ripple through her. "It just gets better and better, Em. Better and better.... Ahh, that's it. Rock against me, sweet. Just like that...."

Emma had long ago decided that lovemaking must feel good, but she had never dreamed it would feel like another plateau of existence altogether. She had never imagined that embarrassment would vanish, and shame along with it. That she could actually clutch a man's head to her breast as she whimpered and rubbed against him.

Gently, with exquisite care, Gage drew her nipple into his mouth and sucked. Her response was instantaneous, a soft moan escaped her as she drew taut against him. God, he loved the way she responded. There was something to be said for inexperience, something to be said for the joy of wakening a woman who had no preconceptions or misconceptions.

His own body felt as if it were about to explode. The need was stronger in him than he could remember ever feeling, the urge to bury himself deeply in her welcoming heat almost enough to override his last scruple.

But not quite enough to override the last scrap of his sense. He had no way to protect her from pregnancy. He had thought about going out that afternoon and buying some condoms, but he had talked himself out of it. As long as he couldn't risk impregnating her, he would retain some self-control. For her sake, far more than his own, he had resisted temptation.

Now, knowing he could not go any further than this without taking an unconscionable risk, he was able to batter down his desires just enough to maintain control. He would give her what she needed because he had aroused the passion in her, but he would take nothing for himself but her pleasure. Damn, Dalton, he thought sarcastically, aren't we the noble one? Because he was enjoying this at least as much as Emma, even knowing how he was going to ache later, when he put her aside. He was enjoying every single little bit of this, reveling in sensations he had believed he would never feel again—feeling every one of them more intensely than he had ever dreamed possible.

He moved his mouth to Emma's other breast, teasing and tormenting her there with exquisite care until she was sobbing for breath and pressing herself against him in a relentless search for release.

"That's it, Em," he whispered encouragingly. Gripping her hips, he encouraged her movements against him. "Oh, that's good, Em. That's great. It feels so damn good!"

"Gage?" His name was a frightened question, and she stiffened.

"Easy, babe. Easy. Let it happen . . . oh, honey, it'll feel so good. . . ." He moved her hips, forcing her to climb the last few terrifying steps to the pinnacle. "Come on, Em," he said roughly. "Come on . . . just let it happen. . . ."

"Gage!" It was a short, sharp cry as she arched one final time against him, then collapsed on his chest.

He held her, stroking her from head to hip, murmuring gently to her as he took an incredible, simple pleasure from holding her like this. It was even possible to ignore his own aching loins and the shaft of pain in his lower back in favor of the warm comfort of her skin against his. Such a precious feeling, he thought, the touch of skin on skin, her chest to his. So damn precious.

"You're beautiful, Emma. Beautiful, warm and passionate," he whispered as he held her. "I wouldn't have missed that for the world. Not for the world."

For a long, long time Emma lay drowsily in his arms, more replete than she had ever felt. His stroking hands on her back assured her of her welcome on his lap, and the contact of their bare chests was a warm intimacy that made her feel even more satisfied. But gradually she began to think again.

"Gage?"

"Hmm?" His hands never paused as he enjoyed the smooth line of her back and the warmth of her against his palms.

"That was the Big O, wasn't it?"

A soft, amused sound escaped him. "It sure looked like it."

"I don't think it could have been anything else. I never imagined it was like that."

"It's not the kind of thing anyone can really imagine." Wrapping his arms around her, he squeezed her. "Fantastic, isn't it?" He was feeling warm and generous and very saintly at the moment, he realized. Kind of a high for hell's own archangel to be so selfless. He almost laughed aloud at himself.

"Mmm." She stirred a little and looked up at him. "But what about you?"

That was one question he'd been hoping she wouldn't ask. Damn Miss Emma and her honesty. "Don't worry about it, Red."

"But—"

He cut her off by placing his fingers against her lips. "Emma, don't. I don't have any way to protect you." As an excuse, it was one of the best. He somehow thought that if he tried to take the high moral ground on this one and claim he didn't want to take a virgin, she would try to talk him out of it. The pregnancy argument was one she couldn't counter.

"Protect me?" It didn't connect in her muzzy mind. "From what?"

"Pregnancy," he said, beginning to feel the early twinges of desperation. She was innocent, he reminded himself. Unaccustomed to thinking in such terms.

But suddenly she stiffened against him, and all the warm relaxation he had felt and enjoyed in her was gone.

"Emma? Emma, what's wrong? You can't honestly think I'd take a chance like that with you. You don't want to get pregnant—"

"I wish I could!" she said with sudden fierceness. Her hands turned into fists on his shoulders, and she sat up, struggling to escape from his lap.

"Emma?" He caught her by the waist and ignored her struggles to get away. "Emma, what do you mean?"

Tell him, commanded a voice in her head. *Tell him now.* He would go away then. He would go away before she started to care any more than she already did. Before it was too late for her heart and soul. And just as suddenly as she had gone wild, she grew utterly calm.

"I can't get pregnant," she said tonelessly. "The attack damaged me so badly that ... I'm barren."

His hands relaxed at her waist as shock ripped through him. Before he could absorb what she had said, before he could do anything at all, she twisted from his hold and fled.

Chapter 7

Several times Gage came to her bedroom door and knocked. "Emma, talk to me. Call me names, tell me what a slug I am, but for God's sake, talk to me."

Each time Emma listened to him but felt no desire to answer. She lay on her back in the middle of the bed, staring up at the jewel-like colors the Tiffany lamp cast on the ceiling. Some pains ran so deep that they made you numb, she thought distantly. She felt numb right now. Numb to everything.

"Emma, come on. Open the door. I'll bring you some of that Earl Grey tea I found in the pantry. Emma?"

She ignored him, and after a while he went away again. She didn't think he'd given up, though. No, he would come back later and knock on the door. Maybe she should shout something at him, tell him to drop dead or get lost or something. He'd opened the wound. He'd awakened all the feelings she had learned to suppress. He had turned her into an aching, wanting, needing woman when she wasn't a woman at all anymore.

She wondered if she could stand it.

* * *

Gage stood staring at the closed door of Emma's bedroom and wondered why it always seemed to turn out this way. Karma. It had to be karma. There had to be some reason why everything he touched turned to ashes, why pain dogged his every step. He'd tried to make the woman feel good, truly good, and instead he'd managed to rip open her deepest wounds.

The door had a solid core, he realized as he stared at the dark, varnished surface. It was the good old-fashioned kind of door, not the thin, modern kind that he could put his fist through.

So he would just have to do something. No way was he going to leave Emma alone to sink into despair. Damned if he could understand this hang-up women had with babies, anyway. He loved kids, sure. Had loved his—scratch that. Nothing wrong with kids, but he couldn't understand this insane passion to have them. How could you love a kid you had never even held yet? How could you be so sure you'd want the little bugger before you knew whether he would even be tolerable? Women were in love with the *idea* of having kids, but as a man, he couldn't begin to understand it.

But he *could* understand that women felt that way, and he could understand that he had just stumbled on the reason why Emma avoided men. Now she was lying in there as raw as a gaping wound, and he'd done that to her. It didn't matter that he hadn't meant to. He'd done it. Now he had to figure out how to fix it.

No, not fix it. There was no fixing this one. But he couldn't leave her alone with it. Nobody should be alone with that kind of pain.

But the solid oak door stood between them.

So he'd pick the damn lock.

Turning, he limped toward the stairway and then climbed the steps slowly, glad there was no one to see him. His back was kicking up pretty bad right now. Why the hell hadn't he stayed in the apartment above Mahoney's? Then he could have limped down the stairs, had a couple of shots and gone for a long walk into oblivion. Instead, he was limping up these damn stairs to get his case of lock picks and worrying about a woman who wouldn't even talk to him.

Yeah, it had to be karma. He must have sold his soul in another lifetime, too.

Forget the long walk, he thought when he reached the top of the stairs. Sweat beaded his brow, the cold sweat of pain. A long, hot bath would be the ticket right now. But no. He was going to climb down those stairs, paying for at least half his sins in the process, and then he was going to shake Miss Emmaline Conard until her teeth rattled.

And probably work up another twenty years of bad karma as a result.

He swore loudly, succinctly, and turned into his bedroom. The picks were in the bottom drawer of the dresser, of course. Under the jock strap he figured would cause any blushing old maid to slam the drawer shut before she looked any further. Not that Emma had pried, but when he'd first moved over here, he hadn't known her at all. She might have been inclined to snoop. Now he knew the thought would never even enter her head.

Unfortunately, now he had to bend to get to them. Holding his breath against the inevitable agony, he bent down to retrieve the small leather wallet. On the way back up, he groaned. He couldn't help it.

He must be out of his mind, he thought. Absolutely, positively out of his ever-loving mind. Why was he getting involved with this woman's problems? Sure, it was nice not to have to live with the noise and stale-beer smell above Mahoney's, but he'd come here for quiet, not an emotional marathon. He'd come here, too, because a woman had looked at him with frightened green eyes and told him that she would feel safer if he shared her house with her.

He'd almost lost sight of that. But maybe all her fears were related to her returning memories and not to anything real at all. The balloon thing was a typical juvenile stunt, and even the decapitated rabbit didn't go far beyond the pale. He could just imagine some smart-aleck sixteen-year-old boy bagging the rabbit with his shotgun and then getting the idea of scaring the old-maid librarian. It wasn't necessarily anything threatening at all.

But his instincts pricked uneasily, and that business about the dagger in her dreams being like the one in the photograph...well, it was too soon to dismiss Miss Emma's fears. He couldn't imagine any reason on earth why anyone should want to harm her, though. But then, a sicko never needed a reason.

Gritting his teeth, he limped back down the stairs. Maybe later he would break down and take one of his pain pills. He almost never took them, because he had a healthy fear of addiction, but it had been months since the last one. Maybe tonight he would give in.

Her bedroom lock was as old-fashioned as the door, with a big keyhole and a simple double-tumbler arrangement. He picked it without any difficulty at all—other than straightening from his squat. He groaned as he did so and shoved the door open.

"Get out of here, Gage," Emma said flatly. There was no expression in her voice at all, not even irritation.

"Don't think so, Miss Emma," he said just as flatly. He closed the door behind him and limped over to the bed. She was lying in the middle of it, staring at the ceiling, and she hadn't even bothered to fasten her clothing. Now, with him staring down at her, she seemed to be unaware that a tempting strip of satiny skin and the soft curve of one breast were visible. That troubled him. She should have clutched the edges of fabric together and glared at him.

He sighed and yanked open the snaps of his shirt. The sound of popping snaps drew her wary gaze to him. "Just don't want you to feel underdressed, ma'am," he said and threw his shirt aside.

Turning, he reached for the comforter at the foot of her bed and unfolded it, snapping it once sharply as he spread it over her. Then, pretending to ignore her, he sat on the edge of her bed and yanked at his boots. That drew another unwilling groan from him.

And then he nearly jumped out of his skin, because he felt the soft touch of warm fingers on his back.

"Your poor back," Emma whispered. "Your poor back."

"Everybody's got scars of one kind or another, Emma. You ought to know that by now."

"How it must have hurt."

"Actually, it didn't hurt at all until a week later." He got his boot off, then turned and slipped under the comforter beside her. Without a by-your-leave, he tugged her into his arms and held her close, chest to chest, thigh to thigh.

"I'm sorry, Red," he said gruffly. "I sure as hell didn't mean to hurt you."

"I know that," she admitted. "You aren't the one who hurt me. It's just . . . sometimes . . ."

"I know. Sometimes it hurts too much to bear."

She nodded and allowed herself to relax against him.

"I've got a great idea, Em," he said a few minutes later.

"Hmm?"

"Why don't you just go to sleep? If you have any nightmares, I'll be right here. And tomorrow things will look better. Or so they keep telling me."

"But what about you?" She *was* feeling drowsy, drained by the day's events and all the emotional turmoil.

"Red, I'll be a happy man if I just don't have to move again until dawn. Especially if I don't have to climb the stairs."

"I'm sorry you hurt," she said sleepily.

"I'm sorry you hurt, too, Emma. Now go to sleep."

During the night, Gage awoke in a state of flaming arousal to find himself and Emma tucked together like spoons. Her bottom nestled warmly against his aching loins, and his arm was wrapped snugly around her as his hand cradled her bare breast. In fact, he thought sourly, the only part of him that wasn't aching and throbbing was his back, for once.

The light was on. He had left it on in case Emma awoke, because he didn't want her to come awake from a nightmare in the dark with a strange man holding her. It illuminated her hair, catching the gold highlights and setting them on fire. Such beautiful hair, as soft as silk. It brushed his chin and chest like wisps of dreams that could never be.

He sighed and tried to relax his internal tensions. The nights were always the deadliest hours for him. Things had a way of creeping past the strongest guard and pouncing without warning. On the nights when sleep eluded him, he walked hard and fast, just as hard and fast as he walked when pain flogged him.

But tonight he didn't want to leave Emma alone. He knew what it was like to be afraid to sleep because of the nightmares, and he knew what it was like to awaken alone and have to struggle your way back to reality without the anchor of a familiar voice. Tonight, at least, Emma wasn't going to have to face that.

He owed her one, he thought. Maybe he even owed her a couple. For the last several days he had avoided thinking about Miss Emmaline Conard and his response to her, but here, alone in the night, with her close and warm in his arms, he could scarcely avoid it.

Her generosity of nature wasn't something he was used to. If Miss Emma hadn't dragged him into her house for brandy the night he walked her home, he could have kept her safely pigeonholed as one of the local characters—odd, amusing, but not someone he would have gone out of his way to become acquainted with. Since coming to Conard County he'd gone out of his way to become acquainted with very few people. Micah Parish, Ransom Laird, Jeff Cumberland…just a very few men who knew what it was to face the abyss.

And now Miss Emma. Miss Emma, who hadn't known him from Adam but had dragged him into her warm kitchen and offered him brandy because he hurt. Miss Emma, who had let him fall asleep in her living room and then served him the best dinner he had eaten in years. Emma, who forgot all her caution and wisdom every time she thought he might be hurting.

Like earlier this evening. Even in her own pain she had reached out in response to his. Surely that made her more unusual than rubies and diamonds? More precious than

gold? Even his oldest and closest friends got uneasy and
eager to get away when they were reminded of what had
happened to him. It was one of the reasons he'd packed up
and accepted Nate's invitation to come to Wyoming. He
couldn't stand the way gazes slid away from him and conversations suddenly became brittle whenever somebody said
the "wrong" thing. People had been tiptoeing around him
as if he were some kind of time bomb. Or some kind of unpredictable invalid.

Out here, he pretty much got left alone. Mahoney would
pour him a couple of shots without trying to analyze him.
Nate gave him enough interesting cases to keep him busy
and never hinted that maybe Gage wasn't up to doing
something. Folks on the street nodded politely when he
limped by, and they'd even gotten used to his disfigured face
finally, so they didn't notice it one way or the other. The
good ladies in the Good Shepherd Bible Study Group tit-
tered that he looked like hell's own archangel, but even that
seemed purely amusing to him—especially since they giggled and blushed like young girls whenever he spoke to any
of them. And Maude, who owned the diner, always made
sure there was a fresh wedge of pie for him when he stopped
in.

It was as close to normal as he had come in a long time.
As close as he could ever get, he supposed. A man who had
spent fourteen years of his life working almost continuously undercover eventually forgot how to really be part of
anything. Survival demanded that you appear involved
without actually getting involved, that you participate while
always remaining an observer. It meant changing person-
alities like a chameleon changed colors. In the end, maybe
it meant losing yourself.

Sighing again, he pressed his face to Emma's neck. Her
scent was hypnotic, fresh and womanly, totally natural and
utterly erotic. The comforter that cocooned them caught the
aroma and surrounded him in it. Her breast was warm and
satiny beneath his palm, and he had the worst time convincing himself not to take advantage of the fact. Emma was
sleeping, a sign of trust he couldn't betray.

GUARANTEED

PLAY "ROLL A DOUBLE" AND GET AS MANY AS FIVE GIFTS!

HERE'S HOW TO PLAY:

1. Peel off label from front cover. Place it in space provided at right. With a coin, carefully scratch off the silver dice. This makes you eligible to receive two or more free books, and possibly another gift, depending on what is revealed beneath the scratch-off area.

2. You'll receive brand-new Silhouette Intimate Moments® novels. When you return this card, we'll rush you the books and gift you qualify for ABSOLUTELY FREE!

3. Then, if we don't hear from you, every month we'll send you 6 additional novels to read and enjoy months before they are available in stores. You can return them and owe nothing, but if you decide to keep them, you'll pay only $2.71* each plus 25¢ delivery and applicable sales tax, if any*. That's the complete price, and—compared to cover prices of $3.39 each in stores—quite a bargain!

4. When you subscribe to the Silhouette Reader Service™, you'll also get our newsletter, as well as additional free gifts from time to time.

5. You must be completely satisfied. You may cancel at any time simply by sending us a note or a shipping statement marked "cancel" or by returning any shipment to us at our expense.

Cautiously he moved his hand to safer ground, on her tummy, and then he closed his eyes, willing himself to sleep. The gripping, clenching, burning pain had for the moment let him go, and now would be a great time to sleep.

Except that he couldn't seem to sleep. He didn't feel especially drowsy, but he didn't feel especially like getting up, either. Instead his mind drifted, for once, into safe channels, carrying him back to his youth, when his refuge had been the city library. He could stay warm there on the coldest winter day, get cool there on the hottest days, and escape entirely on the worst ones.

In retrospect, the librarian hadn't been a dragon at all. Mrs. Scott had insisted on quiet, common courtesy and respect for the books, and on a couple of occasions she had spoken sharply to him for forgetting where he was. Overall, though, she had encouraged his love of reading. Looking back, he could see that when he had finished one book, she had been ready to hand him another. She had started him on the Hardy Boys, led him on to Monte Cristo and the Three Musketeers, and helped him to wade through Walter Scott. Even Captain Blood and the Scarlet Pimpernel—whom he held responsible for making him think undercover work was romantic—even they had been introduced to him by Mrs. Scott.

Mrs. Scott, he sometimes thought wryly, was therefore ultimately responsible for Gage Dalton and his funny notions of honor and duty and loyalty. Responsible for his even crazier notion about making the world a better place. Boy, he'd lost that one the hard way. There was a real war out there, and a few DEA operatives sure as hell weren't going to win more than a couple of skirmishes. Battling drugs was like battling Medusa. Every time you lopped off one snake head, there was another one right there. And in the process something inside you turned to stone, because there was just so much ugliness a man could stand.

And the fact that he could even make that comparison he owed entirely to Mrs. Scott of the vast bosom, the overwhelming perfume and the orthopedic shoes. In retrospect

Gage even allowed she might not really have hated him after all, despite her frequent frowns and sharp reprimands.

But never in a million years would he have envisioned
himself with the hots for a librarian. Or have imagined lying in bed holding one like this. In his mind librarians had
been pigeonholed with nuns and Attila the Hun.

Well, that was just so much hogwash, anyway. Most of
the preconceptions he had developed in his youth had blown
away with time and experience. This was just another one.
Emma had a few dragonish, stereotyped librarian charac-
teristics, but beneath all the defenses he had found a shy,
generous, warm, loving and very passionate young woman.
One who deserved something a hell of a lot better than hell's
own archangel.

Besides, he wasn't ever again going to sign on for that
roller-coaster ride. Once was enough. No man in his right
mind would take risks like that a second time. No way.
Hell's own archangel had safely locked up his heart and
thrown away the key.

Another sigh escaped him, a heavier one this time. He
opened his eyes to fill them once more with the enticing
flame of Emma's hair and the pale satin of her cheek, and
then he gave himself up to sleep.

The knife glittered evilly, coldly gold, threatening, the
blood-drop ruby like a malevolent eye. Voices whispered,
laughing, fractured, a steady background to a lost, frightened whimper. Slowly, so slowly, the dagger lifted. Higher
and higher it rose, then plunged downward in a swift, de-
stroying arc.

"Emma!"

The scream rose from so deep in her that it left her insides raw, then erupted from her throat with shattering
force.

"Emma!"

She sat bolt upright. Her eyes snapped open and stared
uncomprehendingly at the familiar sights of her own bedroom. Grandma's room. The judge's room.

"Emma?"

That ruined voice was now as familiar to her as her own, and it was a lifeline in the darkness of her soul and mind. She turned and threw herself into Gage's waiting arms.

"It's okay," he whispered achingly. "It's okay, Emma."

If she had been alone, eventually she would have calmed herself and restored her self-control. But she was not alone. Now, right now, someone was there to take care of her, and it was like permission to give up the struggle. For just a few minutes she could lean on someone else.

And she did. Before she could gather her wits or her resources, she was clinging to Gage, and huge, silent tears were running down her cheeks. "I can't stand any more of this," she whispered brokenly. "I can't."

There wasn't a damn thing to say to that, Gage thought. He'd been at just that point more than once himself, the point where one little thing more would shatter you like glass.

"I know the feeling," he said rustily. "Come on. Let's get out of here."

Slowly, she leaned back a little and looked up at him from big, wet eyes. "Get out of here?"

"Take a walk. Walking is great therapy, Red. Works out all the kinks, tires you out good, and gets you back on an even keel. I promise."

"It's cold out there," she said in faint protest.

"So bundle up. Don't tell me you don't have the clothes, Emma. You've lived here all your life."

Not waiting for an answer, he turned away and lowered his feet to the floor. He had to bite back a groan when his back filed a protest, but he had a lot of practice at it.

"Ten minutes, Red. If you're real good, maybe we'll drive down to the creek and walk there."

Emma glanced at the digital display on her clock radio. Three in the morning and he wanted to go for a walk along the creek bank? She glanced around the room once more as he disappeared through the door and decided that maybe walking in the dark was a more inviting prospect than staying here any longer.

She started to crawl out of the bed, and that was when she realized her blouse was still open and her bra unfastened. Oh, Lord! Emma, Emma, what's come over you? How could you have...?

And then, like a burst of light in the night, memories came to her, reminding her of how Gage had made her feel last night, how intimately he had kissed her and how tenderly he had held her. How he had insisted on coming to her despite her locked door, and had held her through the night. She remembered waking once or twice to feel him pressed so warmly to her, remembered that once his hand had been cradling her breast.

He had given her care and tenderness and the most exciting and sensual experience of her life, and she was reacting like a prude. Like an old maid. Like Great-aunt Isabel, who had told her to carry a book with her everywhere, to sit on in case she should ever be obliged to sit on a man's lap in a crowded bus. Considering there were no buses other than school buses in Conard County, the advice had been singularly useless. Emma had crowed with laughter for weeks every time she thought of it. A book, for crying out loud.

Good grief, was she actually beginning to *think* like Great-aunt Isabel?

The thought brought her scurrying off the bed toward her closet, where she definitely had adequate clothing for the cold night air. She promised herself not to have another prudish thought, to be honest about how much she had enjoyed everything Gage had showed her.

And to be honest with herself, at least, about how much she wanted to experience it again.

The temperature had fallen into the teens, and their steps crunched crisply on the undisturbed snow along the bank of Conard Creek. Emma's initial chill, which had come as much from the early hour as the cold, had worn off as they walked, and she began to enjoy the unearthly beauty of the night. The light from the waxing moon was strong, silvering the sparkling snow and frost.

There had been a time when she had loved to walk at night, summer or winter. The attack had changed all that. Drawing a deep breath, she forced her thoughts away from that direction.

"Feeling better?" Gage asked presently.

"Much. This was a good idea." In fact, his suggestion of a walk had yanked her out of the dregs of her nightmare faster than anything else she could think of could have. From the moment he had suggested it, the miasma of horror had faded rapidly.

"You know," Emma said a little while later, "I often wonder about my ancestor, the one who first came here to homestead."

"Why?"

"I wonder about his ego. I mean, look at it—Conard County, Conard Creek, Conard City. Do you have any idea how embarrassing it was at times to grow up as a Conard?"

"Nope." He glanced down at her, a crooked smile drawing up one side of his mouth. "Where I come from, they didn't even have Dalton Street."

"There's a Conard Street on the east side of town," Emma reminded him.

"I noticed it."

"Maybe I can talk the city council into changing it to Dalton Street. Would you like that?"

"No. I like my low profile."

"I'd like to know what a low profile feels like. Anyhow, I figure Edgar Conard must have been an egomaniac. If I'd been the first person to settle out here, I think I would have given everything Indian names."

"Some of those unpronounceable words that are sixteen syllables long?"

Emma gave a small, quiet laugh. "Maybe. Anything but Conard."

"I don't think you ought to be embarrassed about it, Em. It took a special kind of person to be a pioneer. Maybe a little ego was a necessary trait for survival."

"Maybe."

"You could use a little ego yourself."

The remark sounded casual, but it didn't strike Emma that way. At the implied criticism, she grew defensive. "What's that supposed to mean?"

He stopped walking, obliging her to do the same. His hat shadowed his face from the revealing moonlight, but her upturned face was mercilessly exposed. "It means that you're not worthless, whatever you keep telling yourself," he said quietly.

"Oh, now we get amateur psychology?"

He considered turning away right then. If he just walked into the night, Emma's problems need never trouble him again. And he sure as hell didn't want to get involved. But he couldn't walk way, he realized, because no one else in Conard County knew what Emma's problem was, and no one but him would have the gumption to confront her about it, anyway. She pretty much had all the rest of them cowed, except for a few sleazeballs who didn't have the sense to know better.

"No amateur psychology," he said quietly. "I never read a psychology book in my life, Red."

"Then what the devil are you babbling about?"

He almost smiled. Emma, he knew, wasn't one to speak so bluntly or discourteously under most circumstances. He had her on the defensive but good.

"Working undercover," he said, resuming their walk, "requires a pretty good understanding of human nature."

"Really."

"Yes, really. My life depended on being able to size up an opponent with only a little bit to go on—the way he stood, the way he talked, a couple of things he said. I was pretty good at it."

"Indeed."

He couldn't suppress an amused smile. "Indeed," he mimicked. "The fact that I'm still alive proves it."

This time she didn't make any smart comment at all.

"It's not book knowledge I'm talking about," Gage continued presently. "It's a gut instinct for what the other person will say or do because of the kinds of hang-ups he's got. It's a knack for knowing what buttons to push—or not to push."

"So you're pushing my buttons?" Rage began to simmer in her. She didn't like this at all.

"Nope. I don't manipulate people I consider to be my friends. I'm just trying to tell you that your self-opinion is about a hundred percent too low."

"What makes you such an authority?" she asked waspishly. He was treading in sensitive territory, and she didn't at all like it.

"The fact that I'm not you," he said easily. "The fact that I can evidently see all the good things you can't. Lady, you've got a lot of sterling qualities. Quit underestimating yourself. End of discussion."

Sterling qualities, she thought as she traipsed along beside Gage. It sounded like something her father would have said. She had a lot of sterling qualities, did she? Well, what about the not-so-sterling ones? The slightly tarnished or downright damaged qualities? So what if she had a few sterling qualities, or even a lot of them?

"Sterling qualities" sounded like something you would say to a homely girl who had once again been passed over for a date. It was the kind of reassurance a parent spouted when a child was convinced no one in the world loved her. It was not the kind of thing a man said to a woman he was interested in. It was, in short, a consolation prize.

The understanding at once relieved her and disappointed her. On the one hand, she had tasted temptation and found it sweet. On the other, she was scared to death that if Gage held her close too many more times, he would walk away with her heart in his pocket. And he *would* walk away. He might be perfectly kind and understanding about her sterility, but when it came to an enduring relationship, he would be looking for a whole woman. What man wouldn't?

Therefore, she told herself, it was far better that he think of her sterling qualities rather than her other ones.

"Emma?"

She looked up from the snowy ground she had been fiercely studying as they walked and realized that she had left Gage behind. She turned immediately. "Are you all right?"

"Every time you get perturbed you go into double-time," he said wryly. "Unfortunately, since I broke my back, I haven't been able to move that fast for long."

"You broke your back?" Forgetting her own problems for a moment, she hurried back to his side. "In the explosion?"

He gave a short nod.

"Lean on me if you need to," she offered as she reached his side. "I suppose it's a miracle you can walk at all, then."

"Maybe." He didn't like leaning on anyone, and he couldn't quite swallow the idea that anything in his miserable, hellacious life might ever have been a miracle.

"What causes the pain?"

"Nerve damage, old muscle damage. Sometimes I think it's pure orneriness."

If that was meant to be humorous, Emma couldn't see it that way. When he didn't drape his arm around her shoulder, she began walking at a slower pace. He moved right beside her.

Emma wondered sourly if Great-aunt Isabel had been complimented on her sterling qualities.

Probably.

Emma stood before the Christmas tree, staring up into its unadorned branches as early-morning sun poured like warm honey over it. She was dressed for work but had a few minutes yet before she needed to go. Gage had been gone for hours, but she had half expected that. He wasn't a man who wanted to get close to anyone. His desire to keep his distance would protect them both.

But the distance, while it was protective, didn't answer questions, and she had at least a couple to ask this morning.

What had happened to make Christmas such a time of grief for him? Why had he gone to so much trouble to make sure she had her tree, then sat here surrounded by light strings and wept the horrible, silent tears that in a man like him must spring from the deepest well in his soul? And then, she saw now, after she had gone back to work, he had forced himself to come in here and string the lights on the tree.

Once you start giving ground, lady, it's hell to get it back. Her memory of him saying that was vivid, and it probably explained the tree and the lights. He was trying not to give any ground. Or possibly trying to regain some he had lost.

For a moment Emma seriously considered getting rid of the tree. Instead, she moved the Kennedy rocker into the study and put away the box of decorations that had been intended to grace the mantelpiece in there. Gage would have this haven until the holidays were past.

Turning to leave the room, she found herself staring at the black leather couch. Lord! The brandy had certainly loosened her inhibitions, but, unfortunately, it hadn't dulled her memory any. Vividly, in embarrassing detail, she could remember everything she had done. Everything Gage had done. Every luscious touch and kiss and sensation.... Oh, Lord!

Quite apart from her sense of horror over her conduct, her body experienced an exquisite, clenching thrill at the very memory of what had occurred. Yes, she told herself tartly, it was a very good thing that Gage wanted to reestablish some kind of space between them. Apparently she was quite capable of succumbing to temptation. In fact, she was more than eager to succumb. It must come from too many years alone, she told herself. It was merely a reaction to... to sensory deprivation. Yes. That was it.

Oh, Emma, she thought gloomily moments later, you know better than to lie to yourself. What had happened with Gage had happened because he turned her on. Didn't she practically drool over the sight of his buns in his jeans? Never in her life had she noticed a man's physical attributes that way. Never. What was this? Some kind of delayed adolescence?

Still shaking her head over her own behavior, she slipped on her parka and reached for her purse. Maybe, instead of checking out the latest thriller for the weekend, she should check out a romance. There was a lot she didn't know about such things, and it occurred to her that a better understanding might do her some good.

The phone rang just as she was opening the door. Sighing, she dropped her purse on the counter and reached for the receiver.

"Hello?"

Silence answered her. The silence of someone on the other end, listening. Perhaps they hadn't heard her.

"Hello?" she repeated, louder. "Is anyone there?"

Again no answer. Well, Emma thought, there must be something wrong with the line.

"I can't hear you," she said into the phone. "The line must be bad. Goodbye."

She felt a little foolish talking to an empty line like that, but it could have been any of her friends, and she didn't want to be rude. Although in all likelihood, she admitted as she climbed into her car, it was probably one of those horrible telephone sales people who were nice until you told them you weren't interested.

She backed out of the driveway, but just as she was about to wheel into the street, she looked back at her house and gasped.

There, in hideous, brilliant color, on the fresh snow between her car's tire tracks, where she had parked overnight, was a huge patch of scarlet that looked exactly like fresh blood.

"How close are the herds now?" Gage asked him. "Would you hear a chopper if it came in to swipe another of your head?"

"I might, if the wind was blowing the right direction. It's sure as hell a sound I'd recognize anywhere."

"Micah's getting back from his honeymoon tomorrow," Gage observed. "I'll see if I can't get him out here on Sunday. He'll be able to read a story in those tracks."

Jeff nodded.

"In the meantime, don't let anybody go out there. We don't want to lose any evidence."

"Damn straight," Jeff said tautly. "Wasn't so long ago we hanged rustlers."

"At least now we know for sure it's rustlers."

Jeff glanced at him and grinned unexpectedly. "Yeah. I was starting to look out for little green men."

"Don't laugh. There're plenty of these mutilations that aren't so easy to explain."

"I know, but I'm happier than a pig in mud that mine *are*. At least there's hope we can put a stop to it. Hot damn!"

After they landed and drove back to Jeff's ranch house, Gage declined the offer of breakfast. He needed to get back to the sheriff's office and find out if Brian Webster had called about the photograph yet. Sally had promised that she would have Brian call just as soon as he received the photograph, and since it was now late morning on the East Coast, he must have gotten his mail for the day.

It was 10:30 when he pulled up before the sheriff's office. Emma, he thought, was probably deep in her work at the library. Placing books on shelves, perhaps. Or making new entries for the card catalogue. There must be a dozen things a librarian did that he had no idea of.

He was trying to imagine them as he stepped into the offices, and also trying not to get too impatient about whether Brian had called. He might have a class, of course, or some meeting to keep him from calling Gage right away.

"Gage?" Velma snagged his attention from the dispatcher's desk. "Gage, you better get up to Miss Emma's.

She hollered for Sara a little while ago, and now Sara's hollering for the crime-scene team. And that includes you.''

Gage froze. "Emma?"

"She's all right, boy, except for her nerves. As I understand it, there's blood all over her driveway, though. Not hers," Velma added swiftly when she saw the look on Gage's face. "It's not *her* blood. Nate has already headed over there.''

Her last few words trailed after him as he headed out the door.

Emma was standing with Sara, the sheriff and another deputy at the edge of her driveway. The convergence of three sheriff's Blazers with flashing lights had drawn some of her neighbors out of their houses to watch from a distance, but no one came too close when they saw that Emma was all right. Later they would undoubtedly all take a moment to drop by and speak with her.

Gage's black Suburban growled to a slushy halt behind Nate's Blazer, and that was when Emma felt the last of her terror seep away. Gage was here. She didn't even try to argue with the irrational feeling of safety that swept through her in a warm tide. Gage meant safety, and that was a gut instinct that knew no logic.

He met her eyes from across the twenty feet of snow that separated them. The contact was almost electric, and it hurried his limping steps toward her and the cluster of lawmen. She was pale, he thought, but not afraid. No, her hazy green eyes were sparking with anger.

"Will you look at that?" she demanded angrily of him when he reached her. She pointed at her driveway. "Will you just look at that?"

Reluctantly he tore his attention from her small, delicate features and looked to where she pointed. Blood stayed crimson on snow, and this blood was a ghastly crimson. Bright. Jarring. Threatening.

Someone had used blood to draw a five-pointed star inside a circle on the snow between the tire ruts in Emma's driveway. Gage recognized it instantly, then recognized the tightening in his gut as honest-to-God dread.

"It's a pentagram," he said. And in each of the five star points had been written a letter: E-M-M-A-C.

Emma C, Gage thought, as the fist in his belly tightened its grip even more. Someone was threatening her. Someone was deliberately trying to terrify her. There was no question in his mind now that this went past an ordinary teen-age prank. He glanced up at Nate. The sheriff's face was like carved granite.

"We need samples of the blood," Gage said. "What about footprints?" Suddenly he faced Emma. "You were parked right there last night, weren't you?"

She nodded. "I saw it when I backed out of the drive-way. I don't understand how somebody could have drawn something so intricate under my car, though."

Gage shook his head. "That little car of yours could be picked up and moved by a few average-size people. I've done it." He scanned the ground, seeing instantly that everything was too trampled to yield any useful footprints. "I wonder when it happened, whether we were even here...."

Nate arched an enquiring brow, and Sara glanced at Emma, a suspicious curve to her mouth.

Nate spoke into the tense silence. "Where might you have been?"

"We went for a walk down by the creek early this morning," Gage said. "I guess we were gone more than an hour. It doesn't matter. They had plenty of time to pull this stunt, regardless."

"It wouldn't take a whole lot of time, or even make much noise," Nate agreed. "I guess somebody's a little mad at you, Miss Emma."

"It certainly looks that way," Emma said sharply. "Whoever it is must be about fourteen years old. This is ridiculous, Sheriff. Juvenile. How can they possibly think they'll scare me with a stupid pentagram in the snow?"

Gage squatted, ignoring a sudden, shearing pain, and studied the symbol. "I wonder if that's cow blood."

"Hell," said Nate. "I didn't even think of that."

Sara spoke. "I don't see why there should be any connection between the mutilations and Emma, though."

"Why not?" Nate growled. "Damn near everything seems to happen around this county lately. Why not rustlers who get their jollies by scaring maiden ladies?"

"Rustlers?" Emma repeated, refusing to let Nate's reference to maiden ladies disturb her. "You've decided Jeff's cattle are being hurt by rustlers?"

"A strange kind of rustler," Sara remarked. She looked at Gage. "What did you find at the Bar C this morning?"

"Helicopter skid tracks. Our villains are human for sure."

"Well, at least that's settled," Nate said sourly.

"Did you ever doubt it would be?" Gage asked.

"Not really. But at least I have concrete reassurance now for all the worried ranchers. I'm not equipped for space wars, son. That much is obvious."

Still squatting beside the pentagram, Gage glanced up and surprised them all with a grin. "What, no laser guns and particle beams?"

"Nope. Just a couple of automatic weapons."

"I'm glad you all find this so amusing," Emma said tartly. "Well, if everyone's satisfied, *I* have to get to work. No one else will open the library!"

She would have loved to stalk over to her car and drive away in high dudgeon, but two of the sheriff's vehicles blocked her car in the driveway, so she had to content herself with stomping into the kitchen. Her reaction was a little silly, she supposed once she was inside and warming up with a fresh cup of coffee, but she honestly didn't think any of them were taking this seriously enough.

Yes, it was juvenile, just as the rabbit and the balloon had been juvenile, but the combination of the three things gave her the uneasy feeling of being stalked. Nor was the thought that someone really wanted to terrify her exactly an easy one to live with.

The idea that someone in the county might actually want to do more than frighten her or annoy her was unthinkable, but Emma knew the unthinkable happened. For her, such possibilities were far from remote. She had been the victim of violence once before in her life, and that made it all the harder for her to dismiss the possibility of it now.

Irritated, annoyed, frightened, she paced the kitchen with her mug in her hands and listened to the rustle of voices at the edge of her consciousness, felt the internal pressure of memories she wanted to keep buried, glimpsed the flashes of gold from the corners of her eyes.

She wasn't going to open the library today, she decided abruptly. To heck with it. Nobody would come today, anyway, except possibly Mr. Craig, and she could call him and tell him not to. There was no story hour to worry about, no scheduled event, and today she wouldn't even have had an assistant. Friday was the quietest day of the week.

Giving herself no opportunity to change her mind, she phoned Mr. Craig and told him she had a touch of stomach virus and wouldn't be opening. He was sympathetic and told her that he hadn't planned to come in, anyway.

"There's snow in the forecast again, Miss Emma," the elderly gentleman told her. "Can you believe it? I don't think I recall this much snow so early in a winter in at least fifty years. It's a good day to stay indoors and off the roads."

"I believe that's exactly what I'll do, Mr. Craig."

She changed from her gray wool slacks and blouse into jeans and a navy blue flannel shirt, then went into the living room to decorate the tree. It took some doing, but she refused to look out the kitchen window to find out what the sheriff and Gage were up to. If they wanted to treat this cavalierly, she didn't want to know about it. When she had first seen that pentagram, something deep within her had turned cold. Anger had briefly squelched her fear, but now she felt afraid again.

What was it? she wondered as she knelt before the twinkling tree and adjusted the red velvet skirt. Most people lived ordinary, pleasant and relatively uneventful lives, didn't they? Of course, she reminded herself before she could sink into the quicksand of self-pity, that was precisely what she had been doing for years now—leading a quiet, uneventful life.

Sighing, she climbed to her feet and began to open the boxes of cherished ornaments. Some were as old as her family's history in Conard County. Some were as new as last Christmas. Each year Emma continued the family tradition of purchasing one or two new ornaments for the tree. Last year's brass angel would join all the memories from Christmases past and, eventually, all the soon-to-be-created memories of future Christmases.

One of the first ornaments she lifted from the box was a ceramic angel garbed in a white-and-gold gown that had been handsewn by her grandmother. As she turned with it in her hands, she saw Gage hovering in the doorway.

"My grandmother made this," she said impulsively, holding it up for him to see. "She was ten at the time. It still amazes me when I look at these tiny little stitches. I never would have had the patience."

Gage stepped reluctantly into the room, his gaze moving from her face to the angel and back again. "It's beautiful," he said rustily. "Aren't you going to work?"

"I've decided to take a sick day. It'll be the first one in three years. I'm entitled, don't you think?" Turning toward the tree, she looked for a good branch for the angel.

"I don't want you here alone."

Emma shrugged one shoulder, pretending an indifference she didn't feel. "I'll be fine. Nobody's going to bother me in broad daylight."

Gage sighed and stepped closer. "Broad daylight doesn't cover the inside of this house. If someone got in here, no one would know you were in trouble."

"I'm still not sure why you think anyone wants to get in here. We've had a few juvenile pranks, that's all."

"So far." He came another step closer. "Listen, I sent that photo of the dagger to a friend of mine back East. He's a college professor, and he's a recognized expert in weaponry. I'm expecting him to call today and identify that knife for me. I need to get back to the office to find out if he's called yet. If he hasn't, I'm going to call him."

Emma turned slowly to face him, the angel still in her hands. "You sent him the photograph?" she repeated, her breath catching painfully. "I thought...I thought..."

"You thought I'd dismissed it," he said heavily. "I couldn't, Emma. Not when it upset you like that."

She looked down at the angel and realized that her fingers were crushing the white satin and gold braid. "You think it's part of this other stuff."

"It may have been the opening move. I don't know. I just know it bothered you, and I'm not going to rest until I find out why."

If Emma thought hard—very, very hard—she could almost remember a time when someone had taken any of her feelings that seriously. When someone had made her feel that she mattered enough. When someone had cared enough. Her throat tightened painfully as she stood there looking down at the angel. Funny that a total stranger made her feel cherished in a way she hadn't felt since childhood.

"Emma, why don't you come with me to the office? I'll help you with the tree when we get back. It won't take long."

It would nearly kill him to help decorate the tree, she thought, raising her head so she could look at him. She had learned a lot of things about Gage Dalton in one short week, but this was the first time she realized he was noble. He would ignore his own anguish to take care of her. He might be an archangel, she thought now, but he sure as heck didn't belong to hell. He was battered and nearly broken from trying to make things right. Battered, nearly broken—and completely unbowed, because here he was taking up his sword again, determined to make things right, this time for her.

He stood now, hips canted to one side, minute movements betraying his pain-induced restlessness as he waited for her to agree with what he thought best.

He was a hero, she thought, swallowing hard. A genuine, real-life hero. The kind that nobody noticed, because they did the hard, dirty jobs quietly. She swallowed again. "You can call from here, if you want. I don't mind."

"I need to make a couple of calls, not just one."

She shrugged a shoulder again. "Whatever you think best."

Unexpectedly, he held out a hand to her. Emma hesitated only an instant. Carefully setting the angel down on the box, she closed the space between them and gave Gage her hand. Leather creaked as he pulled her to him and then wrapped her in powerful arms, in leather and the male hardness of him.

"Come on, Em," he said huskily. "We'll get it all straightened out, I swear."

She could have stayed there forever, she thought longingly, just filling her senses with him. The leather beneath her cheek was still cold from the outdoors, and the scent of the winter day clung to him. But beneath that smell of cold and snow there was the aroma of Gage, a mixture of man and soap that was heady and somehow satisfying.

"Come to the office with me, Em."

She sighed. "Okay."

He held her a moment longer, as if he, too, was reluctant to break away, and then he let her go.

"Just grab your jacket," he said. "The Suburban's already warm."

Emma looked up at him. "You're so sure I'll be able to get into it with you?"

He gave her a small, crooked smile, a smile that conveyed a surprising warmth. "Sure. We got you into it last night, didn't we?"

Emma closed her eyes, remembering the ride to and from the creek. She was sure she had taken five years off the life expectancy of her cardiovascular system. Surely a heart wasn't meant to beat two hundred times a minute? And her fingers still ached a little from the way she had hung on to the door handle. Frankly, she didn't *want* to do it again.

"Okay," she said. "Okay." Maybe this time it would be easier. And it was Gage, after all.

Getting into the Suburban with him *was* easier this morning. The instinctive panic eased after the first jolt, not entirely letting go, but making the ride a far sight easier on her. Gage was good, too, doing nothing to prolong their time together in the cab and talking all the way, trying to distract her. And this time, when they parked, Emma didn't scramble out as if demons were chasing her. She didn't exactly linger, but she climbed out with some dignity.

Velma Jansen greeted her pleasantly, but with a speculative look that made Emma think she might be in for some quizzing from the ladies of the Bible Study Group come Sunday morning. Velma was nothing if not a ringleader among those women, Emma thought.

Velma spoke to Gage. "Ed is driving the samples up to the lab. They'll get them today."

"Thanks, Velma." Gage touched Emma's elbow. "My office is back here."

"Why is Ed driving the samples to the lab?" She saw the wreath on Gage's door and wondered at it as he ushered her to a chair.

"Because it's Friday. Everything will get hung up for another two days if the samples don't get there until Monday. This way we should at least know what kind of blood it was—if it was blood."

Emma stared at him. "It sure didn't look like anything else."

"Smelled like blood, too," Gage agreed. He reached for the phone and punched in the lab's number while he watched Emma survey his office. "Herm Abbott, please," he said into the receiver. "Gage Dalton, Conard County Sheriff's Department."

Books, Emma thought. He had so many books. These had official-sounding titles, all of them related to law enforcement and investigations. She'd never really thought about it, but it appeared that law enforcement required a great deal of study.

"Hey, Herm," Gage said, "Gage Dalton here. No, I realize you haven't received that last carcass yet. I was calling because one of our deputies is hand-carrying some blood samples up to you. I'd like to know as soon as you figure out whether it's human or animal, and if it's animal, what kind."

Emma watched him shift in his chair as he sought a comfortable position for his back and wondered how he could stand it. She would probably cut her throat if she hurt all the time.

"I'll be at home for the rest of the day," Gage said, winding up his conversation. "Let me give you the number." He recited Emma's home phone number. "Thanks, Herm. Talk to you later."

He hung up and paused with his hand on the receiver. "Now to call about your dagger."

"It's not *my* dagger," Emma reminded him.

He started punching in another phone number. "Em, darlin', if that dagger didn't have something to do with you, I wouldn't give a damn about it. I sure as hell wouldn't have bothered Brian Webster with it. He's got more important— Hi, Sally. Gage. I got a note that Brian called?"

There was, Emma found herself thinking as she watched him, a whole world out there that knew more about Gage Dalton than she did. The woman he was talking to now, for example. He spoke as if they were very old friends, asking about her husband and her dogs, and then giving her Emma's number for Brian Webster to call him back in a couple of hours.

When he hung up, Gage swiveled his chair toward Emma, catching a pensive, possibly sad, expression on her face. "Brian'll call me as soon as he gets out of his meeting, maybe a couple of hours. Let's you and me go get some lunch at Maude's."

He didn't want to go back and face that Christmas tree, Emma thought. Initially he'd used the phone calls as an excuse to get her out of the house, and now lunch would be another excuse to stay away for awhile longer. She opened her mouth to tell him that he really didn't have to help with the tree, that if it bothered him so much she would gladly throw the darn thing away, but something about his expression silenced her. It wasn't exactly pain that caused the tension around his eyes, or anything else she could really name. Whatever it was, it made her feel strange. Edgy. Impatient.

"If we go to Maude's for lunch," she said finally, in a smothered voice, "we'll wind up being an item."

"We're already an item, Red. Velma warned me yesterday. People are talking. Are you going to be hanged for a sheep or a lamb?"

The question was vaguely challenging, almost daring her to leap into his arms, but the tension around his eyes had eased, and in their stormy gray-green depths she saw a sparkle of amusement—an amusement that echoed her own over the fact that she had used the same comparison herself only a few days ago.

"You mean I'm still a lamb?" she asked, and then wished she could die as soon as the incautious words escaped. What *was* it about this man that kept shattering all her prudence?

Gage had risen to his feet, and now he leaned across his desk toward her, giving a melodramatic leer. "You, m'dear, are most definitely still a lamb. Take my word for it."

He watched the color bloom in Emma's cheeks and felt a smile grow on his own face. He couldn't remember the last time he had seen a woman blush, and certainly not one Emma's age. She was priceless. Absolutely priceless.

He drove them to Maude's. It was only two blocks, an easy walk, but he wanted to give her more time in the car with him. She had come a long way already, and he figured that each and every time she climbed in with him, she took another step away from the fear.

If Maude had heard of saturated fats, she hadn't allowed it to change her cooking habits. She still served all the old standbys, from fried eggs to fried potatoes, and every item on her menu exploded with equal amounts of grease and flavor. Maude's cooking was a sin meant to be enjoyed, and Emma had long since learned to treat it that way. On the rare occasions when she ate here, she banished all thoughts of her waistline and her bathroom scale.

"I'll have the steak sandwich and fries," she told the waitress. "And coffee."

Gage ordered the same, and then, as the girl walked off, he shifted uncomfortably, trying to find a better position on the bench in the booth.

"Doesn't anything help?" Emma asked him.

He looked at her and slowly, ever so slowly, the corners of his mouth lifted. "Yeah. One or two things make me forget it for awhile."

Emma felt her color rising again. "Don't."

"Okay." He shouldn't be teasing her, he warned himself, and not just because it embarrassed her. He'd gotten too close to her last night, and he owed it to them both to back off before things went any further. It wasn't as if he had anything to offer her. And it wasn't as if she would want it, even if he had. Nor was she experienced enough to keep her emotions from getting tangled up if she had an affair.

So many excellent reasons to keep clear, every one of them inarguable—except that every cell in his body wanted to love this woman. Every inch of him ached to hold her and know her. She was warm, passionate, unspoiled. Loving her would be a fantastic, mind-blowing experience, he was sure. It would be unlike any experience in his life. He had only to remember how she had responded to him yesterday to know she would be as potent as any drug, and just as addicting.

But he didn't deserve her. And she sure as hell didn't deserve him.

And he felt guilty as hell for even thinking of such things.

He eased around again on the bench, trying to find that elusive point of balance that minimized the pain. He wouldn't find it, of course, because it didn't exist. It only felt as if it *ought* to.

"You don't have to help me decorate the tree this afternoon," Emma said after they had been served. "I know it . . . bothers you."

Gage's head lifted sharply, and he studied her, wondering how much else he had betrayed without realizing it. Of course, he had been sitting in front of the tree crying like a two-year-old yesterday when she came home for lunch. Not that he was ashamed of crying, because he wasn't. Some things sure as hell deserved tears. Some things deserved every tear a man could shed.

"I'll help," he said flatly, meaning to close the subject. Some things deserved tears, and other things simply had to be faced.

"You're impossible, Gage Dalton," Emma said tartly. "You won't cut yourself any slack at all, will you? And you don't care in the least how it makes the rest of us feel to be unable to spare you the least little thing!"

"I don't deserve to be spared."

The stark words caused Emma's breath to lock in her throat. His face gave away nothing, but it didn't need to. He didn't deserve to be spared? Oh, my word...

Aching for him as she had never before ached for anyone, Emma would have given the sun, the moon, the stars and the rest of her life to vanquish Gage's demons. She couldn't imagine that a man like Gage, a man so clearly upright and honorable, should have any real justification to feel that way, and it appalled her to realize that he believed he did.

"Years and years ago," Gage said presently, "I got stationed in a backwater Florida town. I grew up in Chicago, and in the army I stayed pretty much on post except when I went to classes at the university. You can't imagine what a shock it was to me, Em. Conard City is big-time compared to this place the DEA sent me. There were about a hundred people and not even a single stop sign. I'd had no idea there were places like that."

"Why did they send you there?"

"Some drug operation was flying cocaine in from South America, and we suspected they were landing near this town. My job was to be sufficiently disreputable to get a job of some kind in the organization."

He looked up from his steak suddenly and surprised her with a rueful smile. "Talk about getting your eyes opened. I was a hotshot street fighter from the big time, and suddenly I was in another world. Another planet. Another race. A twelve-year-old kid who lived up the road used to bring me squirrels for my supper. He hardly went to school at all, but he kept his mother and ten kids in meat by shooting squirrels and snaring rabbits. For me it was like stepping back centuries in time. I quit being cocky real fast. Those people knew how to survive in ways I'd never imagined."

Emma nodded encouragingly, wanting to hear more about him and not caring whether there was a point to it.

"It took about eighteen months to infiltrate the smuggling operation, but in the meantime I learned a lot. I learned that the world didn't have to be dog-eat-dog, and that a man has an obligation to his neighbors. I learned that even when it's tough, it's possible to survive without giving up the high moral ground. Without becoming an animal."

He sighed and pushed his plate aside. "A man has to accept responsibility for his life, Emma, no matter how hard it gets. That's what sets him apart from animals. Would you like some pie?"

A man has to accept responsibility for his life. Emma pondered that enigmatic statement all the way home, wondering just what Gage felt responsible for.

The fully decorated tree sparkled and twinkled in the living room like a fairy-tale vision. Gage stood beside Emma and wondered how he'd gotten through it. He had, though. Every time he had thought of turning tail, he'd reminded himself of Emma getting into the car with him. If she could do it, so could he.

And he was still here. His throat ached with grief, and his heart hammered on the edge of panic, but he was still here.

"It's beautiful," Emma said, then sighed, wondering why she kept bothering. Since her father had died, Christmas tended to remind her of all she had lost and all she lacked. Right now, looking at that beautiful tree, she wanted to cry her eyes out.

The phone rang, and Gage stiffened. "Brian. At last."

"Take it in the study," Emma suggested swiftly. "There's paper there for taking notes if you need to."

"Thanks." He was already headed that way.

Emma hesitated, longing to follow him but feeling he was entitled to his privacy on the phone. Finally her upbringing won. She headed for the kitchen to get some coffee.

It was now shortly past four, and the afternoon was darkening into evening. Snow had begun to fall earlier, but now, for the first time, she noticed they were in the midst of a blizzard.

Pulling back the café curtains, she flipped on the back porch light and looked out at her driveway. Her car was already vanishing under four inches of fresh powder, and all traces of this morning's events had been buried beneath a pristine blanket. Wind whipped the icy crystals around in a chaotic whirl and drifted the snow against the garage door. A sudden gust rattled the kitchen windows and doors, and she heard the house groan before the onslaught.

Mr. Craig was right. It was turning into a very unusual winter. A bad winter. Having lived all her life here, her thoughts turned immediately to the ranchers who would have to cope with this. Freezing winds and heavy snow meant all kinds of deadly problems for many of her neighbors.

She kept a weather radio on her counter, and she turned it on now, listening to the winter storm warning, the stockmen's advisory, the forecast for six to eight inches of fresh fall by midnight.

"Sounds bad."

Gage's voice startled her, and she whirled around to face him. "It's going to be awful for the ranchers."

"For the cops, too."

Emma nodded. "Was it your friend?"

"Yeah. Is that coffee any good?"

"I just made it."

He pulled a mug from the cabinet and poured himself some. "I'm not sure what kind of help we just got, Em, but I guess we know more than we did."

"What do you mean?" Unconsciously, her hands knotted together.

He leaned back against the counter and crossed his legs at the ankle. Lifting the mug, he took a deep swallow and sighed with pleasure. "Damn, lady, you make the best coffee."

"I buy the best beans. Gage, what did he say?"

"He said the dagger in the photo is a very poor copy of a dagger once used by Turkish *hashshashin.*"

"What's a *hash*—whatever."

"*Hashshashin.* The word is Arabic, I believe. We derive the word assassin from it, and the word hashish, which pretty much tells the story. Brian said that back during the Crusades these *hashshashin* were some kind of secret sect. Anyway, the dagger is just a very poor copy, so it sure wasn't sent as part of a fund-raising drive."

Emma pulled a chair out from the table and sat. "I don't think I like the sound of this."

"Me either, if you want the truth." He took another swig of coffee.

"A pentagram and a copy of a knife once used by a secret sect of drug-crazed killers," Emma said after a moment. "Gage, this isn't a very funny joke."

"If it's all linked." But his gut was telling him it was. "You've seen that dagger before, Emma. Haven't you?" It sounded more like a reminder than a question.

She drew a sharp breath and looked slowly up at him. "I think so," she said. "I think so, but I can't remember for sure. When—when I first saw the picture I felt as if I'd just been punched. But, honestly, I can't place it."

She wrapped her arms around herself as if she felt suddenly chilled. "Why would anybody...? Wasn't once enough?"

The anguish of her question cut him to the quick. The truth of it, though, was that he now believed she was being stalked. Nobody made a copy of a centuries-old dagger for a joke. Uppermost in his mind when he had hung up the phone had been the question: who on earth would want to stalk Emmaline Conard? It wasn't even as if she had a disgruntled former boyfriend.

And then he had realized. Her reaction to the dagger had been the answer.

Emmaline Conard was being stalked by the man who had nearly killed her ten years ago in Laramie.

Chapter 9

The storm continued to build as the evening deepened. Windows rattled ceaselessly, and the old house became noticeably draughty. Blowing snow nearly obscured the lights of the houses across the street and next door.

Emma pulled the curtains closed across the bow window behind the Christmas tree, then curled up on the couch with a book. Gage had vanished into the study directly after dinner, explaining that he needed to make some phone calls. Nearly two hours had passed, and now calls were beginning to come in for him. She wished she didn't think it had something to do with what he had learned about the dagger.

In fact, she wished she could just concentrate on the book until she was too tired to do anything but sleep. Instead, she kept feeling that something was about to pounce on her from the dark. Instead, her mind kept drifting back to what had happened between her and Gage yesterday. Caught between fright and yearning, she was too restless to read, and almost too restless to sit.

The things Gage had made her feel were too wondrous for words, and she was honest enough to admit she wanted to feel them again. She would give almost anything if he would just walk into the room right now and take her into his arms. She wanted his kisses and touches, wanted to feel again all those marvelous, dizzying feelings. And surely, after last night, he must realize she was willing.

But he was no longer interested, and the realization cut her to the quick. Her inability to have children had turned him off, too. She could place no other interpretation on the brotherly way he had been treating her since. After all, now that he knew she couldn't get pregnant, what else could be holding him back from taking advantage of her obvious willingness? Only the fact that now that he knew she wasn't a whole woman, he no longer found her to be attractive.

The understanding made her ache, but she forced herself to face it. She prided herself on her honesty, and it would do her no good to build castles in the air, anyway. In the long run, she told herself, it was far better this way. If he made love to her because she was "safe," or avoided her because of it, it made no difference in the long term. Either way he would move on. And either way Emma would continue to be alone.

So maybe it was infinitely better if she didn't get a clearer idea than she already had of all that she was missing. Yes, of course it was.

Just remember, she reminded herself, the fable of the shoemaker and his daughter who were perfectly happy until the rich man invited them to live as he did for a day. As it stood now, Emma had an idea of what she was missing, but she didn't *know*. If she and Gage ever made love, she would know beyond any shadow of a doubt. And the knowledge could blight the rest of her life.

Gage hung up the phone once again and reached up to knead a knot out of his neck. He'd set the ball rolling, and now he could only wait to see what started coming back. Friday night, especially right before Christmas, was not the best time in the world to start bugging law-enforcement agencies for vague bits of information. The law might never sleep, but on a typical Friday night it was too busy handling trouble to want to handle routine requests for information.

Laramie PD had been cooperative enough, he guessed—after he had managed to work his way up the chain of command. They had promised to pull the file on Emma's case and express it to him in the morning. He could have asked them to fax it, but he was afraid somebody at the office might see Emma's name and let her secret out of the bag. Better to wait for express mail.

He'd also managed to persuade a friend at the drug agency to pull a wild-card search on the national crime computer. If a Turkish dagger or references to the *hashshashin* had turned up in any crime reports in the past fifteen years, he ought to know by tomorrow night.

And by tomorrow night he should have a pretty good idea who in Conard County had a criminal record. Then he could start *really* investigating.

Sighing, he leaned back in the chair and closed his eyes a moment, waiting for the clenching pain in his lower back to ease up a little. He guessed he'd better call Nate at home and tell him what he was up to. Nate would be justifiably annoyed if he thought Gage was circumventing him, but he would also understand Gage's reluctance to do all this at the office, where someone might overhear. Nate would recognize the need to protect Miss Emma's privacy. And Nate, unlike some of his deputies, could be trusted not to gossip.

He sure didn't want Emma to hear about any of this. She was already edgy enough without knowing what Gage suspected, and edgy was good enough to keep her cautious.

And last night. He swore and shifted in the chair, trying again to ease his back. The woman was as sweetly tempting as a frosted cupcake, totally vulnerable to the new feelings she had discovered, eager enough to make him hard just thinking about her.

He never should have touched her. Yesterday, when she had comforted him, he had succumbed to the closeness and his own long-unsatisfied needs, but last night, after pumping brandy into her, he should have been able to withstand the temptation. He hadn't been weakened by grief then.

There was no excuse for the way he had lifted her onto his lap—except that he had wanted her. Except that he hadn't been that turned on in years, if ever. Except that Emma Conard was enough to tempt a saint, never mind hell's own archangel.

His crooked smile was self-mocking. From the moment he had set eyes on the woman, starchy and bristly as she was, he had wanted to sink his flesh into hers. He kept having the most incredibly arousing vision of her stretched out on white sheets beneath him, a sheen of perspiration glistening on her creamy skin. He could imagine holding her hands above her head while he licked . . .

"Damn!" He sat bolt upright and forced that fantasy back into a dark dungeon at the bottom of his brain. Thinking that way was only going to get both him and Emma into trouble. Time to call Nate and get his mind back on business. Reaching out, he lifted the receiver from the cradle.

"Gage!"

Emma's cry brought him instantly to his feet. He dashed for the study door and flung it open just in time to catch her as she came barreling through.

"Emma? Emma, what's wrong?" He could feel her shudder wildly as he held her, and she clutched at his sweater as if she wanted to climb right into him. "Emma?"

"Oh, Gage, he was wearing a mask. A horrible, hideous mask!"

Gage stiffened. "Who was wearing a mask? Who did you see, Emma? Was someone at the window?"

She shook her head jerkily. "No . . . no . . . I remembered . . . Oh, God, I can't stand this! I can't stand it!"

He drew her more snugly into his embrace and cradled her head against his shoulder. "You remembered something else?"

She nodded. "I could see him," she whispered shakily. "Just his head, and that horrible mask. And I knew I was . . . hurt . . . and I couldn't move. I was scared. So scared!"

The wise thing, he thought, would be to take her into the kitchen, fix her a stiff drink and keep the table firmly between them while he encouraged her to talk it out. Instead, he began backing her toward her bedroom. What this woman needed now had nothing to do with common sense and caution.

"Get yourself tucked in, Emma," he said, releasing her slowly when he had her standing beside her bed. "I'll be back in five minutes with the brandy."

"But—" She lifted frightened, doubtful eyes.

"Trust me, Red. Just do it. I'll be right back."

With shaking hands, feeling weak and sick as if she were ill, Emma changed into a flannel nightgown and crawled into the bed that had been a haven since childhood. With the covers drawn to her chin, she watched wide-eyed as Gage returned and perched beside her.

"Here," he said. "Take a stiff belt."

"Didn't we do this last night?" she asked shakily, not certain she could survive a rerun.

"Just drink the damn brandy, Emma." Scowling, he shoved it into her hand and urged her hand to her mouth. "I've traveled this road, lady. Take the brandy. Then you're going to talk until you lose your voice or you fall asleep."

She coughed as the brandy burned her throat, but she drank the full shot before she handed him the glass. "Why talk?" she asked a little hoarsely. Her eyes grew even wider when he stood and yanked his belt off his black jeans.

"Because you're not going to be able to think about anything else until you've worn this to death." He knew that for a fact. Some things honestly had to be talked to death. He eased down beside her on the bed, on top of the blankets, fully clothed except for boots and belt. "Light on or off?"

"On," she said. "Please."

"Okay." Reaching out, he tugged her, blankets and all, into his arms. "Close your eyes and talk, Em. Tell me what you remembered. Tell me how you felt. Tell me how you feel about it right now."

For a little while she didn't say anything at all, but he understood her hesitation. The things that hurt the worst, the deepest wounds and scars, were the hardest to talk about.

They were also the ones a person most needed to put into words.

He stroked her back through the blankets from shoulder to hip, and once or twice he pressed a reassuring kiss on her temple. To think he'd been a grown man before he had understood just how important it was to hold somebody close when they hurt. Before he had understood that a kiss and a hug could really heal some hurts.

"I'm mad," Emma said quietly.

"I should certainly think so," he rumbled soothingly.

"I'm furious."

"Maybe mad enough to kill." He felt her hand tighten into a fist on his chest.

"Maybe," she agreed hoarsely. "Oh, Gage, how could anyone do such things? How could anyone...?"

"How could anyone hurt *you* like that?" he completed. "Beats the hell out of me, Emma. It always has and always will. Sometimes people are careless, and I can understand that, but deliberate violence—hell, I don't understand it, either."

"He must have been sick."

"Probably."

She fell silent again, and except for the small movements her hands made against him, he would have thought she slept. He wondered if she had any idea that she was practically petting him, and thought not. She was locked in her memory. He remembered how obsessive it was possible to get with each piece as it surfaced, how you twisted it and turned it and tried to fit it into the jigsaw pattern that was beginning to emerge. How you tried to remember the missing pieces around that one recovered memory. How you feared what else might surface.

"He was wearing a mask," Emma said again, a long time later. She sounded calmer now. Felt calmer. Gage made her feel safe, and the brandy had taken the edge off her anxiety. "Why do you think he wore a mask?"

"I don't know. A precaution, maybe, in case someone saw him." *Or maybe he didn't want Emma to recognize him?* "What kind of mask was it?"

"One of those translucent Halloween things that looks almost like a real face." She shuddered and wiggled a little closer to him. "I could almost see him inside it. Almost. It's like if I could just focus a little more clearly, I'd be able to see him."

He ran his hand down her back again, soothingly, and then took the clip from her hair so he could burrow his fingers into it and massage the tension from her scalp. "Don't push it, Emma. Believe me, it'll come in its own good time."

"I wish it would just go away."

"I know. I know." Yeah, he knew. He ached for her, ached for what she was going to face. And he found himself hoping that the blows to her head had concussed her enough that her memories of that night would always be incomplete. Some things should never be remembered. He knew all about those things, too. Emma stirred and started speaking again, her voice little more than a whisper.

"When...when I woke up in the hospital, it was—I don't know how to describe it. It was as if—"

"As if you woke up in somebody else's body in the middle of somebody else's life," he supplied.

Slowly she turned her face up, and after a moment he looked down at her, meeting her concerned green eyes. "You *do* understand," she said with relief. "The last thing I remembered was being in class, and suddenly I was in the hospital with my arms and legs in casts, and bandages... What about you?"

His hold on her tightened. It was something he tried not to remember, tried not to think about, but he felt he owed it to her. "I was pretty much out of it for a couple of days, I guess. I didn't remember the explosion. The last thing I remembered was...well, right before it happened. It wasn't until a couple of weeks later that I started to recall. It was something I didn't want to do, either."

"Do you...do you think there's any reason to remember? I mean, is there any point at all in remembering? Or is it all pointless?"

He'd wondered that himself and wasn't sure he'd ever gotten an answer. "I don't know, Em," he said finally.

"Honest to God, I don't know. Maybe it's healing of some kind. I just don't know."

Compared to what she had forgotten, he had forgotten very little. Just a few minutes of time that he'd been able to paint with horrifying clarity in imagination. He hadn't needed to remember those moments, least of all the enraged, sick feeling when he had found he couldn't move and had lain there facedown, helplessly listening to his own screams and smelling his own flesh burn. Or the moment when a neighbor had come running and kicked snow on his back to put out the flames. Or the moment when they had lifted him onto the stretcher and he had seen the burned-out hulk of the car. The burned-out hulk of his life. Remembering those minutes had seemed so utterly pointless, except possibly to give reality to the loss. To engrave forever in stark clarity the moments when his life had ended.

"They told me about it when I woke up," Emma said. "They said I'd been attacked and beaten very badly. Both my arms and legs were broken, and I had a fractured skull. It wasn't until later that they told me he had stabbed me, too. He...um...carved some kind of symbol into my stomach."

"My God!"

"My father had it removed by a plastic surgeon before I even came out of the coma. You can hardly tell it was there now. It was...um...a...a..." Suddenly she was gasping for air and clinging to him so hard that her nails dug into his skin even through the thick layer of his sweater. "A—a pentagram!"

Shock nearly froze Gage's blood. "My God, Emma, why didn't you tell me this morning?"

"B-because I forgot. I g-guess I'm good at forgetting. I just remembered that...."

He crushed her to him and gave up any hope of remaining detached or uninvolved with Emmaline Conard. He was involved already. Involved so deeply that his gut was burning with a hunger for revenge and his soul was aching with an impossible need to comfort.

There was no doubt now, he thought grimly. No doubt at all. She was being stalked.

And now Emma knew it, too.

The storm howled savagely outside, and the old house groaned and creaked before its onslaught. Emma had been asleep for hours now, and Gage sat up slowly, moving cautiously as he always did after staying in one position for very long.

"Don't go."

Emma's sleepy voice caused him to turn and look down at her. Her eyes were drowsy but open.

"I just need to go to the bathroom," he told her. "I'll be right back. Need anything?"

"Water, please."

"Coming right up."

What she needed, he thought as he left the bathroom and headed for the kitchen, was something to laugh about. Something to make her forget all the dark things for a little while. Trying to think of something, he took a minute to check all the locks and peek outside. Snow was drifting deeply against the cars in the driveway. Sure as shootin' nobody would be going anywhere in a hurry.

He filled a glass with ice water and took it back to Emma. She was sitting up, propped against the pillow, wide-awake now.

"Thank you," she said when he handed her the glass.

He sat on the edge of the bed, facing her, wishing he could remember a lousy joke or two, wondering, What now?

"You'll probably think I'm a great big chicken," she said shyly after a moment, "but I really don't want to be alone. Not since I remembered that . . . pentagram."

"I don't think you're a chicken, Red. In fact, I was wondering how to tell you that I don't think you ought to be alone." She needed an archangel now, the real thing, one of the ones who were immortal and invincible and who couldn't succumb to temptation. Because she was a delectable sight right now, and he was in mortal danger of succumbing.

That beautiful red hair of hers spilled all over the pillow and gleamed in the lamplight. The nightgown, for all its thick flannel, framed her breasts in a way that left deliciously little to the imagination, and he didn't need to imagine anyway. Just last night he'd touched and kissed those breasts, had sucked on those raspberry nipples until she had groaned and clutched him close. No, he didn't need to imagine when reality was so much better than pretend.

He also didn't want to take advantage of her, so when she finished the water, he set the glass on the night table and returned to his position beside her—on top of the blankets. He was touched more than he wanted to admit when she immediately snuggled close, expressing her trust in the most convincing way possible. It played havoc with his willpower and made his body feel like one great big throbbing ache—and reminded him that he didn't want to betray her trust.

"I'm sorry," she said a little while later.

"Sorry? For what?"

"You need your sleep. It isn't fair to ask you to stay with me like this."

"Fair?" He repeated the word, tasting its bitterness. "Babe, *fair* is an invention of children and wishful fools."

The harsh way he spoke caused her to tense. He had terrible things in his past, too, she reminded herself. She hadn't thought about it before, but it must have been very difficult for him to listen to her tonight. After all, he, too, had painful memories, and everything she had said must have reawakened all that for him.

In fact, she told herself sternly, for much of this entire week she had been too absorbed in herself and her own inchoate ghosts to remember that this man was dealing with some pretty powerful ghosts of his own. Still vivid in her mind was the sight of the tear streaks on his face yesterday when she had found him, and equally vivid was the horrible twisting sensation she had felt in her belly when she had witnessed so starkly and unexpectedly his pain and grief.

There were things he hadn't told her, terrible things. She sensed them roiling in his mind, sensed them in the way he tried to wall himself off. It was awful to think that she might have stirred all those things up and made them fresh for him.

"No," she said presently, "life isn't fair, is it? But that doesn't mean we shouldn't do what we can to *be* fair."

"One small candle flame in the dark, huh?"

He sounded so cynical, so hard, and maybe in some ways he was, but Emmaline Conard knew there was more to him than that. Much more. Hadn't he been there for her each and every time she'd needed someone this week? Hadn't he readily hugged her and comforted her and listened to her? Wasn't he here right now, holding her through a long, dark night?

He said he'd been raised on the streets like a wild dog, but she found him to be one of the most humane people she had ever met. One of the most caring. Because it took caring to take the risks he had taken as an undercover agent in memory of a long-dead brother. To take those risks to make the world a safer place for people you didn't even know. It took caring to feel the kind of grief she had seen in his eyes yesterday.

And you didn't need walls when you didn't have anything to protect.

Slowly she tipped her face up and leaned backward, trying to see his face. After a moment he looked down at her and their eyes locked, hers green and soft, his dark and stormy. Ever so slowly, feeling as if she were mired in molasses, she reached up and pressed her soft palm to his scarred cheek.

She spoke quietly, achingly, a catch in her voice. "You've been hurt so badly."

"So have you." He tried to sound indifferent. He tried to *feel* indifferent. Somehow he couldn't. This woman's caring was shining sadly in her eyes, and the touch of her palm on his hideously disfigured cheek was a blessing he hadn't understood he wanted until this very moment. He tried to pull away, but somehow he couldn't do that, either. He couldn't even move the couple of inches that would take his cheek from her hand.

She held him captive with a single, simple touch.

Emma saw the tension come to his eyes, felt it creep into his muscles as he lay still beside her. He continued to hold her, but something was happening. Something was making him look wary, like a dog that's been kicked once too often, then shies away from the very touch it wants.

She felt that look in the very depths of her being, felt that wary yearning as a reflection of her own deepest fears and needs. All these years she'd been avoiding what she most wanted for fear she might get kicked again. All these years she had been alone because she didn't dare not to be.

Wasn't that incredibly stupid?

Gently, with all the empty, lonely feelings and needs rising in her, she moved her fingers on his scarred cheek. Tenderly she caressed him, trying to tell him that maybe, for just this little while, they didn't have to be lonesome.

Gage's breath locked in his throat. She didn't know what she was doing to him. She didn't have the faintest notion; she was too damn innocent to have any idea. Emma thought she was comforting him, when in fact she was pushing him right over the edge.

And it was going to take only the tiniest push, he realized with angry resignation. Yesterday, between them, they'd built the fire, and nothing had yet happened to throw water on the flames. They were licking at his loins right now, fueled by her soft touch, by her feminine scent, by the sight and feel of her in his arms.

He didn't want to do this, he thought furiously. He was going to hate himself later. He was going to curse his weakness and damn his loss of control. He was going to feel like the lowest slime and the cruddiest sleaze.

But he wasn't going to be able to stop himself.

He looked so angry, Emma thought. She might have been frightened, except that the hands holding her remained gentle as they stroked her back through the covers. Had she made him angry by touching his scarred cheek? Had it bothered him to be reminded of it? Concerned, she started to take her hand away, but just as she moved, he turned his head and pressed a kiss into the palm of her hand.

Emma caught her breath and stared wide-eyed up at him. And suddenly she was free. He didn't move, he just let go of her. Not an inch of him touched an inch of her any longer. Her hand hovered over his cheek, as if frozen there by his kiss.

"Emma," he said softly, in his husky, ruined voice, "if I touch you again, I won't be able to stop." That much conscience and control he had left, just enough to give her a chance to escape.

She didn't move, didn't flinch. She simply stopped breathing and continued to stare up at him with eyes that grew bigger and darker with each passing second.

"Tell me to go," he said, not knowing how to make it any plainer. If she didn't seize her chance to escape, he wasn't going to let her go. He was no gentleman. To the bone he was a rough, ruthless street fighter, and he wore the outward trappings of civilization for convenience. His soul had been meant for a Viking or a cossack, not for a world where men needed to confine their appetites, needs and inclinations in a social straitjacket. He had accepted the constraints as a necessity, but now they were slipping from his grasp, ripped away in a whirlwind of rising passion.

She didn't tell him to go. The pulse in her throat fluttered wildly, and she drew a deep ragged breath. And then…and then her hand settled once again on his cheek, like featherdown, so light and soft and warm. The touch made him shudder, and he felt the impact of it all the way to his frozen soul.

She had no idea. She couldn't have any idea. She was innocent, too innocent to see the violence and raging hunger in him. Too innocent to know what he might be capable of. Too innocent to realize that it wasn't wise to want to give herself to a man who was capable only of taking.

But he was no saint to turn from what was so generously offered. He had given her a chance to back away. Now it was too late—for both of them.

He reached for the blankets and stripped them away from her, flinging them to the foot of the bed with one swift movement of his arm. Only the nightgown shielded her now, and it was no barrier against the hand that suddenly cupped her breast, or the powerful thigh that was suddenly thrown across hers.

"God, I want you," he breathed raggedly against her ear. "Damn it, Em..."

Why did he have to sound so angry? she wondered hazily. Somehow, even with all the layers of cloth yet between them, he made her feel as if he was wrapping her in his body and absorbing her into himself. As if she was being inexorably drawn into the darkness he seemed to carry with him. And dimly, as she felt him tremble and press his hips achingly against her, she sensed the pure white heat that was at the core of the night that surrounded Gage Dalton.

He didn't want to feel. He didn't want to need. He didn't want to lust or hunger or yearn. He had fought his way up to the dark, icy edge of the abyss called despair, had found a precarious ledge where he could feel almost nothing at all, and now... and now...

Oh, God, she was making him *feel!*

Emotions exploded in him with all the devastating force of a volcanic eruption. Rage scalded all the frozen places, melting ice that held the wolves at bay. Pain poured through the cracks, agonizing and fresh, making a joke out of all his denials and defenses. He had admitted he grieved. He had faced that, accepted it, and from time to time even indulged it. But he had never faced any of the other feelings about what had happened, and right here and now they burst from confinement in a maelstrom of torment.

And Emma suddenly looked like a lifeline.

Gage's face told Emma she wasn't about to enjoy the gentle seduction she had once childishly imagined for her first time. She wasn't even to enjoy the tenderness he had showed her last night when he had guided her through her first real taste of passion and fulfillment. No, she thought weakly, it wasn't going to be like that at all.

He looked so furious as he stood beside the bed and pulled his sweater over his head. He looked so... hurt. He was in mortal pain, and she didn't think it was his back this time. No, not his back.

He reached for the snap of his jeans, and some little voice in Emma's mind, some last little voice of reason, told her to get out of here now. And then, before she could consider things logically, some floodgate in her heart opened, pouring the golden warmth of understanding through her.

In an instant she left behind the last romantic notions of her youth. She understood suddenly that a woman's body could do more than give pleasure and then children to the man she loved. It could give him forgetfulness. Or reassurance. Or welcome. It could help mend hurts he couldn't speak of. It could tell him that someone in the world cared for him, cared deeply enough to take him inside her. It could, for awhile, wrap him in security and shelter him from life's cruelties. It could give him all those things men never asked for and seldom admitted they needed.

What Gage needed from her tonight, she realized as he yanked down his zipper, had little to do with pleasure. And whatever it was, she longed to give it to him.

She gasped softly when he thrust his jeans and briefs down, letting her see for the first time in her life a man in the full grip of desire. He was so... big, she thought weakly. It simply couldn't work.

Gage kicked his jeans aside and then suddenly threw his head back, standing rigid, his hands locked into fists, his expression a tortured grimace. *First time...* whispered the cool voice of reason, barely heard through the gale in his head. *Her first time...* He shuddered, clawing inwardly for some remnant of self-control, some last decent impulse to cling to.

"Emma." His ruined voice was grittier than usual, forced past the tight knot in his throat. He made himself look down at her, some corner of his mind noting that she looked like a virginal sacrifice in that damned white flannel. "Emma, I don't think I can—" His throat closed, shut down by a hunger that just kept growing despite everything.

He was beautiful, she thought, losing her fear in her own rising heat and need. So beautiful, like a dark angel. Unlike the hair on his head, his body hair wasn't silver but a dark chestnut brown. It decorated his chest in a masculine swirl and then arrowed straight downward to the most potent part of him. And there... Emma caught her breath and looked up into his anguished face.

"It's all right, Gage," she heard herself say gently, as she held out a hand. "It's all right." At that moment she felt like the earth mother, all bountiful, all understanding, all giving. He was welcome to whatever he needed from her.

Gage made a strangled sound and was suddenly beside her, suddenly hauling her into his arms and then into the curve of his naked body. "Em...oh, God, Em..." He shuddered violently when he felt her soft warm palms on the naked, scarred skin of his back, on the naked, scarred skin of his buttocks.

"It's all right," Emma murmured. "It's all right." And somehow she believed it would be, whatever happened now. The next few minutes might be unpleasant for her, but they hardly mattered next to Gage's need.

Her first time... The words rolled around in his head, and he tried, he really *tried,* to bring her with him. Grasping at the straws of restraint, he lifted her gown over her head, taking care not to pull or tear it from her. When she at last lay completely bare before him, he saw the incredible shyness in her green eyes, in the warm rush of blood to her throat and cheeks.

"Beautiful," he said hoarsely. "Beautiful." He trailed his gaze over her from head to toe, feeling his body harden and throb even more urgently as he traced each graceful curve. The breasts he had touched and kissed last night were full without being large and crowned in strawberry pink. Her nipples were already knotted and hard for him, beckoning to him. Not yet.

He trailed his gaze lower, to the incredibly narrow nip of her waist—damn, how could she be so slender, so fragile?—and lower to the thatch of fiery curls that drew his entire body like a powerful magnet.

Damn! *Her first time!* Another time he might have appreciated that. Now he could only see it as a potential hazard.

He turned his head back up and found her watching him, shyness warring with eagerness on her face. Holding on to a last, rapidly charring thread of control, he bent his head to kiss her.

The instant his hot, rough tongue touched hers, Emma was caught up in a whirlwind of escalating sensation. She became exquisitely aware of each place her bare skin touched his, and each touch fueled the yearning in her and made her press closer and closer to his heat, his strength, his hardness. Oh, yes, suddenly she needed that, too.

His hands were impatient, almost rough, as they swept over her, but she didn't mind. Oh, no. His impatience fed hers, made her feel wanted, made her feel wonderful that he wanted her enough to be impatient, to be rough. She didn't mind at all that he needed her as fast as he could get her, that he was driving toward his goal with little tenderness and only a modicum of consideration for her. She didn't mind at all, because there was nothing, absolutely nothing, as heady or as satisfying as being wanted this badly.

For the first time in a decade she felt like a woman. He had given her that, and it didn't matter a tinker's damn whether he gave her anything else. For him, for these brief minutes, she was woman enough.

Then his fingers slipped within her slick folds. She gasped, electrified by the unexpected sensation. He didn't say anything, just kept rubbing her there in a way that soon had her arching toward his touch and clinging to his hair like a lifeline.

A low growl of laughter escaped him, and he closed his mouth over her breast as his fingers continued to stroke, to delve, to test both her readiness and her inexperience.

Emma groaned, forgetting all her fantasies about being a bountiful earth mother, forgetting what it was she was understanding, and became hostage to the feelings he was giving her. Pleasure splintered again and again within her, and she wondered why the nerve that was directly connected from her nipple to her womb had never showed up in any anatomy book. Because each and every time he sucked on her breast, her insides tightened in a wild, delightful spasm.

And his fingers...oh, his fingers were wicked, teaching her hungers and needs and sensations beyond imagining.

When he parted her legs and knelt between them, she had long since forgotten that she didn't think this could work. All she knew was that it *had* to work. Somehow. Anyhow. Any way.

She felt him probe where no one but he had ever touched her, and then she felt him entering...oh, my word, how he stretched her....

A sharp, searing pain jerked her out of her haze of arousal. She drew a sharp breath but swallowed the instinctive cry and stared up into Gage's grimacing face.

It didn't feel very good, she found herself thinking, wondering if he was just going to keep pushing deeper and deeper. She wanted him out, now, before this feeling got any worse. Oh, my word, surely something was going tear?

She had known it would hurt the first time, but she hadn't been quite prepared for this feeling of uncomfortable fullness, this feeling of being stretched too far, of being sundered in two. Did women really learn to like this?

He stopped pushing inward, and she released a relieved sigh when he started to pull out. But then he plunged again, and again, and again, and she could tell he was totally absorbed by something happening inside him, so all she could do was endure....

A hot tear fell on her cheek. And then another. And another. While he climaxed, Gage Dalton wept.

Chapter 10

Nothing looked any different, Emma thought as she stared past Gage's head at the spangles of color on the ceiling. The storm still howled outside, the Tiffany lamp still cast its colors around the room, the floor hadn't cracked open to swallow her, and the ceiling hadn't caved in.

Except now a man's heavy weight lay limply on her, his body still joined to hers. Except now she knew the sights and sounds and smells of sex. Except now she was free of some invisible barrier that only at this moment did she realize had been a burden. She was no longer a virgin, and she was fiercely glad of that fact, even if she hadn't found the pot of gold at the end of the rainbow. Some women never did. She had read enough to know that much.

Her shoulder was wet where Gage's tears had fallen. It had been a brief, silent storm, over almost as soon as it happened. She hoped that his hurt had eased a little.

And she was afraid, mortally afraid, that he would get up now and leave her. Never had she felt so exposed, so vulnerable, so utterly defenseless. And she suspected he felt the same. He had exposed himself, his anguish, his need, his loss of control. Right about now he was probably wishing he could vanish into thin air.

Regrets, Gage thought, were the manure of life, littering every damn byway and walkway. She was probably feeling them, he was *certainly* feeling them, and right now he felt as raw as if he'd been skinned.

What he regretted was that he had not given her a better experience. What he regretted was that his knapsack full of guilt and remorse was going to keep him from giving her what she really needed for the long run. He couldn't give Miss Emma love, but he sure as hell could have given her good sex, and he hadn't even done that.

He had felt those moments when she had wished he would pull away from her. He had sensed her discomfort, but he had been too far gone to stop. He'd been afraid of that, and it had happened. Now, what the hell could he do about it?

He sighed heavily and raised himself on his elbows so he could look down at Emma. At once she closed her eyes, and color rushed rosily into her cheeks.

"Look at me, Red," he said huskily, catching her face between his large hands. "Come on, look at me."

Her eyes fluttered reluctantly open, and the color staining her cheeks darkened. Gage gave her a lopsided smile.

"It doesn't get much more intimate than this, Em."

Impossibly, she felt the tug of a smile at the corners of her mouth, even as she wanted to hide her face in his shoulder. It couldn't get much more intimate, she thought. She was so completely, exquisitely aware of everywhere their bodies touched, of how he fit even now between her legs, part of him still possessing her. She was aware of textures, of smells, of pressures, of sounds. Nothing was as intimate as this.

"I'm sorry it wasn't any good for you, Emma."

"I didn't say—"

He cut her off with a quick, soft kiss. "You didn't have to say. All I did was hurt you."

"Just a little," she protested. "Besides, at first..." Her voice trailed off, and her blush heightened again.

"At first I got you really turned on," he murmured huskily. "I know. You're fire in a man's arms, Emma. You can't have any idea how good it makes a man feel when a woman responds to him like you do.''

Oh, but she could, she thought, remembering the heady moments when Gage's hunger had thrilled her so. She knew exactly what he meant, and just thinking about how he had trembled for want of her was enough to make her feel hot and weak all over again.

He saw the flash of comprehension in her expression, heard it in her suddenly quickened breathing. Good, he thought. Good. He hadn't killed her desire. She was still halfway there and hoping.

He brushed another kiss against her lips, and one against her collarbone. Then he moved his hips against her, lightly, as if by accident, and smiled when he heard her swiftly drawn breath.

''That's it, Em,'' he whispered roughly in her ear. ''Now that more pressing matters are out of the way, let's take care of unfinished business.''

He rocked his pelvis against her again, slowly, and then again. Emma was amazed to feel herself rapidly spiraling back up to the heights she had just crashed from so disappointingly.

''It'll be good this time, Red. Just relax and let it happen.'' He shifted, covering one of her breasts with his hand and gently brushing his thumb back and forth across the nipple as he continued to rock against her. And amazingly, he felt himself harden as if he were fifteen again and not an ancient thirty-eight. ''Put your hands on my butt, Emma,'' he ground out. ''Hold me like you did before.''

She did, loving the feel of those powerful muscles flexing beneath her palms as he moved against her. He was still inside her, filling her more and more with each movement, but this time it didn't feel quite so frightening. No, it was beginning to feel good.

''Does it hurt?'' he asked breathlessly.

''No...no...''

''Good...?''

''Mmm...'' She was lifting now, rising to meet his thrusts instead of passively accepting them as she had before. Her head began to roll restlessly, and her hands tightened on his buttocks until he felt the sting of her nails. That zapped through him like electricity and dragged a groan from his depths.

"Gage!"

He recognized that sound. It had become engraved on his soul the night before when he had brought her to the peak the first time. He slipped his hand down between them and touched her, drawing another cry from her. "Oh, Em, it's good, isn't it? Just let it happen in its own sweet time. Just... let it..." He was gasping like a marathoner on his last mile, doubtful he could hold out much longer. She turned him on like he'd never been turned on in his whole life. He wouldn't have thought he could...

He felt it happen. She came apart beneath him with a wild upward surge and a cry that pierced his heart. Her arms tightened around him, her legs wrapped around him and Miss Emmaline Conard held hell's own archangel in a timeless moment wrested from heaven.

At two in the morning Emma sat chin deep in the big, claw-footed bathtub, surrounded by scented bubbles and rising steam. Opening one eye lazily, she benefited from the sight of Gage's backside, buck naked, as he leaned into the mirror and tried to scrape stubble from his cheek with her razor. He didn't appear to be self-conscious about his scars, once he realized they didn't repel her, and she was glad. She hated to think of the pain he had endured, but those scars in no way diminished him.

"Damn," Gage muttered. "What is it with women's razors? How the hell can you use them when they're so dull? How do they *get* so dull?"

"There's a fresh one under the sink," Emma said lazily. She decided that she absolutely loved being a fallen woman. It was wonderful to laze around here in her bubbles and listen to a stark-naked man gripe about razors. Yes, she could easily grow addicted to this kind of intimacy.

Gage turned, razor in hand, and looked down at her. "Are you laughing at me?" He pretended to scowl. "I'm only shaving for you, you know."

"I know." Her cheeks felt raw, another sensation she really didn't mind. She wondered if women stopped getting beard burn with time, or if that was always a problem. She gave him a beatific smile. "And I told you where to find a fresh razor."

He tossed the razor down and wiped his face with a towel. "I'm done anyway, Red." A moment later he was kneeling beside the tub, catching her chin with a finger to turn her face up to him. "How do you feel?" he asked huskily. "Really."

"High as a kite," she admitted honestly.

Something in his face, some kind of tension, let go. "Yeah?" he said softly, then leaned toward her to brush a light, gentle kiss against her lips.

Her hand rose from the soapy, scented water to touch his cheek, and she thought how wonderful it was to be able to touch him so freely. How absolutely marvelous it was to have left pretense behind and to be able to honestly express desire. How phenomenally liberating it was to be desired in return. The euphoria would fade, she was sure, but she wouldn't trade these moments in time for anything in the whole world.

Gage's voice was huskier than usual. "You about done, Emma?"

"You could join me."

He flashed an unexpected grin. "I might if that water didn't smell like roses. Of course, the scent will probably get all over me anyway."

Emma's breath locked in her throat, and she felt as if she were drowning in his stormy eyes. "Will it?" she whispered.

"You bet," he whispered back. "All over every damn inch of me. This night isn't over yet, lady. Not by a long sight."

She wanted it never to be over. Never, ever. It would end, of course. Beneath her euphoria an honest part of her accepted the end as inevitable. But for now, for tonight, she wanted to live in a fool's paradise where a man could love her despite her infertility, where dreams could come true and morning never came.

"We're snowed in," Gage murmured as he brushed kisses against each of her eyelids, against her cheek and chin. "Nobody's going anywhere come morning. You don't have to open the library."

"That's right." Her agreement was breathless, the merest whisper as spiraling desire began to coalesce like a warm weight at her center. Instinctively she brought her knees together beneath the water.

"And I wouldn't want to leave you wondering," he murmured against her ear.

"Wondering . . . what?"

"Whether the second time was a fluke."

She gasped as his tongue speared into her ear. A shiver raced down her spine to join the growing heaviness between her legs. He'd said something, hadn't he? Was she supposed to answer?

"No, Miss Emma." His voice was little more than a rough growl. "I want you to know for sure that sex is just about the best thing a man and a woman can do together. I don't want you ever to doubt it."

Emma gasped and arched instinctively as his hand closed around her breast beneath the water. The bath salts made the water slick, and his fingers slipped silkily over her skin as he sought her nipple. She gasped again when he found it, then tilted her head to the side so he was able to nibble his way down to an exquisitely sensitive place on her neck.

"You should wear your hair down, Emma," he said huskily, his lips leaving a hot trail from her ear to her shoulder. "It's like something out of a fairy tale, all gold and red like fire." Catching her swollen nipple between thumb and forefinger, he tugged gently on it and listened with satisfaction to the soft whimper that escaped her.

He could hardly believe it, but he was throbbing again, nowhere near critical, but definitely hungry enough that he didn't want to stop. How did she do this to him? How had she dragged him out of the frozen wastes where he'd been hiding and made him once again a man?

Hell's own archangel had been a particularly apt appellation, he thought now, as he savored each moment of Emma's growing response. People who thought of fire and brimstone didn't know. Hell was a cold place. Colder than the arctic wastes. Emptier.

Her flame was warming him, and damned if he could pull away now. Not yet. Later, but not now. Like a wolf drawn by fire, he just kept circling closer and closer to the warmth, hungry for light, for laughter, for...

He choked the thought down and focused on Emma. Lovely Emma with her wild mane of hair caught up in a gaudy clasp, her neck as pale as dairy cream rising above the slowly evaporating bubbles. Now he could see the breast he was fondling, and he felt his loins tighten even more in reaction.

"So sweet," he heard himself say roughly as another soft whimper escaped her. "God, Emma, you're the sweetest thing...."

Leaning forward, ignoring the viselike pain in his back, he pressed a deep, wet kiss on her mouth as he sent his hand foraging lower beneath suds and water. When he found her soft silky curls she arched upward, tight as a bowstring.

Gage broke off the kiss, breathing heavily now himself. "Isn't it time to get out of there, Red? Before I get in there with you and prove that an old man with a crippled back ought to know better?"

She drew a sharp breath, and her sleepy-looking eyes opened slowly. "Would you?"

"I'm getting damn close to it."

She smiled slumberously. "That makes me feel good, to hear you say that."

Suddenly smiling himself, he leaned closer and nipped her earlobe. "So it makes you feel good to bring a man to his knees, does it?"

"Just you, Gage. Only you."

The words sounded a warning in the back of his mind, but he ignored it. He figured he was earning enough bad karma tonight to turn him into a snake for at least five lifetimes to come. That being the case, he was damned well going to enjoy it.

Standing, oblivious to his own nudity or its impact on her, he grabbed a towel from the rack and then held a hand out to her.

"Come on, Venus," he said. "Time to rise from the sea foam."

All of a sudden Emma felt shy again. Somehow it suddenly seemed impossible to stand up, leaving the concealing bubbles behind, while this man watched her.

"Come on, Em," Gage said, lowering his voice to a deep, coaxing tone. "Promise I'll close my eyes."

Her gaze flew to his face and found him grinning almost wickedly. He looked so young, suddenly, she thought with a pang. Young and carefree.

"Your bubbles are almost gone, Red. There isn't a whole lot I can't see right now. Come on."

Blushing profusely, unable to look at him, she rose from the tub and kept her face averted as the water sluiced from her.

"Damn," Gage said softly. "Damn, you're gorgeous." And somehow, he was going to make Miss Emma believe that, he thought as he studied her blushing face and the way she refused to look at him. He needed to make her believe that.

Stepping forward, he wrapped the towel snugly around her and helped her out of the tub. Then, taking the devil's own time about it, he began to rub and stroke her dry. It wasn't long before Emma forgot her momentary shyness and succumbed to the incredible pleasure of being treated as if she was precious and desirable. And beautiful. He made her feel so beautiful, which she surely was not.

"I'd carry you," he murmured huskily in her ear as he dropped the towel and drew her full, bare length against his. "I'd sweep you off your feet and carry you to bed like Rhett Butler, if I could."

He was referring to his back, and Emma hastened to reassure him. She leaned even more into him and pressed a kiss on the smooth skin of his shoulder. "I always figured I'd be terrified of falling. Not good for the mood."

He chuckled quietly and began backing toward the door. "This is nice. Oh, have I got plans for you, Miss Emma." He whispered a suggestion in her ear and felt the tremor of response ripple through her. "Ah, you like the sound of that...."

His voice was doing as much to her as any of his touches, she realized. There was something incredibly sexy about a man talking quietly in your ear, whispering of the things he'd like to do. Making suggestions that would have caused Great-aunt Isabel to swoon. Poor, dear Aunt Isabel, Emma thought dreamily as she and Gage tangled together on cool sheets. The poor woman had missed so much.

Emma didn't want to miss a bit of it. Not even the tiniest little thing. Spurred suddenly by appetites she had only just begun to discover, she pressed Gage back on the bed and straddled him on her hands and knees.

He looked up at her, a crooked smile on his face. "What's this?"

She leaned down and kissed him lightly on the lips. "I want to find out what turns you on."

A soft laugh escaped him. "Lady, *you* turn me on. The way you walk, the way you smile, the way your breasts bounce when you laugh...I don't think there's one thing about you that doesn't turn me on. If there is, I've been too turned on all week to notice it."

He captured her breasts in his hands and rubbed his thumbs over her nipples, drawing a long, low sound from her. "That turns me on, too," he murmured. "The way you respond. The way you sound."

"But I want to please you," she said when she could find breath.

"You do, Emma. Oh, baby, you do." But he understood. She wanted to be active, not just passive. She wanted to participate. She wanted to draw from him the same sounds he drew from her. So he told her what he liked. And then endured the exquisite torture of having her try it all out.

And, oh, how it excited her to excite him. When she licked his small nipple to a hard point and sucked on it, drawing a deep moan from him, she felt a tug of pleasure in her own center every bit as strong as if he had been sucking her breast. When he guided her hands to his arousal and taught her how to stroke his silky length, her insides clenched again and again in a deep, wrenching throb of pleasure.

Somehow, at some point, it had become impossible to tell who was giving and who was receiving, who was touching and who was touched.

When Gage eased her onto her back and scooted down to bury his face in her musky, dewy core, she was prepared to give him anything he wanted, because each new experience only sent her higher and higher in the excruciatingly wonderful spiral of passion.

The touch of his tongue electrified her, a sensation so powerful that it bordered on pain. She tried instinctively to pull away, but he caught her hips in his powerful hands and held her still.

"Let me, Emma," he said roughly. "Let me taste you."

Oh, my word! she thought hazily. His touch, his voice, his demand, they all added fuel to the fire. She had never dreamed that simple, ordinary words could be so erotic.

"Yes," she said hoarsely, totally unable to say no. "But it hurts...."

"Not for long. It's just so new...Emma, sweet...so sweet..."

The sensations were so new, so sharp, so exquisite, that she reached the brink swiftly and then stalled there, unable to find her way over. Writhing, she clawed the sheets, and then, in a moment so intense it seemed to halt time in its course, she tumbled over.

She would never forget, she thought dazedly. She would never forget the way her thighs had clamped around his head, holding him to her. Never forget the low sound of triumph he had made when he knew she had reached the apex. Would never, ever forget the instant when he slid up over her and slipped into her, causing a deep, clenching thrill to spear through her. Would never forget the way he lifted her hips to him and made her climb the peak one more time, this time with him.

She would never forget the way he felt when he collapsed on her and lay tiredly against her, his muscles quivering, his breath gasping. She would surely never forget the sound of his name on her lips or the sound of hers on his as they slowly slipped back into reality.

And most definitely, most assuredly, she would never forget the moment she realized she loved him.

Lying on his side, Gage watched Emma sleep. Her silky, curly hair cascaded like wildfire over the pillow; her golden eyelashes shadowed her pale cheeks. In repose she looked remarkably fragile and delicate, in marked contrast to her waking manner of strength and competence. From the outside, no man would ever guess how soft, how warm, how utterly vulnerable, was Emmaline Conard.

He'd been lying there for what seemed ages, just watching her. The throb of pain in his back was persistent, but it seemed unimportant beside the tightness in his chest, a tightness born of unaccustomed emotions. Miss Emma had opened old wounds simply by giving herself to him. He shouldn't have allowed her to do that. He couldn't allow her to keep on doing it. He couldn't ever again be responsible for anyone else's well-being. No way. And he couldn't allow his own internal walls to be torn down, his defenses to be breached. They were the only things that stood between him and madness. Or so he sometimes thought.

If he had half a brain, he would get out of this bed now and make it clear that this night would never happen again. Let her know that nothing would come of this. Make it clear that she wasn't to count on him for anything. Show her that he could only give her pain.

But he stayed, and in the soft light from the Tiffany lamp, he watched her sleep. *Titania*, he thought, a crazy thought but one that seemed suddenly apt. A fairy princess with flaming hair and incredibly delicate features slumbered trustingly beside him, and for this little while he allowed himself to forget that he didn't deserve her trust.

Tomorrow, he thought with a shudder, tomorrow would be soon enough to return to hell.

Reaching out, he touched a soft curl. He never lost control, but he had lost control tonight. Emma and a couple of nurses from long ago were the only people on the planet who had seen Gage Dalton completely stripped to raw feeling. He should feel uneasy, threatened, embarrassed, that she had seen him shaking with need and almost out of his mind with hunger, but he didn't. Somehow he felt his vulnerability was in safe hands with Emma.

He felt *he* was in safe hands with Emma. It was a strange feeling for a man who had never counted on anyone but himself, a man who was accustomed to having others turn to him for safety. Not that he was able to provide it, but he had always sure as hell tried to.

Aching, trying to swallow feelings that seemed to be determined to be felt tonight, he tried to think of sex and not of needs. He tried to put the night down to rampaging hormones, not loneliness, not tenderness, not caring.

Yet Emma had given herself to him with tenderness and caring, whether he wanted to face it or not. She had held out a hand to him when he had been caught in a tempest of unchained needs and hurts, had told him it would be all right at a time when she should have been afraid and seeking his reassurances.

He wanted to accept all that she was offering him, but he didn't deserve it. He would never deserve the promises he had seen in her eyes after the last time they had made love. So tomorrow he was going to have to find some way to put distance between them, some way to let her know that nothing more could happen between them.

Somehow he had to stop things before he hurt her any worse than he already had.

"Gage?"

Aw, hell, he thought, he should have put on a shirt. He was standing in the kitchen in his unbuttoned jeans, watching the snow drift deeper in the dark driveway. Dawn was approaching, but it was impossible to tell. The blizzard still raged, blowing snow against the windowpanes with an icy rattle, burying Emma's small car, coming close to burying his Suburban.

She was standing in the kitchen doorway, hesitating because he hadn't responded when she called his name. He could feel her back there, could feel her eyes on his scarred back, could feel her wondering why he was standing in the kitchen in the dark like this.

"The coffee's hot," he said finally, not knowing what else to say. He kept his back to her, hoping she would take the hint.

"Is your back hurting?"

The concern in her voice was like a claw in his conscience. Damn it! He didn't deserve her caring. And she sure as hell didn't deserve the cost of that caring.

"No more than usual."

Emma edged into the kitchen, uncertain how to handle this. She had hoped this morning would bring an easiness between them, a warmth. Maybe that they would make love again. She had suspected it wouldn't be like that, and had known for certain when she found him gone from the bed.

The question was whether she should let him deal with this in his own way, or whether she should let him off the hook by telling him that she was aware there was no future for them. At least, she thought that was what might be troubling him.

Looking back at last night, she could clearly see what it had taken to break down his resistance to making love to her. She had, after all, seen him stand beside the bed, shaking from head to foot and battling his own needs. She had heard him offer her a chance to get away. She had witnessed the strength of the forces that had buffeted him.

He hadn't *wanted* to make love to her. He had *needed* to. And later, when he had been so sweet, he had been giving her something he believed he owed her.

The night beyond the windows was surprisingly bright, the light of streetlamps diffused by the glittering snow into a pale glow. That cold glow poured eerily into the kitchen. Emma felt around in the cabinet for a mug and poured herself some coffee, wondering if she should just act as if nothing had happened between them.

It was Gage who broke the strained silence. "There's no future in this, Emma."

"I know." She *did* know. She knew with agonizing clarity that no man would want her for long. She had known it for a decade now. But he didn't seem to hear her.

"I can't—" He broke off, unable to find words.

Emma pulled out a chair at the table and sat, watching his back, aching for both of them with a depth and fatalism that astonished her even as she felt it. They were doomed, she thought. Both of them doomed by circumstances beyond their control. Was it so wrong to seek what comfort they could from one another?

Several minutes ticked by in a silence punctuated by the rattle of snow against the glass and the low moan of the wind as it whipped around the house. Finally Gage tried again.

"I don't have a future to offer you, Emma," he said roughly.

She knew better than ever to have hoped for any such thing. "I didn't ask—"

He interrupted. "I used up my brownie points with heaven a long time ago, if I ever had any."

Confused, she tried to see him more clearly. "What do you mean?"

"Just that. I've been condemned to hell."

"Gage, what—"

"Do you know what hell is, Emma?" His voice was quiet, controlled, belying the anguish his words conveyed. "It's an endless, bottomless, icy void. An infinite emptiness of the heart and soul. A gaping chasm that was once filled by everything and everyone you loved."

Emma drew a long, shuddery breath as she began to understand. "Tell me," she said unsteadily.

He tilted his head back and closed his eyes, clenching his hands into fists at his sides. He had to do this, he thought desperately. For both of them. He had to say it, and she had to hear it, before it was too late. Because he was too damn tempted to take what she offered.

"It was just before Christmas," he said, his voice low, and rougher than she'd ever heard it. "My wife and I had just finished decorating the Christmas tree."

Wife? Emma's heart began to beat painfully.

"We got the kids into their snowsuits...."

Kids? Oh, my God! She wanted to run, hide, knowing she didn't want to hear any of this. Not any of this.

"The youngest was just two months old," Gage said almost dispassionately. "We had two little girls already. Sandy was four, and Karen was two. And then we had Tommy. My wife was so thrilled with him. She'd wanted a boy from the start. I kind of liked having little girls, myself. Jan, my wife, said they had me wrapped around their little fingers. I guess maybe they did."

"Gage..." What could she say? What could she do to stop the coming agony? Not a thing. Like a doe caught in headlights, she simply waited for the impact.

"We were..." He cleared his throat. "We were going to leave the kids with a friend of ours while we went shopping. We got everyone into the car, and then I remembered I'd left the diaper bag by the front door. I went back to get it...." He swallowed painfully. "I was halfway up the walk when the car bomb went off."

Emma closed her eyes, wishing she could somehow make this all go away for both of them.

"A piece of debris hit me in the back," he continued, his voice completely expressionless. "I fell facedown in the snow and couldn't move. I heard the roar of the fire behind me, I knew... but I was paralyzed. I couldn't help. Something hot fell on my jacket and set it on fire, and there wasn't anything I could do for them.... It was too late, anyway, they told me later. They all died instantly...." His voice broke, and he fell silent.

Presently Emma drew a shaky breath. "And the screams?" she asked, remembering what he had told her.

"My own," he said. "A neighbor managed to kick snow on me and put out the flames. I understand I didn't stop

screaming for three days. I don't remember most of it." He
drew a long, rough breath. "I *do* remember looking at the
car when they carried me away. I remember—" His voice
broke. "I remember knowing my life was gone."

Emma flew across the kitchen and slipped her arms
around him from behind, knowing only that enough was
enough. No one should have to bear such things alone. No
one should have to be so utterly without comfort.

"Emma, I told you...."

"It's all right, Gage. You told me. I heard you. That
doesn't mean I don't care. That I won't care." She pressed
her cheek to his back, feeling the line of keloid tissue that
defined one of his many burn scars. She drew a shaky
breath, trying to ease the tightness in her throat, and blinked
back helpless tears. "Did they catch the person who...
bombed the car?"

"Yeah."

"Who was it?"

"You know, Em, that's the really great thing about it. It
was one of the brothers of a drug kingpin I helped put
away."

"Why is that so great?" His sarcastic use of the word
puzzled her.

"Because I was directly responsible for the deaths of my
wife and three children."

Emma gasped, stunned. The bitterness of his voice left
her no doubt that he meant it, and she began to see very
clearly the depth of the problem here. "How...how do you
figure that, Gage?"

"It's simple. They died because of my job. No two ways
about it. If I'd been a mechanic or a carpenter, they
wouldn't have—they would have—" He couldn't go on.
One more word and he would start crying. He'd cried
enough.

"Oh, Gage, no!" The words were a horrified whisper. He
couldn't believe that. He couldn't!

"Believe me, I've had a lot of time to think about it. I
knew the dangers. I was just a damn fool to believe they
would be directed only at me. And there are still a few peo-

ple out there who would like to get at me. So that's it, Emma. I killed my family. And I'll be damned if I'm going to put anybody else in that position. Or put myself through that again.''

She longed to argue with him, to insist that bad things just happened, that no one was to blame except the perpetrator. Her own life was proof of that. But she sensed that Gage wouldn't believe it. Couldn't believe it. He felt guilty for the deaths of his wife and children, and no simplistic argument was going to alter his feelings.

She told herself to turn away now, that this briefly born relationship was doomed for too many reasons, beginning with his guilt and ending with her infertility. But it was already too late.

Sometime in the last two days she had passed the point of no return. She had given him what she had given no one else, but that giving had been merely symbolic of a commitment she had already made. For her, it was already too late. Since the pain was going to be unavoidable, she made the decision to take what she could from the moment.

She stepped back from Gage and took his hand. ''Come on,'' she said, tugging gently. ''Come back to bed.''

''Emma—''

''I know,'' she said softly. ''I know. It's just a one-night stand. Maybe a two- or three-night stand. Nothing more. I know. It's okay, Gage. I promise.''

Even as he was letting her drag him back toward the bedroom, he knew he was making a mistake. For her sake, for his, he ought to go upstairs right now. But she kept whispering that she understood, that he wasn't to worry, that no harm could come from a few stolen moments together. Like a siren, she drew him.

And, like a man, he followed.

Chapter 11

"I've been hearing things, old son," said the gravelly voice of Sheriff Nathan Tate over the telephone. "Maybe you'd like to tell me what the hell is going on?"

Gage leaned back in the leather chair behind the desk in Emma's study and looked out the tall window at the gray sky and blowing snow. The blizzard still raged, and the morning was waning with no sign of the storm's passing yet apparent. "I meant to call you last night, but something came up. Are you at the office, Nate?"

"I wish. No, son, I'm at home, hiding in my shop, hoping Marge and the girls don't run out of videotapes to watch. I got a phone call from Laramie. Some Lieutenant Doherty of the LPD, wanting to know if you were really one of my people. Something about a file on an old case you asked to have expressed out here. I admitted ownership of an investigator named Gage Dalton and seconded your request to have the file come by mail, not fax."

"Thanks, Nate."

"Don't mention it. So, what's going on?"

Gage hesitated, reluctant to expose Emma, but not knowing how he could avoid it now. "I don't know if you heard what happened to Miss Emma years ago when she was a student in Laramie."

"Actually, yes, I did. The judge told me about it, but I don't think he told another soul in the county. How did you find out?"

"Emma told me."

"I was under the impression she didn't remember anything about it."

"She's begun to remember quite a bit, Nate, and she's scared."

"I don't blame her." The sheriff sighed heavily. "So why did you want the file?"

Gage hesitated only briefly. "You know all these incidents—the balloon, the rabbit, the pentagram—I don't think they're pranks. I stopped thinking that when I saw the pentagram yesterday—"

"Well, so did I," Nate interrupted. "Give me something I don't already know."

"Last night Emma told me that the bastard who assaulted her in Laramie carved a pentagram on her stomach."

Nate swore. "It might be unrelated."

"I don't think so. There's something else that happened that you don't know about. Last week Emma received a photograph in the mail. It shook her up badly, which made me curious, so I sent it to a friend of mine back East. He says it's a poor copy of a dagger used by Turkish *hash-shashin* in the Middle Ages."

"But—"

"By itself that doesn't mean a whole lot, Nate, I know. But why would somebody go to a lot of trouble to duplicate something like that? Why would they send it to Emma?"

Nate drew a long breath. "To scare her," he said heavily. "Just like they did with the rabbit and the pentagram."

"That's what I'm afraid of. Hell, that's what I'm convinced of. I asked an old buddy of mine to do a search on the national crime computer system for other crimes that are similar in any way to Emma's assault, and I'm waiting for information on anyone in the county who has a related criminal record. In the meantime, I don't think Miss Emma should be alone.''

The silence grew protracted as Nate pondered what Gage had told him. "I'm with you," Nate said finally. "Keep a close watch on her. Is there any other information I can get for you?''

"There's probably no connection between what's been happening to Jeff's cattle and whoever is stalking Miss Emma, but I have to admit, ever since that decapitated rabbit turned up, I've been wondering about it. Anyhow, related or not, I'm still waiting to hear from the FAA about helicopters and helicopter pilots in the area. I guess I won't hear until Monday now, unless you know some cages to rattle.''

"I know the district chief. Let me see if I can roust him out for you. What exactly do you want to know?''

"Whether we've got any helo pilots around here who have criminal records, and what kind of records they've got. Crooks are almost never completely clean, Nate. There's always something that's a tip-off to an investigator, if he just knows where to look.''

"How's Emma taking this?'' Nate asked.

"Other than a few nightmares, she's handling it remarkably well,'' Gage said.

"Well, you tell her I said to let me know if she needs anything at all.''

"I will, Nate.''

After he hung up, Gage continued to contemplate the snowy day beyond the window. At the base of his skull there was a niggling feeling of pressure. He always got that feeling when things were about to start popping on a case. It warned him to watch his step, to take extra care, because things were going to blow wide open.

Now he felt that way and didn't know if his instincts were telling him that the stalker was about to move on Miss Emma, or if he was just feeling that way because of last night.

Too much had happened. He'd been a fool to give in to his needs, a fool to believe that he could ever simply step back and tell Miss Emma that there could never be a future for them. Of course, he hadn't counted on Emma. If he lived to be a hundred, he would never forget the way she had taken his hand this morning and urged him back to bed, as if it were the most natural thing in the world to give herself to a man who wanted to give her nothing at all. As if she understood, as if she wanted nothing in the world more than to give him whatever he needed.

How was a man supposed to resist that?

His conscience niggled at him, but at a level he had long since learned to ignore. Working undercover had numbed him to a lot of things, but in this instance he really wasn't being deceptive or taking advantage. Not now. Not after he had told Emma he had nothing to offer her.

He could, however, be a little angry at Emma for the way she was selling herself short. She deserved a whole hell of a lot more, and he felt like shaking some sense into her, except that there was no way on earth you could really shake sense into anyone. All you could do was satisfy your own need to get things off your chest.

She was an adult, he reminded himself. A mature woman of thirty or so. She was entitled to do this, if that was what she chose. And he didn't have a damn thing to say about it, except as it affected him. End of discussion.

Figuring he couldn't do any more investigating until some information started coming in to give him a direction, he went out to the kitchen, where Emma was making Christmas cookies.

She greeted him with a smile that said she was glad to see him, a smile he didn't feel he deserved. "Have a cookie," she said pleasantly, pointing to the cooling racks on the table. "They're pretty good even without the icing."

He poured himself a cup of coffee and stopped to watch her roll out another batch of dough. "What are you going to do with all these?"

"Serve them at the open house next Sunday. I'll probably need to bake all week just for that."

"Is it worth all the trouble?"

"Oh, I think so. It's really a lot of fun, Gage. Just about everyone comes, and the caroling is so beautiful. It's..." She hesitated, seeking words as she began to cut out tree-shaped cookies. "It's Christmasy. All the warmth and friendship and goodwill most of us associate with the season is there at the open house. To me, it's the essence of the season."

She looked up suddenly, remembering that the season was a painful time for him. She bit her lip and glanced apologetically his way.

"It's okay," he reassured her. Damn, he didn't want the shadows of his life to blight hers. But how could he prevent it, when she insisted on caring?

Emma wished he didn't look so removed this morning. It was as if the past week had never happened, as if Gage had retreated into the frozen place he'd been inhabiting the night he walked her home. Hell's own archangel was back.

And why shouldn't he be? she asked herself as she worked the rolling pin with trembling hands. His losses were almost beyond imagining, and there was no reason on earth why he should ever again risk the cost of caring. But if ever he did take the risk again, he certainly wouldn't do it for a woman who wasn't a woman. A woman who couldn't give him a real family.

Feeling her lower lip tremble, she caught it between her teeth to still it. Lord, she hated to cry. Besides, she'd done all her crying years ago—unlike Gage, who evidently hadn't done his crying at all yet. Instead of giving in to the pain, he'd fast-frozen it in the depths of his soul.

Maybe hell *was* a cold, empty place, as he'd said this morning, but maybe it was also a place a person made for himself. Grief wasn't a cold emotion, but ice wasn't any emotion at all. He would never heal until he raged, and rage was hot, a searing emotion that would surely melt all the ice he hid his feelings in. And then what?

Maybe, she admitted, he was better this way. He might never heal, but perhaps the price of healing was too high.

A long sigh escaped her, relaxing the tension that had brought her close to the edge of tears. She reached for a cookie cutter and began to make rows of bells.

Well, she'd already thrown her heart over the moon sometime in the past week, when she hadn't been paying attention and guarding her own emotions. It was too late to avoid the pain now. So, whether he liked it or not, she would just go right on giving him whatever caring she could. Everybody, no matter how frozen, needed to know that someone in this world cared.

"I guess I should try to move some of that snow in the driveway," Gage remarked. He stood at the kitchen windows looking out at the whirling snow and nearly buried vehicles. The storm seemed to have let up a little. Maybe. And maybe it was just wishful thinking.

"Don't you dare," Emma said mildly. "The boys next door and I have a contract. They'll be heartbroken to lose the money."

"Oh." Probably just as well, with his back. Even after all this time, it was hard for him to accept that there were some things he was wiser not to do. Nor did it help with the caged-lion feeling that was bugging him right now. He needed some good, hard physical activity. Ordinarily he would have gone for one of his endless walks, but he refused to leave Emma alone, and she was in the middle of enough dough to feed a hungry football team. She wouldn't want to stop now.

Jan had used to do this, too, at Christmas. Coming from the streets, just as Gage had, she had carried in her heart an image of what Christmas should really be, a picture-postcard image that she had tried her best to create each year for him and the children.

He drew a long, shaky breath and continued to stare out the window as he allowed himself to remember. The house had always smelled just like this—baking cookies, pine needles, coffee. Secrets wrapped in gaily colored paper and foil had been hidden on the highest shelves in every closet. There had been whispers and giggles, and that last year his eldest daughter had started to grow so excited at the prospect of Christmas that getting her to sleep at night had be-

come a chore. Jan herself grew as excited as any child, and
the excitement had been contagious. He, too, had come to
love Christmas, to love the excitement and sense of magic.

And as he stood there staring blankly out at the stormy,
snowy day, a surprising thought twisted through his sad
preoccupation and turned his thoughts in an utterly different direction.

Emma, too, prepared for the holidays. She, too, created
a Currier and Ives Christmas with her decorating and baking, and she spoke of the good feeling and fellowship of the
season. But she would never have children to create that
magic for. She would never know the excitement of buying
a toy that she knew, just knew, was going to bring excited
shrieks on Christmas morning. She would never know the
anticipation of hiding secrets in closets, or the joy of teaching carols to her own daughter or son.

He had experienced all that. He had lost it, but he would
never regret the precious episodes, the memories, the remembered joy, even if the price had been excruciatingly
high. Emma would never know that. Until he had wormed
past her defenses, she had always avoided men, and now he
thought he knew why.

Shaken out of his self-preoccupation, he turned from the
window. She might never have a family of her own, he
thought, but she sure as hell didn't have to spend this
Christmas alone with a man who was acting like a total jerk.

He reached for a cookie and took a bite. "Fantastic
cookies, Emma," he said.

"They're just sugar cookies."

"Well, they're great. How are you going to manage to
decorate them all by yourself?"

She glanced over her shoulder. "Are you volunteering?"
She expected him to deny it, given his problems with
Christmas.

"Sure. Except that I've never done it before and I can't
guarantee I won't mess up your cookies."

Emma slid another baking pan into the oven and laughed.
"We're not painting the Sistine Chapel here. If I were making just a couple dozen for a special party, I might sweat it.

Making hundreds for a crowd, a smear of icing and a dash of sprinkles will do."

"Smears and dashes are right up my alley."

Smiling, Emma faced him and wondered what had changed his mood so dramatically. Hell's own archangel was gone, replaced by a friendly-looking guy with a crooked smile. Even his gray-green eyes, only moments ago as cold as snow clouds, now looked softer, like a summer rain squall.

"I'll mix up the icing, then, and you can frost while I bake."

A couple of hundred cookies later, Gage realized that something was troubling Emma. She didn't seem to be able to hold still, and if she wiped down that counter one more time, he would be tempted to growl at her. Of course, she had plenty to worry about, and he knew the need for activity when things were worrisome.

"Why don't we take a walk?" he said abruptly. "We can finish icing these things later."

"The sidewalks will be a mess," she said, glancing out the window to see that snow was still falling steadily, though the wind had let up considerably. "I don't remember it ever snowing so much or so heavily."

Gage shoved his chair back from the table and stood, stretching cautiously to ease the stiffness in his lower back. A muscle twinged, and he winced.

"Is your back hurting badly?"

He looked at Emma and shook his head. "Nope. Just a twinge. Well, if you don't want to go walking, I guess we'll have to find another way to distract you."

"Distract me?" She looked puzzled.

"Sure." He took a step toward her and gave her a lopsided smile. "You think I don't recognize the signs? What are you worrying about? Sleeping with me last night? Or about . . . other things?"

Emma felt her breath catch as a strange hot-cold feeling drizzled through her. In an instant he had made her aware of him again, intensely aware of his size, his shape, his masculinity. In a way she hadn't experienced since the first few days, she noticed the breadth of his shoulders and the narrowness of his hips, the long, lean power of his denim-covered thighs. And suddenly her palms remembered exactly how he felt when she clutched him to her in the delicious throes of passion.

He had taught her so much last night, she thought now as her mouth turned dry and her heart sped up, yet there was so much she still didn't know, that she still hadn't tried. She was inexperienced, not ignorant, and looking at him right now, she also discovered she was creative. There were so many ways she still wanted to touch him, so many ways she still wanted to discover him.

Was it only two days ago that she had wondered how people could look each other in the eye once they had become intimate? That didn't seem to be a problem at all. No, her problem was keeping her hands off him. She ached, actually *ached,* to feel his arms around her, to feel the smooth heat of his skin against hers, to feel the coarse hair on his thighs against hers as he fit himself between her legs.

Gage saw the longing in her darkening eyes and felt it like a punch in the gut. Being Mr. Nice Guy to her over the holidays was a far cry from being her lover for an extended period. She'd already gotten under his skin. If he gave her half a chance, she would probably curl right up in his soul and then, when he moved on, become another one of those empty places he could never fill.

"Get your boots on, Emma," he ordered harshly. "We're going out. Now."

Emma wasn't used to taking orders of any kind, and for an instant her temper flared in white heat. But she wasn't blind, and she could see the tension in his posture and the lines around his mouth. "What's your shoe size?" she asked him.

The question was so unexpected and so far out of context that his head jerked backward in astonishment. "What?"

"What's your shoe size? I think your height and weight are close to my father's...well, you're probably thinner. He got a little thick around the middle—"

"Emma, what—"

"The skis will probably be just a tad too long, but not by much. What's your shoe size?"

"Thirteen."

Emma smiled. "Good. Let's go cross-country skiing."

"When I was a kid," Emma said as they drove slowly out of town in Gage's black Suburban, "we had to wax our skis. We always carried a little backpack with all the waxes for different temperatures and types of snow, and as the day wore on and conditions changed, we'd have to stop and scrape and rewax. Waxless skis finally got to be good enough that a few years ago Dad and I bought some. What a pleasure it is to just be able to ski!" And what a pleasure it was to be sitting in the car with him without feeling the violent urge to escape that had always plagued her before. The sense of freedom was exhilarating.

The county snowplows had evidently been working long and hard, Gage thought as he steered them between pristine white drifts. Fresh powder covered the recent plowing, but the road was drivable. "I've never skied cross-country," he warned Emma.

"It's pretty much like walking. I don't go for speed, just pleasure, and where we're going, the ground is pretty level, so you won't have to worry about control. Do you ski downhill?"

"I have, a little."

"You'll probably notice a difference in control, then. These skis are a lot narrower."

At several places along the road turnouts had been plowed so that vehicles could pull over or turn around. Emma finally directed Gage into one.

When the Suburban's engine was turned off, the immense silence of winter Wyoming settled over them. Nothing could be heard but the whispery whine of the wind as it blew snowflakes around in dancing patterns. The sky remained gray, and blowing snow obscured the distance, but the scene held an incredible tranquillity. Gage could almost feel it seep into him, easing his inner tensions.

Emma, too, seemed to be caught up in the quiet. For long moments she simply sat beside him, looking out over the vast, open spaces.

"I needed this," she said presently, her voice low. "That monster stole everything else from me. I don't even feel safe alone in my own home anymore, but he can't take this away from me. Short of murdering me, he can't steal this."

"Emma..." But what could he say? He could barely guess how much she had lost because of that assault and the terror tactics of the past week. Instinctively he started to reach out to offer comfort, but he caught himself before he touched her. If he touched her, he feared, he might never be able to let go.

She turned and gave him a wan smile. "Will you catch him?"

"I sure as hell intend to."

Her smile faded, and she studied him intently for several seconds. "Thank you," she said. "Thank you for staying in that house with me, and for caring what happens." She looked away and drew a deep, shaky breath. "This was a great idea," she said with forced brightness. "Let's go skiing."

It was a lot easier than he had expected. The stride and poling went naturally together, and since Emma was in no hurry, he was soon whooshing along beside her through the deep fresh snow.

"You can go a lot faster on a prepared track," she told him, sounding only a tiny bit breathless from the exertion, "but I think this is more fun."

"Going where no man has gone before, huh?"

She shot him a laughing glance. "Exactly. Is your back okay?"

"Sure. Actually, stretching out feels good." And the rise of endorphins in his blood, resulting from vigorous exercise, always eased the pain.

There were few obstacles out here—an occasional cottonwood, some brush, once in a while a boulder. For the most part they were simply able to fall into a steady rhythm and just keep going.

The exercise and fresh air were cleansing, Emma thought, as her arms and legs strained and grew pleasantly tired. The silence and the vast openness were healing, and she could almost feel the shadows withdrawing from the edges of her mind for the first time in over a week. For just this little while it was possible to believe that everything was normal and that nothing threatened her.

Eventually they reached Conard Creek, and Emma suggested it was a good time to turn back. Gage hesitated, looking beyond the creek to the rougher terrain behind it, the beginning of the foothills. Huge boulders, looking as if they had been dropped in a heap by a giant fist, rose up from the snow, a hill of nooks and crannies.

"That looks like a great place to explore," he remarked.

"It is. I used to love to come out here when I was a kid. We all did. I don't know how many hours we spent in the summers playing cowboys and Indians, or space invaders. I think our parents were absolutely sick of us asking for rides to come out here, but one of them always gave in and brought us anyway."

"The property owner didn't mind?"

"No, that section is fenced off. There was never enough grazing to make it worth risking his cattle in the crevices between the rocks. This is all Fenster land," she added, motioning with her arm. "I don't think they keep many cattle since the old man died four years ago, but the grandson keeps it running somehow."

"Don Fenster, right?"

Emma glanced at Gage. "You know him?"

Gage shook his head. "Lance Severn's boy mentioned him when I went to get your tree. He said Fenster has a bunch of real creeps staying with him. Have you heard anything about it?"

She shook her head. "Not a peep. It wouldn't surprise me, though."

He looked at her. "Why not?"

"Don was always a creep himself. Even when I was little I hated to be in the same classroom with him. He was always out here, though, and since it was his grandfather's land, we always let him play with us.''

One corner of Gage's mouth lifted. "Where I grew up, that wouldn't have made a bit of difference."

"Well, it made a difference out here. Our parents were pretty strict about being good neighbors. We got up to as much pettiness and quarreling as any other kids, I suppose, but nobody ever got entirely ostracized. And certainly not when we wanted to play on his land." She shivered a little as she began to cool down from her exertion and was grateful when Gage suddenly wrapped an arm around her and shifted so that he was sheltering her from the wind with his body.

"What made the Fenster kid so creepy?" Gage asked. "Was it just the way he looked, or was he one of those who wanted to boss everybody?"

"Oh, he wanted to boss, and he was always spying on everybody. You could always count on Don to squeal to the teacher. But I didn't think he was creepy until we were about twelve. I found him tormenting a dog. Torturing, actually." She shivered again, this time with distaste. "He wouldn't quit it, so I beat him to a pulp. Literally. Twelve-year-old girls are generally larger than boys of the same age, and I was never a shrimp." She shrugged. "He never spoke to me again."

He squeezed her suddenly, hugging her tightly. "I'll bet you were something else, Red. An avenging angel." And he felt as if something icy had just trickled down his back. Don Fenster? He tucked the name away for further investigation.

Since they were both still on their skis, the hug swiftly became uncomfortable, and Gage released her. "Let's cross over," he suggested.

"Uh-uh," Emma said, gripping his hand. "It hasn't been cold enough for long enough this winter. Even if the ice is solid a little ways out, it'll be rotten by the bank. Believe me, you don't want to get your feet wet this far from home."

He smiled lopsidedly down at her. "I told you I was a city kid."

She smiled back, feeling her heart quicken. Surely he was the sexiest man on earth. Every time she looked at him, her body responded in a flash. "Someday maybe you can warn me about city dangers."

"Maybe." He cast one longing glance over the rough terrain, aware that it was definitely the kid in him who wanted to go over there and explore. How long had it been since he'd felt that way?

Turning, they began to ski back toward the road at a leisurely pace.

"So you did all your work for the DEA in the cities?" Emma asked.

"The vast majority of it. The trail of drugs from Southeast Asia or South America has a lot of links in it, and we go after all of them. It's not enough to knock out a single producer or a single transporter or a single deal. We work from all ends of the problem."

"And you always infiltrated some big drug organization?"

"Not always. I did that twice. Most of the time it didn't get anywhere near so involved."

"Why not? I mean, I would think these dealers try to keep things secret so they don't get caught."

"They do, but it's a Catch-22, Emma. They need buyers, and as long as they need buyers, they'll keep slipping up. It's not too tough to find an informant and get him to introduce you as a big buyer. They'll be a little cautious, naturally, but it doesn't last long, because they trust the informant. And once they see the flash roll, it's usually all over."

"What's a flash roll?"

"A big wad of money. Generally, when you want to make a big buy, the dealer insists on seeing the color of your money before he'll even agree to sell the stuff. So you arrange a meeting, flash your roll—sometimes as much as fifty grand—and then he tells you when he'll be able to produce the drugs. That's a big danger point right there. More than one agent has been killed for his flash roll."

"But making the buy must be dangerous, too."

"Not really, unless the dealer insists you use the drugs before you leave."

Emma stopped skiing, and Gage followed suit immediately, stepping carefully backward until they were once again abreast. "What's wrong?"

She looked up at him with huge green eyes. "How do you handle that? If you refuse, they're bound to get suspicious, aren't they?"

"Oh, we've got excuses all ready to use. I'm a great actor when it comes to smoking a marijuana cigarette. When it's something injectable, I just refuse to use the dealer's shooting gallery."

"His *what?*"

"Shooting gallery. His needles and things. It's easy to claim you've gotten sick from using somebody else's dirty needle. Depending on the situation, there're probably a dozen different excuses. And if your excuse doesn't work, you just drag your heels, because you know your backup is right outside, and if you don't come out by a certain time, they're going to come in after you."

Emma shook her head, studying him with frank amazement. "I don't know where you find the nerve. And you miss it, don't you?"

Gage looked away, focusing his attention on some point made invisible by the steadily falling snow. "Maybe a little," he said after a moment. "Working undercover is a drug addiction, an addiction to adrenaline. I refuse to be addicted to anything."

Turning again, he looked at her just in time to see her shiver. "Come on, Em. You're getting chilled. Let's keep moving."

Back at the truck, Emma wasn't able to get her skis off. Somehow, despite the exertion that had kept her feeling warm, she had managed to become slightly hypothermic, and her coordination had suffered.

"Let me, honey," Gage said, squatting before her to release the bindings. Then, just as soon as she stepped out of them, he rose and steadied her with an arm around her waist. "You need to warm up. Just get in the truck. I'll take care of this stuff."

Honey. The word drizzled through her like honey itself, warm and sweet, touching places that had long felt cold. If only he meant it, really meant it. But it had probably slipped past his guard out of some old habit. And besides, she knew she would never really be anyone's honey.

He opened the door and helped her up onto the passenger seat. "I'll come around and start the engine. We'll get you warmed up."

It wasn't until a few minutes later that she began to shiver in earnest, the sudden, uncontrollable bursts that came from deep inside despite her efforts to relax. Gage loaded the skis and poles into the back, whistling as he did so. Shivering or not, Emma smiled with pleasure. Never in her wildest imaginings had she pictured Gage whistling. She liked the sound, liked the way it made her feel inside to know that for now, at least, he was feeling cheerful.

When he joined her up front, he brought a wool blanket and insisted on wrapping it around her. His movements were surprisingly gentle, making her feel suddenly on the edge of tears again. It wasn't until a person went without it that she knew just how much she missed having someone care. Bravely, she blinked back the moisture.

"This is crazy," she told Gage, to cover her roller-coastering emotions. "I never get hypothermic from a little exercise in the snow."

"You're worn out after this week, babe," he said with gruff gentleness as he caught her chin in his hand. With infinite care, he brushed a kiss on her chilled lips. "You've been having nightmares, you've been worried and scared, and then last night I only let you get a couple hours of sleep...maybe. You're exhausted, Em. Maybe you ought to think about taking a nap."

He drove slowly back to town. Gage was evidently in no bigger hurry to get back to that house than she was, Emma thought. Nor was there any need to hurry. The Suburban's heater was soon blasting enough hot air that her shivering stopped and the blanket became stifling. When she cast it aside, Gage flashed her a crooked smile and turned down the heat.

"Better?" he asked.

"Much. Thanks."

When they arrived back at the house the Haroldsen twins were just finishing up with their small snowblower and a shovel.

"We'll have to come back tomorrow and do it again, Miss Emma," Todd Haroldsen told her, "but we figured you'd want your car uncovered so there's some hope of getting to church in the morning."

"Thanks, guys. I really appreciate it. Can I interest you in some cookies?"

It was never difficult to interest two fifteen-year-old boys in food, especially junk food. Emma was almost laughing out loud a few minutes later when the twins disappeared with their booty.

"That was a major part of the Conard County high school football team, right?" Gage asked drily.

Emma chuckled. "And a good share of the basketball team, as well."

While Emma went to change, Gage slipped into the study and closed the door. His first call was to Nate Tate at home.

"Did you get anywhere with the FAA?"

"Sorry, old son, but the man's in Kansas City to see his first grandchild. Not much cage rattling I could do."

"I guess not." He swiveled the deep leather chair and looked out the window at the failing day. Unless he was mistaken, a thin golden beam of sunlight was slanting across the yard, looking every bit as beautiful and welcome as a rainbow after a storm. "It looks like the storm is breaking up."

"Yep," Nate answered. "I'm looking out my shop window right now. It's clearing over the mountains. It'll be a clear, cold night. And that reminds me. Micah called from Denver. He and Faith won't make it back today because their flight was delayed. Said he'll be back in the county sometime tomorrow."

"Good," Gage said, and meant it. He could use a little of Micah's preternatural instincts right now. "Jeff Cumberland's about fit to be tied, and I promised to bring Micah out to look at those helicopter tracks—"

"Which are now buried beneath the snow," Nate growled.

"Unfortunately. But it'll probably calm Jeff a little to know Micah's back on the case."

"I don't think anything short of a hanging is going to calm Jeff," Nate rumbled.

"Maybe not. What can you tell me about Don Fenster?"

The sudden change of subject took Nate by surprise, and it was a moment before he responded. "Don Fenster? What the hell has he gone and done now?"

"You mean he's in the habit of doing things?"

"We sent him up the river a few years back for armed robbery. Before that there were a couple of other things, but he always got probation. Anyhow, the armed robbery was the worst thing he ever got up to. He came back to live with his granny almost two years ago, and as far as I know he's been quiet. Why?"

Gage didn't answer. "What other things did he get up to?"

"Oh, hell, let me think. It was a long time ago, Gage. Joyriding. He 'borrowed' Jill Cranston's pickup when he was still a senior in high school. Judge Conard gave him a week in the county hoosegow and six months' probation, I think. He got picked up a time or two for shoplifting in his younger days. I don't know. He was a thorn in my side back then, but until the armed robbery he was just like any of a dozen other troublemakers his age. I don't recall that I worried unduly about him, just that I tried to keep him from annoying everybody else in the county. About the only thing that really strikes me in retrospect is that nobody liked him. In fact, most people felt an out-and-out aversion toward him. Why?"

"I don't know, really." Gage hesitated and then sighed. "Hell, yes, I do. Emma told me a little story this afternoon about how she beat Fenster to a pulp when they were both twelve because he wouldn't stop torturing a dog.''

"Damn, I never knew that.'' Nate sounded disturbed.

"I don't suppose anybody but Emma and Fenster ever did. He wouldn't want anyone to know, and Emma's not the type to tell anyone much of anything. She *did* say that Fenster hasn't talked to her once since then. And that strikes me as being...a little odd. It's been at least eighteen years.''

"Yeah.''

For a long time neither man said anything. Between them, the line echoed with silence.

"Let me think about this,'' Nate said presently. "Let me think, and maybe ask a few questions. I'll call you back, but probably not before tomorrow.''

After he hung up Gage rocked back in the chair, trying to ease the growing ache in his back. He was relieved, he realized, to have shared his uneasiness about Fenster. It wasn't much to go on, a fight between two kids nearly twenty years ago, but it was the first motive he had seen anywhere for why anyone on earth would want to torment Emma. Of course, crazies didn't need motives. The worst of them had absolutely no rhyme or reason to what they did. Someone like that might be involved, but his gut didn't believe it.

It was a crazy, all right. One with a motive. One with a grudge that hadn't died in at least the ten years since he'd attacked Emma in Laramie.

There was a quiet knock at the door, and Gage looked toward it. "Come on in, Emma.''

The door opened slowly, and Emma peeked around its edge. "I'm sorry to disturb you.... ''

"Hey, I'm sorry I closed the door. It's your house, Em. I just needed a moment to make a phone call.''

"That's all right.'' She stepped into the room, and the way her hands were clasped before her gave Gage an uneasy feeling.

"Is something wrong?'' he asked.

"I'm not sure,'' she admitted. "Gage...I think someone was in the house while we were gone.''

Chapter 12

"I told you, I only *think* somebody was in the house," Emma snapped a short while later. "If I could absolutely pinpoint the reason, I would!"

"*Something* had to give you the feeling," Gage argued.

"I know." Emma threw up a hand and nearly glared at him. "Quit badgering me. It's nothing I can exactly put my finger on. I just *know*. As if . . . as if I caught a whiff of an odor and can't quite place it."

Gage frowned. "Maybe that's it. Maybe you *did* catch a whiff of someone else's odor. It'd be subtle enough to elude you, but definite enough to give you this feeling. . . ."

Relieved that he was evidently going to give up pressuring her to show him something that was out of place, Emma leaned back against the foot of her bed and unfolded her arms.

"You didn't get the feeling anywhere but here?" he asked.

"Here and in my bathroom. I haven't been upstairs, and now I doubt if I could tell anything for sure. My imagination is going hog-wild right now."

"Let's go up anyway," Gage said grimly. "Together. I don't want you out of my sight, Emma."

Emma was agreeable. She didn't want to be out of his sight, either. There was little, she thought, quite as horrible as the feeling that someone had invaded your home without your permission. The sense of violation was inescapable.

"I don't think anyone's in the house now," he said as he took her hand and began to climb the stairs, "but stay behind me anyway."

"Why don't you think anyone's here?"

"Because, as long as we've been back, either he'd have taken some action or we'd have heard something." That wasn't necessarily true, but for now he was counting on it.

Emma realized he was trying to reassure her, but she didn't overlook the way he kept close to the wall as they climbed and encouraged her to do the same.

There was little light at the top of the stairs. All the doors were closed, shutting out the last of the evening sun. When Gage flipped the wall switch, yellow light cascaded from the overhead fixtures.

The hall was L-shaped, and Gage led her swiftly past the closed door of his bedroom on one side and the closed door of the bathroom on the other. Rounding the corner, he headed for the bedroom at the very back of the house. There he opened the door slowly and peered in. Nothing in sight. The bed concealed nothing; stripped of any concealing fabrics, even the shadows beneath it were in plain view. A hazy golden evening light filled the room, brightening it. Gage drew Emma in with him and kept her to one side while he investigated the walk-in closet.

"Nothing," he said.

"This was my parents' room when I was little," Emma remarked. It seemed so barren and empty now, she thought a little sadly. She hated to come up here, because every time she did, she remembered when it had been decorated in the bright, primary colors her mother had so loved. "No one has been in here," she said with conviction. "Whatever it is that caused me to feel uneasy in my bedroom isn't here."

"Maybe he didn't come upstairs at all, then. Maybe he found out what he wanted to know in your room."

Emma raised troubled eyes to his. "Maybe," she agreed. "Let's check the other rooms to be safe."

The next two rooms were the same, empty, barren of anything except Emma's memories of her childhood and her brother. The front bedroom, the one Gage had taken as his, had always been the guest room.

It was there they found the evidence that someone had indeed been in the house.

The bottom drawer of the dresser was open, one side tugged out a little farther than the other. On the floor beside it lay the heap of jockstraps Gage had intended to deter Emma from snooping. And there, in plain sight, lay the item he had been hiding. A word escaped him on an anguished breath, a word that might have been a curse or a prayer.

Emma's breath stuck in her throat as she saw the framed color photograph. Gage—a younger, dark-haired, unscarred Gage—looked up proudly from a position behind two grinning little girls and a woman who held an infant. Beyond any shadow of a doubt, this was Gage's lost family.

For an endless moment Emma thought she would never breathe again. Pain seemed to swallow her, reminding her that he had lost what she would never have. His heart had gone to the grave with this woman and his children, and even if it hadn't...

Somehow she took a breath, and then another. Her heart began to beat again, a painful, throbbing rhythm of loss and compassion. Turning, she looked at Gage and saw the stark agony of his expression as he looked down at the photo.

And then something in his face stiffened, and his shoulders straightened. He looked at Emma. "I'm calling in the crime-scene team."

"For an open drawer?" For a violation of his privacy, his sanctuary, his grief? "What will they do?"

"Ransack this place looking for fingerprints or anything else."

"Oh. But I didn't notice anything else—"

Gage interrupted. "Emma, that man didn't come in here just to drag out a photograph of my family. He wanted something. We need to find out what."

Three hours later the last of the sheriff's crime-scene team trailed out the door. They'd found what the intruder had come for, and now Emma stood in her living room, staring blindly at the Christmas tree and trying not to think about the crude doll they had found hanging in its branches. A voodoo doll, badly mutilated, with unmistakably red hair. And no fingerprints. Not a one but hers and Gage's.

Shuddering, she flipped the switch and turned off all the lights. She hadn't seen Gage in the last hour, and suddenly she needed desperately to see him. He made her feel incredibly safe even when he was trying to keep her at a distance.

Thinking he must still be upstairs, she climbed wearily and turned into his open bedroom. He was there, standing by his dresser, looking down at the open drawer that held the photo of his family, a photo now dusted with black fingerprint powder. Her whole damn house was covered with the stuff, but this disturbed her as the rest didn't. It upset her, somehow, to see Gage's memories of his family tangled up in her mess.

Coming to stand beside him, she looked down at the photo. And then some instinct seized her, driving her to bend and lift the photograph into the light where it belonged. Gently, she dusted the black powder away with her sleeve and set it on the dresser.

For a minute, perhaps longer, there was no sound in the room save Gage's ragged breathing as he tried to absorb his own pain.

"They're beautiful," Emma said finally, the words painful on her lips. "Your wife was lovely. So pretty."

He said nothing, but she heard him stop breathing.

"And your daughters," she continued gently, "look so much like you. How old is your son in this picture?"

She thought he might not answer, that he might be so locked in his grief that he didn't even hear her.

But then, every syllable rusty, he answered in a low voice. "Two weeks. Just two weeks."

"You must have been so happy. So proud."

"We were." But suddenly he turned toward Emma, recognizing that his loss was not the only sorrow in this room. She was looking at the portrait, staring fixedly as if she could grow used to what it implied. And then her gaze lowered to the drawer, to the stacks of photo albums he kept but was never able to look at.

"You must hurt so badly," she whispered unsteadily. "So badly."

"I was lucky," he said, in that instant realizing the truth of it. The understanding was suddenly there as if it had always been there, feeling as if he had known it all along. "I was luckier than most people ever get to be."

Jerkily, Emma lifted her head and looked up at him. "Lucky?"

"It didn't last long," he said roughly. "Just seven years. But for seven years I had it all, Emma. I had it *all*. Some people don't ever get even half that much."

Like her, Emma thought, turning her attention back to the picture.

Like her, Gage thought, her loss piercing him as violently as his own had. All of a sudden he was very much in the present and the past was very much in the past. Emma was here, in need of things he didn't know if he could give her. But there was one thing he could definitely give her, one thing that would drive reality away for a little while. One thing that would make her forget her own sorrows. Reaching out, he took the photo and put it back in the bottom drawer. Then he shut the drawer and straightened, facing Emma.

"Come here," he said. Before she could object, he pulled her into his arms and bent his head until his mouth was pressed to her ear. "I want to make love to you," he whispered hoarsely and felt a ripple of response pass through her as she caught her breath. "I want to kiss you all over, taste you all over. I want to feel you come alive beneath my hands, and I want to come alive beneath yours."

Each word set a spark loose in Emma, and together they ignited a conflagration. Her emotions soared from sorrow to passion in an instant, and a shiver of hunger ripped through her, driving everything beyond the moment into a dark dungeon where it belonged.

"Stay here," he said raggedly. "Right here. I just want to make sure everything is locked up. Wait for me, Emma. Promise."

She opened heavy-lidded eyes and met his intense, stormy gaze. "I promise," she said huskily. "I promise."

He checked to make sure all the doors and windows were locked before he rejoined her in his bedroom. Native caution, learned from hard years on the streets and in the DEA, wouldn't let him forget such details.

Assured that the house was as secure as it could be, he stepped into his bedroom and caught his breath.

The yellowing shades held the night at bay, and she had turned on the bedside lamp. Her jeans made a dark puddle on the floor, a puddle topped by her sweater. Emma lay waiting for him in navy blue lace and satin, in a camisole and bikini panties that were an incitement, an enticement, he hadn't expected from her.

"God, Emma!" He drank her in with eyes that felt starved. "Did I tell you how lovely you are?"

Those were his hormones talking, she told herself, but her skin flushed under the warmth of his gaze, and she felt herself beginning to smile and relax, even as a deeper tension began to grow at her center.

His black sweater, jeans and briefs quickly joined the heap on the floor. He came down on his side next to her, propping himself on his elbow so that he could fill himself with the sight of her. She had freed her hair for him, and he wasn't shy about scooping up handfuls of it and sifting it through his fingers.

"Like fire," he whispered huskily. "Sweet, sweet fire . . . ah, Emma . . ."

At last, at long last, his mouth settled on hers. She was thirsty for him, thirsty for his taste and touch and smell and feel. It hadn't been that many hours since they had risen from her bed, but Emma felt as if she had spent months in a desert.

Her arms closed snugly around him, holding him as he needed to be held, as she needed to hold him. Her palms settled on the scars on his back, feeling the shiny smoothness of the grafts, the ridges of the keloids. A map of his pain and loss, she thought, and felt a wild, almost agonizing need to comfort him somehow, some way.

"Tighter, Emma...oh, God, tighter..."

So she tightened her arms until they began to ache, holding him as if she could squeeze the pain away. His tongue plunged deeply into her mouth, taking possession of her with a hunger that revealed a need far beyond simple wanting.

And she needed him every bit as desperately. The aching, yearning need went deeper than anything physical could have. She loved him, and loving him, she needed him more than she needed to breathe.

"Gage...oh, Gage..." She was incapable of silence, yet unable to say anything but his name. When his mouth closed over her breast, through the satin, she arched upward, begging for more. When he gripped her wrist and drew her hand down to his aching manhood, she curled her fingers around him greedily and relished his smooth, hard heat.

A husky laugh, almost a groan, escaped Gage suddenly, and he moved away from the breathtaking, maddening inexperience of her touch. Suddenly her arms were caught above her head, held easily in one of his large hands. Startled, she opened her eyes and looked up at him.

"You make me crazy," he told her. There was an astonishing warmth in his gray-green eyes, in the faint smile that tugged the corners of his mouth upward.

"Good," she said breathlessly.

"It's good, all right. But things happen too fast that way. I want to go slow. Easy. I want to take my time with you."

She thought she would never breathe again. Every inch of her responded to the lazy promise in his voice, his words, his eyes. Last night had been cast in a web of complex emotions, she realized, colored by so many things from outside. This time it was going to be simple. There were no shadows in Gage's eyes right now, no glimpse of the chilly wastes of hell. All she could see was heat. He was totally absorbed in the moment, totally awake to the sexuality that was steaming between them. For this little while, Gage Dalton wasn't going to be anything at all except Emmaline Conard's lover.

The understanding kicked her heart into overdrive and caused white heat to pour through her veins.

"This blue is a great color for you, Em," Gage said quietly. He continued to hold her arms above her head, but now his free hand came to rest on her satin-covered midriff, halfway between her breasts and her thighs. The touch seemed to shoot sparks through her. "It makes your skin look so creamy I want to lick it. But not yet."

Not yet. Instead he trailed a fingertip up the valley between her breasts and smiled as she undulated helplessly in response. "I want to touch you, Em," he said huskily.

"Touch me," she begged breathlessly.

"Where?" He looked up at her, a wicked sparkle in his gray-green gaze. Hell's own archangel was out on a weekend pass, and he was in a mood to play devilish games.

She caught her breath, and then a soft, whispery laugh escaped her. "Oh, Gage...you know I can't say those things...."

"No? Why not?" His finger trailed slowly up the side of one breast, causing her nipple to harden visibly beneath the dark blue satin. He came close, but he didn't touch the pouting peak. "You want me to do it, don't you? Why is it so hard to say it out loud?"

He was teasing, she thought, catching the gleam in his eyes even as her own internal drumbeat was slowly drowning out the sounds of reason. Helpless to prevent it, she felt her hips arch upward in a search for release. He'd hardly even touched her, yet she was already losing her sanity.

"How am I supposed to know how to please you if you don't tell me?" he asked softly. Slowly, ever so achingly slowly, he ran his fingertip around her swollen nipple, never quite giving her the touch she was needing more desperately by the instant. Emma shivered, and a small moan escaped her, causing Gage to smile. It was a gentle smile, an expression so tender that it pierced her desire and made her throat ache.

"Touch me," she whispered hoarsely. "Touch my breast."

"Yes, Emma," he said just as hoarsely. "Anything you want." He slipped his hand up beneath the satin and cupped her warm flesh with his. Carefully he caught her nipple between his fingers and tugged. Emma arched like a drawn bow. "Whatever pleases you," he murmured hoarsely just before his mouth covered hers and his tongue stroked roughly against hers.

Emma felt as if she were drowning, drowning in his heat, his scent, his touch, his sheer masculinity. All her life she had read of such feelings, but until now she had never experienced them. She had never dreamed how wonderful a man's differences could be, how much pleasure it could give her to feel hair-roughened skin against her, how exciting it could be to feel his hardness against her softness. And then he released her hands.

Led by instinct, compelled by need, she began to explore him with her hands. Everywhere her fingers wandered they found hard, lean muscle sheathed in warm, resilient flesh. Her throat began to ache again, this time with appreciation of Gage's vitality. With wonder that he was sharing it with her. With awe for life and its miracles.

He dragged his mouth from hers and then leaned down to give her swollen lips a gentle lick with his tongue. "I need you, Emma," he said on a ragged breath as he tugged her camisole over her head.

Her breasts tightened even more as cool air brushed across them. Bowing his head, Gage lapped at a taut nipple. Emma groaned deeply and arched upward, forgetting about awe as need swamped her.

"Oh, that's good, Emma." His praise was rough, ragged, hardly more than a groan of approval. "Your breasts are so pretty...so sweet...." He gave himself over completely to Emma's pleasure, and in so doing he answered a need he had only just now recognized. It was a need to drive the shadows from this woman's eyes, a need to bring her something good and beautiful. A need to give himself to her.

"Oh, Emma, sweetheart . . ." He licked and sucked and nibbled as if he, too, felt the pleasure he was giving her. Low in her belly, the knot of need tightened and grew heavier, a pressure that desperately needed an answering pressure.

"Touch me," she whispered. "Please . . . touch me. . . ."

"Where, baby? Where?"

Desperate, she grabbed his hand and drew it downward, pressing it snugly against her satin-covered mound. "Gage . . ." His name ended on a rising note, a plea.

"Yes . . . oh, baby . . . yes . . ."

Her panties vanished, tugged impatiently away, and then his hand was on her, slipping across the aching nub and plunging sweetly into her heated depths. With a cry Emma bucked upward, and Gage groaned.

"Tell me," he urged as his tongue swirled around her ear and sent another shiver running through her. "Tell me. . . ."

But she was past telling, and he was rapidly getting past the point of listening. Again and again she rolled upward against his hand, telling him with her body that it was good, so good, but not enough. Not nearly enough.

The world spun dizzily, and Emma suddenly realized she was above Gage, straddling him. Before the shift could shatter her mood and bring her back to sharp-edged reality, he lifted her and drove himself deeply into her. Oh, so deeply. She caught her breath as pleasure clenched her in its vise.

"Ride me, Red," he commanded hoarsely. "Ride me."

He had warned her that he was coarse, but neither of them had imagined she would like it. And she did like it. The blunt, unvarnished command sent thrills racing through her and moved her far beyond the cloak of inhibition or the reluctance of embarrassment.

Bracing herself with her hands on his powerful shoulders, she began to move, wringing every bit of pleasure she could from them both.

She rode him, hard. All the way to the stars.

* * *

"I may never move again."

Gage's muffled words brought a smile to Emma's lips. She tried to wiggle off his chest, but his arms tightened, refusing to release her. As soon as he felt her relax onto him, he ran his hands downward over her silky back and cupped her soft, round rump. For a moment he pressed her closer. It was a hug, a reminder and a promise, all in one.

"I should make dinner," Emma said, partly because her conscience was pricking her, and partly because she wanted him to object.

He objected. "Forget it. If we get hungry we'll eat cookies. Are you hungry?"

Only for you. She swallowed the words before they could spill over her lips and tell him what he had come to mean to her. Time, she thought, was irrelevant. In one short week she had come to know Gage better than many of the people she saw daily. It wasn't, after all, how many facts you knew about someone that told you the kind of person they were. "No, I'm not hungry," she answered lazily. "We'll be starved later, though."

"We'll worry about it then. I want you to stay right where you are." He squeezed her rump again, gently, and then tugged a blanket upward, covering them both.

"I'm heavy."

"Not that heavy, Red. It feels good to have you all over me like this."

It felt good to sprawl all over him like this, she admitted. Questions hovered in the wings, unspoken fears and the shadow of inevitable loss lurked right outside this cocoon, but she refused to acknowledge any of them. These stolen moments were *hers,* and they would have to last her the rest of her life. She absolutely wouldn't let anything take them from her.

But just as she had that defiant thought, the phone rang downstairs.

"No," she mumbled when she felt Gage stiffen.

"I have to, Em. It might be Nate." He brushed a kiss on her forehead. "I'll come right back."

Sighing, she slid off him and watched as he grabbed his briefs and yanked them on. Wearing nothing else, he trotted from the room.

Lying on her back, Emma stared at the ceiling and tried to pay attention to nothing but how good she felt right now. How beautiful and cherished Gage had made her feel. How every muscle in her body felt as if it was warm and relaxed. Unfortunately, it didn't work.

She told herself that she was prepared to pay the inevitable price of loving Gage, that she was living in a fool's paradise with complete awareness that it was just that. He would move on and she would be alone again, and she would deal with it when it happened. She could handle it, she told herself, and not for anything would she have missed the magic he had given her. Hell's own archangel had spun a fantasy of sparkling sensations and jeweled emotions for her, and the price for that would be her heart. She could handle it. She *would* handle it. And she would never regret it.

But as she lay there alone, waiting for him, the shadows moved closer, reminding her that there was a price. The chill crept into her glow, and sorrow tinged her joy.

The door opened, and Gage approached the bed. Emma found his black briefs incredibly sexy. In fact, every line of him was incredibly sexy, from his broad shoulders to his narrow flanks to his muscular legs. Until this very moment she had never guessed a man could have great legs.

Gage sat beside her and smiled crookedly when her hand rose to dive into the dark swirls of his soft chest hair.

"Was it Nate?" she asked throatily.

"Nope." His smile faded. "It was a breather."

"Breather?" Her hand stilled, and her eyes rose to his face.

"You know, one of those people who calls and then just listens."

"Oh! Oh, I've had a couple of those calls."

"You have?" He frowned. "Emma, you should have told me."

"Why? Could you do anything? Of course not." She gave him a smile that didn't quite reach her eyes. "It's probably some kid I yelled at in the library."

His frown deepened. "It could also be the person who's been pulling all these other stunts. The one who was in here tonight."

She didn't want to think about that. She didn't want to think about that horrible doll or the hate its creation implied. "Gage, he can't hurt me over the telephone."

He shook his head, as if despairing, and then sighed heavily. "No, I guess not. But, Emma, he's escalating. Surely you've noticed."

"Yes." She closed her eyes, and the hand that rested on his chest knotted into a fist. "I've noticed. But what the hell can I do about it, Gage? You tell me. I don't know who he is. I can't hide, I can't run, I can't get even. I just have to wait and count on you being here if he comes after me. There's not one other thing I can do about it! Oh, Lord..."

Gage scooped her up from the pillows and pulled her against his chest. She burrowed into his shoulder and drew a shuddering breath.

"I'll be here, Emma," he said. It was a vow.

The good spell ended during the night. After several days of relatively moderate pain, Gage awoke in the fiery grip of agony. A groan escaped him before he could swallow it, and then he forced himself to lie there facedown and accept his suffering. It was his due, after all, a purgatory of the body to match the damnation of his soul.

"Hell!" The exclamation escaped him on a breath as a fresh spear thrust through his back and into his leg. He should get up. Walk. But he couldn't leave Emma alone. Didn't dare leave her alone. Couldn't risk her getting hurt.

Couldn't risk losing her.

The realization was like a blinding shaft of nuclear heat in the barren wastes of his soul. *Couldn't risk losing her?* Oh, God, he didn't *deserve* her. She wouldn't want him for long. He was so scarred, so damaged, so...ruined. So afflicted with his losses that he didn't seem capable of living for tomorrow. What woman would want that?

No, he didn't deserve her. Didn't deserve her sweetness, her light, her warmth, her caring. Because he had failed his family.

But he wouldn't fail Emma. No, he would be there when she needed him to protect her. That determination kept him glued to the bed when he might have found some relief by rising and walking. Kept him firmly pinned to the mattress when the cold oblivion of the winter night beckoned him with the promise of solitude and miles of empty streets.

It was crazy, he thought, to feel that his body's suffering somehow atoned for what had happened to his wife and children. Even his former boss had taken him to task for his belief that he was somehow responsible for what had happened to Jan and the children.

"If you have to blame someone," Cal had argued vehemently, "blame that damn fool cop who let your real name slip to Joe Valenza. Blame the guy who built the bomb. Blame the guy who wired it to your car. But don't blame yourself for trying to do what was right!"

Cal was right. Intellectually, Gage recognized it. But his aching heart and frozen soul weren't as amenable to logic. It sounded stupid to admit he felt responsible for what had happened. It sounded incredibly egotistical, when he thought about it. He had done nothing that several thousand other agents didn't do daily. It had simply been his misfortune to send Val Valenza up the river. If Gage Dalton hadn't done it, some other agent sure as hell would have. And some other agent would have found a bomb wired to *his* car. The chances of the game. Period.

But if he hadn't been an agent . . .

That was the thought that haunted him. If he had been an electrician or a carpenter or a pharmacist, Jan and the kids would still be alive.

Maybe. If some other chance of the game hadn't gotten them. A car accident. A tornado. A loony like the one who seemed to be after Miss Emma.

Smothering another groan, he turned his head to one side and tried to make her out in the dark. She was there. He could hear her soft breathing, could feel her warmth like a radiance that warmed his frozen places. She deserved better than Gage Dalton. Much better.

But he wasn't able to resist her, he admitted. The sexual tension that crackled between them would have overwhelmed a stronger man than he. And the other things—her gentleness, her caring, her kindness—those things overwhelmed him even more. She had pierced his solitude and poured warm balm over some of his rawest places. She had made him start to feel that maybe it was okay that he was alive. That maybe life would be worth living again. That maybe he was worth something.

He needed her. He needed Emma in ways that had absolutely nothing to do with the incendiary sexual attraction he felt for her. Another chasm was opening in his spirit, another place that would ever afterward be empty.

Because surely Emma could not want to fill it.

A searing razor of pain slashed through his back and startled a soft moan from him. Beside him, Emma stirred.

"Gage?" she asked drowsily.

"It's okay, Emma," he whispered roughly. "Go back to sleep."

She turned slowly onto her side and reached out a hand, finding his naked shoulder with her fingertips. "Do you hurt?"

"Yeah. Nothing unusual. Go back to sleep."

For several moments she remained still, her fingertips warm and motionless on his shoulder. Just as he began to believe she had gone back to sleep, she stirred again.

"Your back?" Her voice was soft, thick with sleep.

"Just the usual, Em. Honey, just go back to sleep."

"I like that," she murmured.

"What do you like?"

"When you call me honey."

"Aw, hell," he sighed, beginning to realize that he was well and truly lost. She liked him to call her honey. Not one week ago she'd hollered because he'd called her Emma. Too familiar, she had thought. And he had answered that calling her "honey" would be familiar.

He sighed again, this time less from reluctance to face what was happening between them than from yearning. "How about sweetheart? Do you mind if I call you that?" Because he sure as hell would like to. *Sweetheart.* He'd never wanted to call anyone that, not even Jan. But that was how he felt about Emma. The admission cost him some savage twinges of conscience, but after a moment they eased, leaving him to face the future unimpeded.

"Yes," she whispered. "I'd like that. If you meant it."

He caught his breath, trying to absorb the emotional impact of what she had just told him. He didn't dare answer, he realized. If he answered, he would tell her the truth, and then she would feel obligated to stay with him. He didn't want soft words and promises made in the warm, sleepy intimacy of a bed in the middle of the night. If ever, if *ever,* he was to take Emma into his life, he had to be sure she was going into it in the bright light of day. That she saw his flaws and his scars, and still thought him worthy.

Emma didn't wait for him to answer. She didn't really expect him to. She wasn't a woman any man would ever call sweetheart, and she knew it.

But Gage hurt, and she cared deeply that he did. Throwing back the quilt, she rose and straddled him as he lay on his stomach.

"Emma?"

"Shh. You need a little rubdown."

Her small hands settled into the small of his back and began to knead strongly, finding the knots and kinks instinctively. Another groan escaped Gage, but this time it was one of absolute relief.

"Ah, God, that's good...." he moaned. "Oh, Em..."

"Shh...just relax. Just let me..."

It was so marvelous, she thought, to feel free to do this. Even one day ago, she wouldn't have dared touch him without invitation. Now here she sat, buck naked herself, on his naked thighs while her fingers dug into him.

She could feel the knots in his muscles, almost rocklike in their hardness. "Is it cramping that causes the pain?" she asked presently.

"Some of it." Oh, man, she had magic fingers, he thought as knot after knot gradually dissolved. "Some of it is from damaged nerves."

"Is this helping?"

"Sweetheart," he said, giving up the battle against himself, "it's heaven."

The endearment settled on her like fairy dust, bringing enchantment to the night, into these precious moments of intimacy. Leaning forward, she pressed a kiss on Gage's back between his shoulder blades, then straightened and resumed the massage.

"Your hands must be getting tired," he murmured.

"Just a little." She was enjoying this too much to quit, despite the cramping of her fingers. It was rare, she thought, so rare, that one person could give another this kind of caring. Her life had been barren of such things for so long now. Too long. She needed someone to love, to worry over, to look after, to care for. Without that, life became a meaningless progression of days.

In the past week her entire life had changed—for the better, she thought. She looked forward to coming home from work in the evenings, knowing Gage would be there. Just being able to share a meal, or relate the day's doings, was a joy.

And now, now she had experienced an intimacy with him that she knew she would always crave, would always miss when it was gone. If only he wouldn't go. If only he would stay and make her part of his life. But what could she possibly offer him that he would want?

Suddenly Gage reached behind him and caught one of her hands. "Come here, Emma," he said softly. "Come here."

When she was stretched out beside him, he caught her hands in his and began to rub them gently. "You'll be sore tomorrow," he muttered. "Your hands aren't used to doing that."

Then, in turn, he lifted each hand to his lips and pressed a kiss in each palm.

Emma caught her breath. "Gage..."

"Hush," he said quietly. Wrapping her in his strong arms, he drew her into the welcoming curve of his body and settled her head on his shoulder. "My back feels a whole lot better now, sweetheart. A whole lot better." He kissed her gently on the temple and smoothed her hair with his hand. "Sleep now, Emma. Sleep."

Sleep carried her away slowly. As she spiraled down into its depths, feeling warm and cared for, she wondered why no one had ever realized that a white knight didn't have to be white. He could be dark. A dark angel. Archangel.

Turning her head drowsily, her last conscious effort was to drop a soft kiss on his smooth, warm shoulder.

Gage felt the kiss. He felt it to the very core of his being. Long after Emma dropped off, he stared into the teeth of the night and wondered why the hell he should have to give her up.

Or if he really did have to.

Chapter 13

Monday morning brought sunshine to Conard County. The fresh layers of snow lay like pristine blankets over everything, but the sun was warm, the air was calm and Christmas was only a week away.

Gage pondered that as he drove Emma to the library and personally escorted her to her desk. He needed to find something to give her, he thought. Something special. Something memorable. Because suddenly he couldn't stand the thought of Emma having a Christmas without one precious memory to store up.

"Promise me you won't go anywhere alone," he said as he helped her out of her parka.

"I promise." For the umpteenth time in the last half hour. His edginess was beginning to make her edgy, too. "Gage, I'm just going to be sitting here at this desk the way I do five days of every week. I *can't* go anywhere, because I get paid to be *here*."

"Okay." He was being ridiculously overprotective. He knew it, but he couldn't help it. You couldn't suffer the losses he had suffered and ever again be entirely comfortable with the safety of someone you cared about. No way. "I'll pick you up for lunch at one."

"I'll be ready." She would be, too. Even though she was pretending impatience, she loved every bit of his concern for her. Where once there was only a cold bleakness in his gaze, she now saw warmth. How could anyone dislike that?

"Okay." Bending, he gave her a quick, hard kiss on her mouth. "Look out, Miss Emma. I'm already hungry for you again. By tonight I'll be crazy with it."

Emma blushed profusely, but she laughed. "Me, too," she managed to admit softly. This kind of frankness was new to her, but she thought she liked it.

Gage astonished her with a broad, warm smile, a smile unlike any he had ever given her. It was a young smile, the smile of a happy man. Emma caught her breath and watched as her silver-haired archangel pivoted and strode from the library.

The report of Emma's assault was waiting on Gage's desk when he reached his office. The Express Mail envelope was still sealed, preserving her privacy.

From everyone but him.

He was reluctant to invade her privacy, even though it wasn't really an invasion. He was a police investigator working on a case, and that meant he had to look beyond every closed door and curtained window in search of information that could be useful. Still, he hesitated. His personal relationship with Emma complicated the ethics of things, but it was more than that, he realized after a moment. Much more.

He didn't want to know what had happened to her. He didn't want to read the callous, jargon-laden descriptions of every detail. He didn't want to read the cold, feelingless report of an event that had wounded Emma so terribly.

It had happened ten years ago, but for Gage, learning this all for the first time, it was going to be fresh. It was going to be today. Deep inside himself, he knew he was going to feel a rage unequaled by any except the rage he had felt over the loss of his family. He knew he was going to suffer a fresh agonizing wound.

But he had to know. He had to know in case there was an overlooked clue. He had to know because Emma was remembering, and somebody in this godforsaken world had to understand the things she wouldn't be able to say.

He opened the envelope.

The photocopies of the police file made a thick stack. At the top was the initial report detailing the discovery of Emma in a trash bin in an alley behind a bar. One of the cooks at the bar had evidently noticed something suspicious in the alley and called to report a prowler. When the police arrived, they found no prowler, but a sound from the bin had drawn their attention. Investigating, they had found Emma. The cook was unable to tell them a thing about the man he had seen except that he was large, heavily bundled in dark winter clothing, and his hair had been concealed by a stocking cap. Not one useful thing.

Following were several pages devoted to the fruitless questioning of others who had been in the area at about the right time. Then came page upon page of medical reports detailing Emma's injuries. Nineteen stab wounds. Countless small burn marks, presumably from a cigarette. A star fracture of the skull resulting from a blow by a blunt instrument. Surgery to remove a clot on the brain. Other operations to repair the damage caused by the stab wounds. Two separate operations to repair shattered bone in one arm. Eventually a hysterectomy resulting directly from sepsis of one of the stab wounds. No evidence of sexual assault.

That was truly odd, Gage thought. This type of violent crime against a woman usually involved sexual assault, as well. Ignoring the way his hands were shaking, he turned to the report by the forensic psychiatrist who had been asked to profile the crime and perpetrator. There was little there that Gage hadn't read before, but one thing stuck out: the psychiatrist believed the perpetrator had been startled before he had fulfilled his intentions, had stabbed her in an attempt to kill her immediately, and then had dumped her.

Emma was most likely alive only because her attacker had panicked.

The file closed on the note that the victim, upon recovering consciousness, was unable to recall the events of that night.

Rage shook Gage, every bit as strong as he had expected and then some. He couldn't stand the thought of anyone treating Emma that way, the thought of anyone hurting her that way. He would have loved to smash something, anything, to give vent to some of his anger, but in the end it wouldn't help at all.

But he couldn't meet Emma for lunch. Not with what he had just read so fresh in his mind. Not when he was so furious he needed to destroy something. He reached for the phone and called her.

"Conard County Public Library. Emmaline Conard speaking."

Even the sound of her voice over the telephone affected him, he realized almost ruefully. Sexy. Sweet. Warm. "Sweetheart, it's Gage."

"Oh, hi!" A smile was suddenly apparent in her voice. "Did you forget to give me some warning or other? Or did you overlook a promise you want me to give?"

Her teasing warmed him, and he felt a silly, cockeyed smile grow on his face, driving his anger back into a darker place. "There're all kinds of promises I want," he growled laughingly. "We'll get to those later. About lunch . . . something came up. . . ."

"Oh."

Damn, she sounded disappointed. But he couldn't face her, not yet. Not for an hour of pretending to be cheerful over lunch. He needed time to cope with his anger and his knowledge of what had happened to her. "Listen, I'll have Sara bring something over for you and keep you company. She'll be thrilled to get away from the front desk."

"Sure, that would be great. I haven't really had a chance to talk to her in weeks. One o'clock?"

"I'll have her call if that's not a good time."

But Sara thought it was a great time. She eyed Gage a little curiously when he suggested she stand in for him, but she didn't comment. But then, Sara seldom offered an opinion about the stupid things other people did, at least, not apart from her job as a deputy.

"Sure," she said, accepting Gage's suggestion amiably. "Emma and I can compare notes about you. That's always fun."

Gage paused in the midst of turning back to his office. "Compare notes?" He caught a gleam in Sara's brown eyes.

"Yeah," she said with a shrug. "Girl talk, you know? Whether you or Ed has the best buns in the department ... Well, maybe we ought to consider Micah, too...."

Gage took a threatening step toward her, which sent her off into a peal of laughter. Smothering his own reluctant smile, he headed back to his office.

Micah showed up moments after Sara left. Marriage agreed with the big Indian, Gage thought as he watched Micah, ordinarily taciturn, joke lazily with Velma and Nate. Gage had only known him for a few months, but even he could see the new relaxation and quiet happiness in that harsh face.

"What's happening with the mutilations?" Micah asked Gage finally.

"Things are getting complicated. Come on back and I'll tell you about it."

Micah and Nate both followed him back, bearing mugs of coffee with them. In Gage's office they settled on chairs while he closed the door and rounded his desk. As briefly as possible, Gage and Nate brought Micah up to date on the events of the past week, including the several things that had happened to Miss Emma. And now, because it was relevant to the case, Gage gave Micah a bare-bones account of the Laramie attack on Miss Emma. Gage didn't know whether to be relieved or disappointed when Micah leaped to the same conclusion linking Emma and the cattle mutilations at the Cumberland ranch. He might have felt easier about Emma's safety if Micah hadn't also felt that the mutilator might be after her, but then, he might also have simply become more worried.

"It would take the same kind of mind, I guess," Micah said. He accepted the psychological profile of Emma's attacker from Gage and scanned it quickly. "Well, hell," he muttered. "What kind of blood was it in that pentagram on her driveway?"

"I was just about to call the lab to see if they've reached any conclusion."

"I'll do that," Nate said. "You fill Micah in on the story about Don Fenster torturing a dog. And that reminds me, I was going to pull Fenster's rap sheet for you."

As Gage told the deputy how Emma had creamed Don Fenster for abusing a dog all those years ago, Micah's brow lowered in a scowl.

"Yeah," he said. "Yeah. There could be a connection. It's sure as hell the only possibility we've got. Maybe we ought to make a little visit to the Fenster place."

"Without a warrant?"

Micah smiled faintly. "I've never needed a warrant to go anyplace I've wanted to go. Never."

Gage returned the smile with a small one of his own. "Not exactly admissible evidence."

"We can get a warrant," Nate said, startling them both as he rejoined them. "Your friend at the lab says the blood on Emma's driveway appears to match that last mutilated steer we found. They're running confirmatory tests right now."

Gage swore. Adrenaline pumped through him in a sudden surge, bringing him to his feet, creating a need to act. "That settles the little-green-men question."

"Easy, Gage," Nate said. "Fenster might seem obvious, but it could be someone else—although, I have to admit, I can't think of anyone nearly as likely off the top of my head. Anyhow, we need to explore possibilities here. Knowing there's a link helps, but—"

Gage interrupted. "Walt Severn told me Fenster has a bunch of his friends staying out there with him. 'Creeps' was the word he used."

Nate appeared struck. "Friends. Creeps. A cult?"

"That's what I'm wondering. Walt said they've been living off the old lady for months."

"I can sure as hell look into it," Micah said. "Quietly. See if there's anything to it."

Nate was beginning to nod; he knew Micah's capacity to pass over the landscape like a wraith, invisible to anyone who didn't know where to look.

Just then Gage's extension buzzed. He picked up the receiver. "What is it, Velma?" he said to the dispatcher.

"Sara just radioed, Gage. Miss Emma's gone from the library, and no one knows where she got to."

Her car was still in the lot behind the building. Mr. Craig had been there all morning, but he confessed he had fallen asleep behind the stacks and hadn't heard or noticed a thing. Emma's assistant, Linda, wasn't scheduled to show up until two o'clock, so that meant Emma's disappearance had left the library unattended. And no one believed Miss Emma would have done that by choice.

Standing on the steps of the library, Gage looked up the street through the gray lace of leafless trees, across the blindingly white snow, out toward the edge of town. Toward the vast barrenness of the wintry landscape.

Such a bright, beautiful day. Once before, on a day like this, he had lost everything. Today, faced with Emma's disappearance, realization struck him like a spear in the chest. Somehow, some way, she had become his life. She had become everything that mattered. And he was losing everything all over again.

"Son." Nate's gravelly growl hauled Gage back. "You and Micah head on out to the Fenster place. I'll have a warrant in my hands before you get there. Check in before you set foot on his property, though. I'll let you know what we're doing to support you."

Gage didn't doubt for a minute that Nate would get the warrant. Everybody in Conard County owed Nathan Tate a few favors. He gave a short, sharp nod and headed down the steps. Micah caught up with him.

"We'll take my unit," Micah said. "I've got an arsenal stashed in the back."

As they sped away from town, Micah at the wheel, Gage squeezed his eyes shut against the painful beauty of the day and prayed for the first time since his world had blown up in his face. He prayed they weren't headed in the wrong direction—what did they have to go on except some far-fetched conclusions?—prayed they wouldn't be too late, prayed Emma wasn't as terrified as she must be, that she hadn't been hurt.

There had been little in his life to persuade him that heaven ever listened, but Miss Emmaline Conard, with her gentle nature and caring heart, had taught him that heaven existed. Even an archangel from hell recognized it when he was faced with it.

Micah offered no false assurances, didn't even seek to distract him with aimless conversation. Micah understood what he was going through, down to the smallest twinge of conscience and the largest stab of fear. He just kept driving, a little too fast, but with steady hands on the wheel.

Oh, God, Gage thought desperately. Dear God, don't let us be too late.

When Tam Tennyson came running into the library a little before one o'clock to tell Miss Emma that somebody had backed into her car, Emma had no cause to doubt him. Tam was one of her favorite children, a six-year-old with carroty hair and freckles. Emma never looked at him without envying the Tennysons.

"The man said he'll wait, Miss Emma. You gotta get the 'surance stuff."

Emma supposed she did. She never imagined it was a subterfuge, not even when she recognized Don Fenster and a strange man standing beside the pickup that had backed into the side of her car. Tam ran off, back to whatever he'd been doing earlier, leaving her alone with the two men in the lot behind the building. It was then that she experienced a prickle of unease, but she promptly dismissed it. She was always feeling uneasy about something lately, and it was broad daylight, for goodness' sake!

"I dented your door, Miss Emma," Don Fenster said, speaking the first words he had spoken to her in nearly twenty years. Stepping aside, he gave her room to look.

Emma bent, surveying the damage, wondering only if she would be able to open and close the door now. Recognizing that Don could have driven off without letting her know he had hit her, she wanted to be fair. "Let's just see if it opens and closes all right, Don. If it does, we'll just forget—"

Before the last words left her mouth, a blanket was thrown over her head, muffling her outraged cry in thick, hot wool. Her hands were seized, and a cord was wrapped around them so tightly that it cut.

"Now you just shut up, woman," a strange voice growled. "You shut up, 'cause I'll hit you every time you squeak." He gave her a sharp cuff for good measure.

She was roughly shoved into a cold, confined place, probably the toolbox in the pickup bed, she thought as shock began to give way to terror.

Don Fenster. Oh, my God, it was Don Fenster. Memory crashed through her, casting her into a prison of horror so deep that everything else receded, like a pinprick of light that grew smaller and ever smaller.

Until the only thing that was left was the dark.

Micah keyed the microphone on his radio and told Velma to let Nate know he and Gage were in place, a half mile up the county road from Fenster's gate.

Velma acknowledged, and Micah clipped the mike to the collar of his jacket. "You got a radio?" he asked Gage.

"Yeah. In my Suburban."

Micah twisted and reached behind his seat. "Here. Take my spare."

"Thanks."

The sun had sunk low, casting golden and pink light across the rippled snow. It looked like a vast sea, Gage thought, all those open spaces with occasional islands of leafless cottonwoods or rocky upthrusts. And somewhere out there was Emma. God, if he ever got his arms around her again . . .

He drew a deep breath, forcing himself to be calm, battering down all the urgent impulses to act. For Emma's sake, he reminded himself, he had to keep a clear head and think his actions through. Last time he had been able to do nothing for those he loved, but this time he was in a position to help. In a position to redeem himself.

What a stupid idea, he thought. What did one have to do with the other?

Suddenly Nate's voice crackled over the radio, bursting abruptly out of the silence. "We got the warrant. Three units are already on their way to help you. The Tennyson kid evidently saw who took Miss Emma. It was definitely Don Fenster."

Gage released a breath he hadn't even been aware of holding. They had come to the right place.

"If you go in there by yourselves, you be damn careful," Nate cautioned. "Walt Severn says Fenster has five other guys staying with him. And if they're running some kind of weird cult, there's no telling how many other people might be involved."

Gage shifted impatiently but kept silent. He'd been dealing with superior officers for too many years to back-talk one now. And, as usual, he would just go ahead and do whatever he felt was necessary.

Micah was evidently of similar mind. "We're going in, Nate. Miss Emma can't wait." With a click, he turned off the radio, then released the Blazer's brake.

"We're on our own," Micah remarked as they rolled forward toward Fenster's gate.

As they had been the night they rescued Faith Parish from her former husband, Gage thought. Hard to believe that had been only a month ago. Then, however, they had been up against only one man. This time they would face Fenster and an unknown number of his cronies.

"I recommend we drive in slowly and openly," he said to Micah. "As if it's just a routine call."

Micah nodded agreement. This was the hardest part of any lawman's job, going into a situation with almost no idea of what was waiting.

They turned onto Fenster's private road and passed beneath a weathered overhead sign that was totally illegible.

"Looks like this guy doesn't put out any more effort than he has to," Gage remarked.

"Nope."

Inside, tension was drawing Gage tight, and unanswerable questions kept trying to crowd everything else out of his mind. He couldn't afford to become distracted, and he certainly couldn't give in to his worry about Emma. His hands tightened into fists on his splayed thighs, and he kept his attention firmly fixed on his surroundings.

The Fenster house was invisible from the road, hidden by dips in the land, but as they came around a bend in the rutted track it came into view. Dilapidated, in need of a good scraping and a coat of paint, it looked forlorn, abandoned.

Fresh tire tracks passed by the house, heading for the barn several hundred yards behind it.

"That must be where she is," Gage said.

"Maybe. But maybe they put her in the house. Let's check it out."

Gage couldn't argue with that, but this was one time when patience seemed to be escaping him too rapidly for his own good. He wanted to tear the door down and race through the house at full tilt.

"Stay here, man," Micah said as he halted the Blazer right in front of the house. "Watch my back while I go to the door."

Gage opened his mouth to insist that he should go to the door, then realized that was a foolish demand. Micah was the uniformed deputy, and it would look a hell of a lot less suspicious for him to walk up to the door.

Gage climbed out of the Blazer and stood waiting while Micah crossed the few yards of snow to the front porch. When he reached the door, Micah lifted his fist and hammered on it in the time-honored way of cops everywhere.

Nobody inside would be in the least doubt of who was at the door, and it was not a sound that could be ignored.

Micah had to hammer a second time, and by then Gage was uptight enough to gnaw his own bones. His back had begun hurting again, a fiery ache that pulsed like a steady hammer blow, but he hardly noticed it in his anxiety for Emma. Just let him get his hands on her again. Just let her be unharmed. He would never let her out of his sight again. He would protect her from harm for the rest of his days.

Finally, what seemed like aeons later, the door swung slowly open. In the shadowy depths of the house beyond Micah, Gage saw a small, very elderly woman, leaning unsteadily on a walker. She wore a flowered housecoat, and her hair was ratty and dirty looking. She simply looked up at Micah as if she didn't know what to make of him.

"Good afternoon, Miz Fenster," Micah said politely. "I'm Deputy Parish. I'm looking for a young woman who turned up missing this afternoon. You wouldn't happen to have seen anything unusual, would you?"

An endless time passed before the old woman's eyes blinked. "Emma Conard," she said, in a voice as dry as ancient parchment. "Don hates her."

Gage tensed and stepped forward. Micah made an almost imperceptible movement, warning him back. "What do you know about Emma Conard, Miz Fenster?" he asked with surprising gentleness. "Can you help us find her?"

"It's those boys he hangs around with," Mrs. Fenster said, her eyes strangely bewildered, almost as if she wasn't sure who Micah was, or of what she was trying to say. "They're evil, all of them, and I've told Donny so many times to tell them to go, but he just tells me to shut up and go back to my room. But they're wicked. Wicked!"

"Emma Conard, Miz Fenster," Micah prompted gently. "What about Miss Emma?"

"I heard them," she said. "I heard them talking about how they were going to... do those terrible things to her. Like they did to the cows—"

"Do you know where she is?"

"In the barn. They took her to the barn." She looked up at Micah with a kind of sad bafflement. "Why didn't you come out here before? He took the phone out so I couldn't call you.... They're wicked...wicked...."

"How many are there?"

"Donny and four of his friends."

The few hundred yards seemed endless as Micah and Gage ran toward the barn. The growl of the Blazer's engine would have given them away, so after radioing Nate, they grabbed weapons and took off at a dead run. Micah cradled a shotgun in addition to the .45 strapped to his hip. Gage carried a second shotgun and a 9 mm Browning. The fresh vehicle tracks made a packed path that was easier to traverse than the deep snow to either side, but it was also more slippery, which impeded them a little. Gage suspected that not even dry ground could have given him the speed he wanted now.

Emma. Oh, God, please . . .

A litany of prayers and pleas ran through the background of Gage's thoughts as he forced himself to focus on what they needed to do now. "Donny and four of his friends" meant that if Walt Severn had been correct, there was another one to worry about. One who might not be in the barn. One who might come upon Micah and Gage at an awkward time.

The shadows of the snow dunes had grown longer and bluer. Evening was fast approaching, and Gage welcomed its advent. Less light would be an advantage for him and Micah as they cased the situation.

The side of the barn they approached had no windows and only one small door in its side. Reluctant to chance being noticed if they opened that door even a crack, they split up, heading in opposite directions in search of some means to see inside. Gage came upon a window at one point, but it opened into a tack room that was empty, giving him no clue as to what the men in the barn were up to. It would be a good way to get inside, though, once they had an idea of where their quarry was located.

On the far side of the barn he found the helicopter that must have been used in the cattle rustlings. It was hidden beneath a ramshackle lean-to against the side of the barn.

He slipped around it and encountered Micah. The bigger man was pressed to the side of the building near another door, and the way he was frozen led Gage to hope he could see inside. Hurrying as quickly as he could while still remaining silent, Gage crept up to him.

Micah glanced at him and then stepped back, motioning him to look.

There was a narrow slit between the door and frame, a place left open by a missing strip of insulation. Gage peered inside, and what he saw froze him to his soul. He could see the vague shapes of men moving about, indistinguishable in dim kerosene light, rendered completely shapeless by long robes. When he shifted a little to one side he saw what appeared to be an altar, draped in black, with a ram's head painted in gold on the front of it.

A whispered oath escaped him. No doubt, he thought. There was no doubt that some kind of ritual was about to be performed. Taking into account the pentagram and the ram's head, he would bet it was some kind of satanism. And Emma was in there. Fear squeezed his heart.

Shifting again, he tried to see in the other direction, and that was when his heart stopped utterly. Emma was there, clad only in her thin work clothes, her hands bound above her head by a rope that hung from a high rafter. Her head lolled to one side, as if she was unconscious, and he couldn't for the life of him see whether her feet touched the floor.

Gage pulled away and leaned back against the barn wall, trying desperately to find some of the detachment that was necessary for what was going to have to be done. Without detachment, he couldn't trust his judgment.

"Did you see her?" he whispered to Micah.

Micah gave a brief, wordless nod.

"She could suffocate that way." It might take time, but when you hung by your arms it became nearly impossible to breathe. Gage had had the experience once, when a dealer had gotten suspicious of him. He looked at Micah. "We can't wait."

Micah nodded his agreement. "There's still one unaccounted for."

"He might already be in there. And Emma might already be dead, or close to it. I found the tack room back there. It has a window we ought to be able to climb through."

"Let's go."

Moving in swift, careful silence, they crept around the corner to the end of the barn where the tack room was located. The sun was now a red sphere above the distant mountains, and a fiery twilight colored the world.

The window proved to be unlocked and gave only a little resistance to being raised. The cold weather had dried all the moisture from the wood and loosened the window in its frame. Gage could hardly believe their good fortune.

Micah insisted on going through first. Gage understood—Micah had had a lot more training for this kind of thing—but he didn't like it. Moments later, though, he climbed through and joined Micah by the door of the tack room. Cautiously he tried the knob and found the door unlocked. The hinges made only the quietest of creaks as he eased the door open.

Between them and the men were six box stalls, three on either side of a wide passageway. The shadows here were deep, concealing, hardly penetrated by the couple of kerosene lanterns Fenster and his friends were using at the other end of the barn.

They were confident, Gage thought, as he and Micah crept down opposite sides of the passageway, keeping close to the stalls. They were laughing and talking in normal voices as they prepared to commit their obscenities. One of them even joked about whether it would be as easy to skin a human as it was to skin a cow.

Gage closed his eyes briefly, praying Emma was unconscious and unable to hear this filth. And then, with a monumental effort of will, he returned to the ledge on the abyss where feelings couldn't reach him, the place where the cold wind kept his soul safely frozen. He couldn't afford to let his feelings interfere now.

Undetected, he and Micah reached the end of the line of stalls. As they'd agreed, Gage squatted in the shadows and waited for Micah to step out into the light and reveal himself. The intention was for Micah to ease his way around, away from Emma, drawing the attention of the five men that way, so that Gage could slip around to protect her.

And unfortunately, until somebody threatened him or Micah, they had to do this by the book. Right now Gage would have liked to burn the whole damn rule book.

That was when he heard the distant *whop-whop* of a helicopter. He cast a look at Micah and received an "okay" signal in return. It must be the sheriff's medevac chopper, Gage realized. Micah would certainly recognize the sound of the Huey. And that meant that Nate and his units couldn't be far away. Just a few more minutes.

Emma must be freezing, Gage thought as he looked her way again. It was cold in the barn, though not quite as cold as the outdoors, and her sweater and slacks were little protection. Her feet were touching the floor, he could see now, but he couldn't tell if she was standing or simply hanging by her arms. He half wished she would move, so he could tell if she was alive, and then was glad when she didn't, because he didn't want her to remember any of this. Not any of it.

The attention of the five men suddenly shifted from their various tasks toward a clatter near the makeshift altar, where one of them dumped the contents of a black bag onto a small table. Gage caught a glint of silver, and then one of them—Don Fenster, he thought—lifted a golden dagger.

It was the one from the photograph that had been sent to Emma. Gage recognized it instantly, even though the photograph had been black-and-white. On the pommel was the ruby—probably just glass—from Emma's dreams.

"I used this on her once before," Fenster said, showing it around as if it were a trophy. "I thought for sure I killed her."

"Drop it!" Micah's voice suddenly cracked through the barn and he stepped around the corner of the stall with his shotgun leveled at the cluster of dark-robed men. Easing around the stall, he edged slowly to the right, drawing their collective gazes from Emma's direction. "You're under arrest for kidnapping. Put your hands where I can see them."

Now! Gage thought, and slipped around the corner of his stall, staying low and trying to keep quiet as he crept toward Emma. The Huey's *whop-whop* was louder now, loud enough to fill the five villains with tension.

"Hold it!" Micah barked.

Gage glanced back to see one of the men suddenly freeze in the process of lowering his arm. He kept moving toward Emma.

"The sheriff will be here in just a minute," Micah said. "It won't pay you to try something foolish."

The door just to one side of Gage suddenly burst open, admitting a blast of cold night air and the missing sixth man.

"Don, Lew, there's a whole crowd of police moving in...." His voice trailed off, and he froze as he saw Micah. Gage rolled onto his back and leveled his shotgun at the sixth man.

"Don't try anything," he said.

The man gaped down at him, then stiffened when he looked into the barrel of the shotgun.

But apparently it was the distraction the other five had needed. They all dived in different directions. Micah fired, and Don Fenster hit the floor bleeding. Micah cocked and fired again, catching another man and putting him down.

"Hold it!" screamed a frenzied voice. "Hold it or the woman dies!"

Gage's attention strayed past the man he was holding at gunpoint to Emma. One of the robed men was holding her shieldlike before him, a knife at her ribs.

Gage lashed out with his foot, bringing the sixth man to the floor, where he was less of a threat. The man holding Emma jumped nervously.

"Both of you cops get out of here or she dies," the man said desperately. "Now."

"Forget it," Gage said flatly. "It's a stalemate. I'm not going anywhere, and neither is the deputy. We're both armed and ready to shoot, and all you've got is that woman. If you hurt her, there's nothing to keep me from shooting you in the groin, is there?"

The man's pale, frightened face grew even paler, but the knife never moved away from Emma. "You won't touch me while I got her."

"Like I said," Gage drawled, "stalemate. But not for long."

Micah had drawn his .45, and now he pointed it upward and pulled the trigger. The startled man with the knife spun around, exposing his back to Gage. It was all the opening Gage needed. Heedless of his screaming back, he rolled forward onto his feet and threw himself at the man who threatened Emma.

Gage caught him around the knees and knocked him to the floor. The knife went spinning out of the man's hands when he fell. He tried to scramble away, but Gage yanked the Browning from his belt and shoved the cold barrel right in the man's belly. "Don't move."

"That goes for all of you," Micah said, his deep voice as hard as steel. "Not a muscle."

The *whop* of the Huey's blades was a loud roar now, and Micah keyed his microphone, telling Nate what the situation was. Thirty seconds later the barn was full of armed deputies and a couple of paramedics.

Gage's only thought was for Emma. He grabbed the knife that only moments before had been shoved against her ribs and hacked at the rope that held her arms suspended.

"Emma? Emma, do you hear me?" She was breathing, thank God, but she was pale, so pale, and as cold as ice. As soon as he got her down, he propped her on his lap and began to rub her icy hands. "Emma, honey, do you hear me? Oh, God, baby, answer me. Please. Just one little sound...."

A small whimper escaped her, and then she drew a deep, shuddering breath. Slowly, very slowly, her eyes fluttered open. Gage looked down into them, seeking the warmth, the caring, the gentleness—the *love*—that was Emma. It was gone. All of it.

He looked down into her hazy green eyes and realized with a terrible sense of dread that Emma had gone far away, had withdrawn to some place deep inside. Some place beyond hurt, beyond fear.

He knew that place intimately, had dwelt in it for years now. With a groan, he held her as close as he could get her and made up his mind to give her a reason to come back.

Because he sure as hell couldn't live without her.

Chapter 14

The Christmas open house had come and was nearly over. Gage watched Emma as she bade good-night to the last of the visitors, then paused in the open door to listen to one last carol from the choir that had wandered the neighborhood all evening. They stood before her steps in a semicircle and sang "The First Noel" with voices growing cracked from overuse and cold, but beautiful all the same.

Emma, too, was beautiful, Gage thought. She wore a full-skirted green velvet dress that emphasized her femininity and brought her fantastic hair to blazing life.

But ever since the night at the Fenster ranch, she had been withdrawn, hardly speaking to him or anyone else. Something had happened, something that had pulled her out of the present and cast her into some painful abyss of the soul. Gage Dalton recognized someone who was wrestling with demons when he saw her. Someone who had been there, too, couldn't mistake the signs.

After her rescue, Doc Randall had put her in the hospital for a couple of days of rest and recuperation. She had suffered from exposure and hypothermia, but Gage knew the real damage was deeper and less treatable.

He was sure she had remembered the details of the attack ten years ago. Nothing else could explain this withdrawal. She needed the time, he told himself, to deal with all those memories. She needed him to be supportive and silent.

But it had been nearly a week, a week during which he'd battled a few of his own demons, and he didn't know if he could face another day without at least a small smile from Emma. He didn't know if he could face another Christmas alone. And he had vowed he would give her a reason to come back. He'd given her time, he'd given her space, and now, no matter how it scared him, he would give her love.

"Emma?"

She turned from closing the door and looked at him. Just as it had all week, her expression looked blank, as if she was only peripherally aware of him.

Something inside him cracked wide open. He couldn't endure another day with this wraithlike woman moving silently, pointlessly, through the house. He wanted to shake her, wake her, make her look at him once again as if he mattered. He took one step toward her, then caught himself up short.

"Damn it, Emma," he said, his voice hoarse with anguish. "I hate Christmas. You know I hate it, and you know why. You know all about it. Are you going to give me another reason to feel that way?"

She blinked. For the first time in days, he believed she really saw him.

"Emma, what happened is in the past. I realize that finally. I need you to realize it, too. I need . . . I need you to make this Christmas joyous for me. I need you to give me—give me—aw, hell, Emma, I need you to give me all the Christmases to come."

He saw his words strike home. A long, slow shiver seemed to pass through her, and she took a step toward him. All of a sudden she didn't look remote. All of a sudden she was very much there. Very much with him.

"I remembered," she said, her voice hardly more than a whisper. A flash of searing agony showed in her eyes. "I remembered being in the car with him... I remembered what he did.''

"I figured you did. God, baby, I would have spared you that if I could have.''

"I know." She gave him a small, forlorn smile. "I'm sorry, Gage. It's just so much, so awful.... I can't have children because of that man!'' The anguish seemed to rip her chest wide open, and tears began to spill down her cheeks. "It's his fault, and now I know it was *him,* and I think of all the times I was in the same room and never knew.... Oh, Gage—''

At last, at long last, she flew into his arms and let him give her the comfort he had ached all week to offer.

"I know, sweetheart. I know. But he's dead now, Emma. You don't ever have to see him or worry about him again.'' Micah's shotgun had taken care of that.

"But I feel so angry," she said into his shoulder. "So angry.''

"I know. I've been angry for a long, long time, and I guess you will be, too. But, Em, are you going to sacrifice tomorrow to your anger the way I did for so long? Or are you going to put it in its place and try to make some good Christmas memories for us?''

Another long, shuddering sigh escaped her. After a few moments she raised her wet face so she could look up at him. Her hand rose instinctively to his scarred cheek, cradling it, remembering just what it was he had lost, and comparing it to her own losses. He was looking at her now with a new expression in his gray eyes. Warmth blazed out at her, warmth and something very like hope.

"But I can't have children," she said, a litany so old it came automatically.

"That's fine. I don't want any. I had mine, and I lost them, and if you want the God's honest truth, Em, I don't think I could sleep another night if I ever again had a child to worry about. In fact, it scares me sh—scares me to death to think of worrying about *you* for the rest of my days. I'll probably drive you crazy, hovering over you all the time, sending out search parties if you're fifteen minutes late....''

A small, reluctant laugh escaped her, just a puff of sound, but it reached him in his very heart. He looked intently down at her and felt nearly swamped by relief when he saw the old Emma peering up at him from sparkling green eyes. For the moment, maybe for all time, the shadows had been driven back.

"Are you trying to tell me something, Mr. Dalton?" she asked primly, Miss Emma the spinster librarian from the top of her head to the tips of her toes. Deep in her green eyes, behind the sheen of tears, was a teasing sparkle that warmed his chilly soul.

"I most certainly am, Miss Emma," he said gruffly. Then hell's own archangel bent to whisper the most seductive words of all into the pink shell of Miss Emma's ear.

"I love you, Red," he said roughly. "I'll love you all my days, and probably far beyond. I need you with every breath I draw. Say you'll marry me. Whatever comes, we can face it together."

"Oh, Gage, I do love you!" Her tremulous sigh filled his ear, filled his heart, filled his soul. With those simple words, she set him free and handed him heaven.

Hell's own archangel had found peace at last.

* * * * *

COMING NEXT MONTH

#487   COLD, COLD HEART—Ann Williams

Rescuing kidnapped children no longer interested rugged
American Hero Jake Frost, but to save her daughter,
Rachel Dryden was determined to change his mind. Could
Rachel warm his heart to her cause . . . and herself?

#488   OBSESSED!—Amanda Stevens

Both shy cartoonist Laura Valentine and undercover FBI agent
Richard Gentry were pretending to be something they weren't. But
complications *really* arose when they realized their passion wasn't
a fake. . . .

#489   TWO AGAINST THE WORLD—Many Anne Wilson

All Alicia Sullivan wanted was a little peace—and *maybe* a nice,
normal, sane man. Instead, she found herself stranded with
secretive Steven Rider, whose mysterious nature was far from safe.

#490   SHERIFF'S LADY—Dani Criss

Fleeing cross-country from a powerful criminal, C. J. Dillon
couldn't afford to trust anyone. But when Sheriff Chris Riker
offered his assistance, C.J. longed to confide in the virile lawman.

#491   STILL MARRIED—Diana Whitney

Desperately worried about her missing sister-in-law, Kelsey Manning
sought out her estranged husband, Luke Sontag. But as they
joined forces on the search, could they find the strength to save
their marriage?

#492   MAN OF THE HOUR—Maura Seger

Years ago, fast cars, cold beer and easy women had been bad boy
Mark Fletcher's style. But he'd changed. Now his only trouble
came in the form of single mother Lisa Morley.

SPRING FANCY

Three bachelors, footloose and fancy-free... until now!

Spring into romance with three fabulous fancies by three of Silhouette's hottest authors:

ANNETTE BROADRICK
LASS SMALL
KASEY MICHAELS

When spring fancy strikes, no man is immune!

Look for this exciting new short-story collection in March at your favorite retail outlet.

Only from

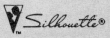

where passion lives.

Take 4 bestselling love stories FREE

Plus get a FREE surprise gift!

Silhouette Books
is proud to present
our best authors,
their best books...
and the best in
your reading pleasure!

Throughout 1993, look for exciting books by these top names in contemporary romance:

CATHERINE COULTER—
Aftershocks in February

FERN MICHAELS—
Nightstar in March

DIANA PALMER—
Heather's Song in March

ELIZABETH LOWELL
Love Song for a Raven in April

SANDRA BROWN
(previously published under
the pseudonym Erin St. Claire)—
Led Astray in April

LINDA HOWARD—
All That Glitters in May

When it comes to passion,
we wrote the book.

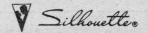

CONTINUES...

Come back to Conard County, Wyoming, where you'll meet men and women whose lives are as dramatic as the landscape around them. Join author Rachel Lee for the third book in her fabulous series, MISS EMMALINE AND THE ARCHANGEL (IM #482). Meet Emmaline Conard, "Miss Emma," a woman who was cruelly tormented years ago and now is being victimized again. But this time sheriff's investigator Gage Dalton—the man they call hell's own archangel—is there to protect her. But who will protect Gage from his feelings for Emma? Look for their story in March, only from Silhouette Intimate Moments.